KU-523-347

Hello Love

Central Library, Henry Street,
An Lárleabharlann, Sráid Annraoi
Tel: 8734333

Leabharlanna Poibli Chathair Baile Átha Cliath
Dublin City Public Libraries

First published in 2017 by
Liberties Press
1 Terenure Place | Terenure | Dublin 6W | Ireland
Tel: +353 (0) 86 853 8793
www.libertiespress.com

Distributed in the UK by
Turnaround Publisher Services
Unit 3 | Olympia Trading Estate | Coburg Road | London N22 6TZ
T: +44 (0) 20 8829 3000 | E: orders@turnaround-uk.com

Distributed in the United States by
Casemate IPM | 1950 Lawrence Road | Havertown | Pennsylvania
19083 | USA
T: (610) 853 9131 | E: casemate@casematepublishers.com

Copyright © Carmen Cullen, 2017
The author asserts her moral rights.
ISBN (print): 978-1-910742-99-0
ISBN (e-book): 978-1-910742-971-6

2 4 6 8 10 9 7 5 3 1
A CIP record for this title is available from the British Library.
Cover design by Roudy Design
Printed in Dublin by Sprint Print

This book is sold subject to the condition that it shall not, by way
of trade or otherwise, be lent, resold, hired out or otherwise circulated,
without the publisher's prior consent, in any form other than that in
which it is published and without a similar condition including this
condition being imposed on the subsequent publisher.

No part of this publication may be reproduced or transmitted in any
form or by any means, electronic or mechanical, including
photocopying, recording or storage in any information or retrieval
system, without the prior permission of the publisher in writing.

This is a work of fiction. Any resemblance between the characters
in the book and actual persons, living or dead, is coincidental.

Praise for *Two Sisters Singing*

'A f.. dessly accurate recapturing of Dublin in the 1940s: Nelson's Pillar, silk stockings, Find.. ers and Switzers, and Caffola's cafeteria, and horses and donkeys drawing carriag.. on O'Connell Street.'

– Mary Kenny, *Irish Independent*

..ike Dennis Potter's landmark drama, *Pennies from Heaven*, the story of Lily Doneghue, a flighty eighteen-year-old UCD student aspiring to be a professional ..., 's peppered with songs that evoke a wayward imagination fleeing reality. The ...were popularised by Carmen's aunt, Delia Murphy.

..novel with a compelling storyline and a charged finish. Where Cullen excels is in ..ly vivid portraits.

-- Alan Murdock, *Sunday Times*

'If you want to wake in the magical countryside of Ireland's past or step into shabby bu.. ..autiful Dublin streets of 1942, then you must read Two Sisters Singing. Our ..roine Lily will draw your irresistibly along as she loves and sings and faces up to what ..t really means to be a sister, in Emergency Ireland. Shining prose from a talented new sh writer.'

- *An Bhradan*

'Carmen Cullen is an excellent dramatist, and these plays for young people, with their har..s-on approach, are vibrant and authentic.'

– *Evening Herald*

'Shining, magical, spell-binding'

– *Adrian Mitchell*

'An original voice emerging on the Irish poetry scene. Worth watching out for.'

– Eavan Boland, *Irish Times*

Hello Love

Carmen Cullen

Prologue

I thought you might like this photograph.

Jacqueline Clancy read the card she'd been sent from her sister Susanna and removed the accompanying black-and-white picture from the envelope. When her eyes rested on the girl in the middle of the family picture those many years ago, she had to try hard to make herself out. At least that was how Jacqueline put it to herself. Only a superhuman effort would allow a sixty-year-old granny connect with the girl she had been, all those years ago. Although Jacqueline's eyes had been drawn to herself instinctively, standing in that upright fashion beside her sister, the child she had once been seemed a stranger.

The child in the picture smiled out at her as if to say, *Here I am. I am smiling at the world because that is what the photographer instructed, and as a matter of fact it suits me to smile. Remember, I was the girl who listened when she was told what to do, even if she didn't like it. After all, there was somebody else in charge of her life, and she needed to be obeyed.* There had been rebellion in her mind also, Jacqueline struggled to think, because her hair had been scraped into a bun at the top of her head for the picture.

The grin might be only barely there, but now Jacqueline could recognise the real her, despite that pasted-on expression. The small girl was standing with shoulders back. She was looking at the world squarely in the face. Whatever happens, I am wide awake and alert, the face said, and reaching out to life, wanting to take it all in. 'I must have had no troubles,' she murmured. Even putting the photograph down that instant, couldn't stop the memories rushing back. A picture of Teddy, her father, flashed into her mind. She knew he was in a good mood, because he was beaming at her, about to swing her onto the handlebar of his bike. She saw him clearly. His coal-black wavy hair was Brylcreemed down. There was an impression of neatness because he secured her between his arms like a piece of precious china in a well-wrapped parcel. He could negotiate busy Tooradulla with his eyes shut, he was boasting to her mother Imelda. At the same time, he winked at her. They were off on their private adventure, and her heart soared.

Lastly, Jacqueline saw the Aravon Hotel, where she had been born. The hotel was smaller than she'd thought it was when she went back to visit in later years, but a palace, with its warren of rooms, to a small child, and dominating the wide main street of Tooradoo, like a frontier-fort in a story of old.

Later that day, Jacqueline changed her mind about leaving aside the photograph Susanna had sent, and put it in a frame. She found a place for it on her writing desk. The desk was barely used for the purpose it was designed, since it was in her busy sitting-room. She'd slotted the piece of furniture in beside a bay-window with sea-views. It had its complement of small drawers for her grandchildren to peer into, and delicate carvings adorned the front and legs. When the sun fell on its smooth writing surface, the mahogany wood seemed to drink in the heat. There were shades of weathered chestnut, and Jacqueline had a dim sense of the despoiled forest from where the original rough wood had come.

That summer was a busy one for Jacqueline. The weather had decided to favour Cloonvara, the seaside town where she lived, and blue waters beckoned. She had resided in this locality for a long time, and had always kept to herself, but in the relaxed atmosphere of heady summer days, she began to make new friends. Still, she kept up her habit of writing her diary, as she had done since she arrived, and her reading.

'The past is another country.' Jacqueline spoke aloud. It was a rainy day during this long summer of bliss, and she'd found herself confined indoors. In the adjacent green spaces, resident trees must be welcoming those heady draughts, but her mood was restless. She sighed and turned her attention to housework. Recently her grand-children had stayed for a week in her much-loved newly converted attic room, and it needed to be cleaned. Carefully climbing steep steps into the freshly carved-out space, she surveyed the disorder left behind. Rain pattered on the skylight. The same window was slightly ajar from her last visit, and traffic from distant streets pen-etrated. She banged it closed and peace swept back. It was a perfect atmosphere for writing and putting off the cleaning: she went to fetch her diary. Downstairs, she picked up her sister's gift to see if the photograph might suit an attic shelf. Returning, the smell of recently installed pine, heightened by the closed atmosphere, attacked her nostrils. She breathed in deeply.

Like their pine surround, the ceiling of the attic must have seemed like an upturned boat to the children when they slept here. At their tender years, they could have no sense of their own futures; how they would strain and toughen up, like sturdy old wood, in the years that stretched ahead. In the course of things, she didn't have many years left herself: she glanced at the impenetrable girl in the photograph. Perhaps it was time to be young again, to bring all that had happened round full circle.

She could be four years old. Jacqueline began to write.

Part 1

Central Library, Henry Street,
An Lárleabharlann, Sráid Annraoi

Chapter One

Jacqueline Clancy loved her father Teddy. That was why she always liked it when they could be together, and disliked it because that wasn't too often. Sometimes he was like the sun: he glowed in a way that made her feel warm, and because he was tall and she was small he looked down at her from a great height.

Jacqueline did not like the people in Tooradulla, the town where she lived, because it was very hard to get her way with them. If she had been bold and managed to sidestep her father's disappointment — because really he didn't know how to give out — she was often the object of dark glances in the town, or at least looks from on high from those who thought children should be seen and not heard, that little people were more of a nuisance, who often got in the way of the busy life of a town.

Jacqueline was a fish in a pond complete with weeds, she could have answered these no-nonsense types. Her pond was filled with delicious clear water, and that was life. Her father was a bevy of thin reeds rising upright to the sky, deeply rooted in the impenetrable depths of the pool, and as constant as the world itself. However far she ventured from his presence, he was always there to come back to. Her mother Imelda, on the other hand, was a songbird who often pecked her daughter into place.

3

The town that Jacqueline lived in might be called Tooradulla, but she called it Tooraloo. It had a main street as wide as a prairie. There was a park beyond the main street that stretched to the edge of the world and further on. The park had a lake where big fish prowled — not like the little minnows who flitted about in her pond. Once, a man had walked into that huge pool of water and never come out, she'd been told, to warn her about the dangers of venturing too close to lake-edges.

Jacqueline might be four at this stage, but if she was ever questioned about her age, she always said she was nearly five. Despite her tender years, if anybody had asked, she knew herself that she was as capable of thought and decision as any adult around her. As it turned out, there was no need to question that realisation, until the day she was grounded and her protestations that she was being treated like a dumb child were not listened to.

If Teddy, Jacqueline's Dad, allowed her to frolic about in the town, bending down to kiss her on the cheek every so often when she made him smile, her mother Imelda was the air she winged about in; to put it plainly. Jacqueline wasn't a fledgling, of course, but somehow the presence of her mother created that sensation. Soon she grew sorry she thought so simply, when, possibly due to something she'd said or done — she wasn't sure — one morning her mother was gone.

It was true that Jacqueline didn't know whether she loved where she lived, or not. It was because she had nothing to compare it to. She knew her home was a hotel and that the nerve-centre of that hotel was the kitchen. The family accommodation was tucked into the corner of the hotel, but upstairs. These family quarters were like a sea-captain's living-space Teddy had once told her about, when he was reading to her from *Gulliver's Travels*. They were the central hub from which everything else radiated. 'Rise and shine,' her father would say when he appeared at her doorway in the mornings, like the giant Gulliver he himself was. She would hop out of the bed and happily pad about, because the captain had given his orders. Where she emerged from every day was remarkably like a ship's quarters too, in the sense that the rooms were neat and compact and everything fitted perfectly into a small space. Every room, that is, apart from the one where her mother received her into her presence. If her father was Gulliver, then at times Imelda was his fairy-tale queen. She was the opposite of the Ice Queen, of course, because to be at her side was to sit up against the warmest fur-clad Ruler of Avalon Jacqueline could imagine. But it wasn't easy to get to that side. Her mother was usually busy, and that was why Jacqueline was not often brought to her. When she was, it was to make sure they could sit and love each other for at least some time during the day.

Jacqueline always felt a thrill of happiness as the time approached when she could be led in to see her mother. Even though her twin brother and sister, Tim and Susanna, and her older brother, Tom, would be present too — the twins probably in her mother's arms, and Tom making car noises with toys as he played on the floor — still Jacqueline felt privileged to be there, because the heartbeat of the world was tick-ticking silently in the room, making sure that the order of things that happened every day would stay the same, marking the beat without fail, in her ever-expanding existence. Shortly after Jacqueline was five, she found out that even the best wind-up clocks can stop.

As well as her mother's sitting room, Jacqueline was also mesmer-ised by the hotel kitchen. A row of pots bubbled on a high range, like cauldrons. In there, she definitely belonged to the land of the little people, cocooned from everything around her because of her low height. Sitting on the convenient slat of wood that extended underneath one of the two long kitchen tables, and watching as feet scurried about, she could calmly observe the lightning speed of it all. From there, she heard her mother's voice call commands, and because she herself was strictly forbidden from being in any part of the hotel other than her family quarters, she would make no comment. It was when she was hunkered down in her underneath-perch one day that Jacqueline came face to face with a beady-eyed lobster that, one day soon, would change her life.

Chapter Two

However much Imelda's presence drew her into the hotel's big kitchen, where shouted commands and snatches of songs flew about in the steam-clouds that gathered overhead, sometimes it turned out for Jacqueline that wanting badly to be in a place just wasn't enough. Her mother had those eyes in the back of her head Jacqueline had heard Teddy refer to once, because Imelda's penetrating voice would travel right to the kitchen door where Jacqueline stood, poised to sneak inside. 'The kitchen is no place for little girls. Go upstairs and play,' she would ring out, and Jacqueline would be forced to step back from the colourful, smells-peppered world.

Pale-faced Kitty, with dreamy eyes, worked in the back-kitchen. She was joined there from time to time by her friend Phyllis. Jacqueline might be ousted from the kitchen, but Kitty always longed to enfold her in her arms and, although she would squirm away, the maid usually managed. 'Isn't she lovely?' Kitty would address the air as soon as Jacqueline appeared in her domain. Immediately the small visitor felt like a precious delicate thing: so rare and refined, she should not be touched. The sensation never lasted, though, because as soon as she was nabbed, Kitty took advantage of her gullibility and tried to glue her to her side.

If Jacqueline resented being in the drab back-kitchen, because she had been foiled in her attempts to locate herself where, often, her mother's cheerful singing pervaded clouds of steamy air, and where, from her low vantage-point, legs sped about with the speed of cutting scissors, Kitty's corner had its compensations. It was gratifying to be so openly admired for one thing, and then there was the mystery that surrounded this nondescript person. One day Jacqueline found out that although Kitty spent a long time in her annex, she had another existence. She wasn't just a girl who covered herself in a dowdy apron and kept her hair pinned back, but a princess who lived in a garret.

It was hard to think of the back-kitchen as a proper room, because it was filled to bursting by a black stove. This ancient cooker was mostly stone-cold: to make matters worse, smuts of black polish flew about when Phyllis set about her job of shining up the guests' shoes arranged in front of her. If the cramped annex was night to the little girl where the other kitchen was day, and Jacqueline didn't like Kitty really because she wasn't the one she needed to be loved by, Kitty also told her things. She had revealed how a boy had tickled her in the ribs and how another one had eyes like sheep, the way he stared at her. She laughed then, and Jacqueline saw that Kitty wasn't tied in the same way to the hotel as she was. She belonged to the world of the town and its people, and she only thought Jacqueline was lovely when she was in the hotel. After that, she had other trees to chirp on, and she longed to be free. The day would come when Jacqueline would long to be free too, but that was in the future, after the lobster had been caught, when the creature was plunged into boiling water, becoming red, and her mother had called out gaily that she was sure she heard it scream.

Chapter Three

The family's Avalon Hotel was as big as a mansion to Jacqueline. Although she was forbidden to, one day she plucked up the courage to explore beyond their own rooms. She wasn't supposed to go adventuring. She was being bold, and as soon as she began her trip, she was afraid. The hotel is not a playground, she had been warned. She didn't like to disobey, but her older brother, Tom, had said not to worry: he had already made an expedition. She didn't have to tell anyone, and so she set out. The hotel had long corridors and when she moved along, a red carpet dulled the sound of her footsteps. In the first passage into the womb of the building — a narrow corridor that could be part of a maze that would trap and expose her for being naughty if she was caught — a door was ajar.

'. . . and eat up little girls for my dinner. Make them pay for not doing what they are told,' she was sure she heard a voice say as she approached.

'She ought to be informed she's a trouble-maker and that she'll be the death of me yet. I sometimes wonder why I couldn't have been given a good child like everybody else,' a woman replied. She was a witch, Jacqueline decided, and the man was an ogre. As soon as she stepped past that door, they would open it wide and peer out, and they would have the same ferocious expressions as wild beasts because she was where she shouldn't be, and she crept back. On the next corridor, Tom's words of encouragement rang in her ears: she decided she wasn't going to give up. She would tell him the story of her explorations, going deeper and deeper into the unknown, and she would make him laugh. 'I never went beyond the first landing,' he would say; although he might doubt her account too, and that would drive her mad.

The end of this second corridor was disappearing into the distance, and Jacqueline peered down. Before she got to the bottom, she would hear her father's voice boom behind her with all the impact of a gunshot. To help her keep on going, she began to make up stories. There was a row of doors ahead. Each one would have a sign painted on it saying, *Welcome. Please come in.* Passing the first door, she created a family of mice, with little mouse faces, who would look at her in a friendly way, delighted to make her acquaintance. Tiptoeing on, she made the next bedroom full of sun, with spiders busy creating a rainbow of webs on the window. She saw how the window had become a face with a voice like her mother's, that said, 'Stay as long as you like. Nothing will harm you when I'm near.'

In the end, as it turned out, reaching the last door to the corridor didn't matter because, just as she was about to run there and turn back, Jacqueline's heart skipped a beat. Straight ahead was a concealed set of steps that curved upwards. A familiar voice reached her from on high, and a door creaked open. It blew wider, and Kitty appeared. Behind Kitty's face, Phyllis peered out.

'Hello, darling. Isn't it lovely to see you? Come into my boudoir,' Kitty's voice tinkled, and the other girl laughed. 'At least come and say hello to Phyllis.' Kitty crooked a finger.

Jacqueline gripped a frail hand-rail and found herself in Kitty's bedroom. The girl of the drab back-kitchen was transformed. Her hair fell onto her shoulders like the shining tresses of Alice in

10

Wonderland. She picked up a brush and began to quickly fashion Jacqueline's own dark locks into a plait. 'With a little make-up, she could be very pretty,' Phyllis sniggered, and looked across into the mirror to aim correctly, to dab some lipstick on Jacqueline's lips. Perhaps they meant well, the pinned-down girl thought, but the hairbrush began to hurt, and she tried to pull away from the relentless brush-strokes.

'Little girls who step out of line and think they're so important nobody can say boo to them should be punished. It doesn't matter that you're the boss's daughter here,' Kitty said, and pinched her when she jerked her head.

'Sit still and we'll be finished soon,' Phyllis said. Jacqueline decided she had a fox's nose, because it twitched and was pointed.

'Phyllis and I are in line for jobs in Dublin. We're leaving the hotel and getting the train and never coming back,' Kitty announced. She flung the brush on the dressing table and twisted Jacqueline round. 'You can come and live with us when you grow up. You won't be living in this town forever, you know.' Jacqueline was sure Kitty had grown a few inches, because she looked much bigger in this low-ceiling attic room.

'I'm not going. I'll be living with my Mammy and Daddy forever,' she said. Any minute now, her mother would call and ask her where she was, but it didn't happen.

Chapter Four

Jacqueline had seen a fire-engine once in Tooradulla. She had observed the spray of water it emitted as she peered from the window of their hotel family-breakfast room, but when she pressed her face closer to the glass pane, it steamed up. The red of the engine became blurred, and she had to rush downstairs. 'A fire is no place for a small girl.' Her father had hustled her off the street when she dashed to his side, but for a moment smoke and water towered and hissed in such a magnificent way, she knew how greedy flames could be.

'It's only a lobster,' she thought one dark morning, not long after her explorations of the hotel, because she'd sat up in bed abruptly, with a dry mouth and sore eyes. She'd had a bad dream. Jacqueline looked around her quickly to make sure she was awake. Even if she was — and her sister's flushed face and chubby legs pronounced it to be true, because Susanna had kicked off the bed-clothes and was plainly there in the twin bed beside her in the room — she was sure the lobster really was still under her bed. It gave itself away, though, despite her sister's reassuring presence, because it made a noise, and Jacqueline imagined baleful yellow eyes in that cave of darkness beneath the bed-springs. It was where all kinds of danger lurked. The lobster was poised to make an attack, and Jacqueline whimpered.

Across the way from her, fingers of sunshine had stolen into the room. Even if she put the pillow over her head, those keys of light were a glaring lemon colour and would poke at her to get up. Tears had come, but she stopped them to think about how she could defeat this dream-lobster. In the end, she made herself so tall, she could turn and scold the creature if it did follow her when she landed on the bedroom floor, and she ran towards her parents' room.

'I've had a bad dream. There was a monster-lobster that could bite me in half,' Jacqueline sobbed, because her tears had returned.

Sometimes she was forbidden to come into this room, and then on other occasions, for no reason, she was allowed. Her parents' bed was like a giant pillow for plopping down on, where there were no rough edges to scrape against, and everything was warm and comfy. Now she eyed it warily. Perhaps if she sidled up, she could slip in and crawl up and lie in the warmth of her mother's side like a baby porpoise, before later easing back into the sea of her own world.

'Is it all right if I come into your bed, Mammy?' She put a fist up to rub her eyes.

'Let me just move over. Come along here,' her mother said. Jacqueline said thank-you to the lobster, silently.

If Jacqueline had her way, she would stay in this bedroom all the time, she'd once decided. She snuggled in between the cleft of her parents. Nobody ousted her. It was as if she could remain this way forever, like arriving in a story-land where all that happened was play. She licked each one of her fingers. They were all there. She wriggled in further. The sun didn't shine on this side of the hotel in the early morning, but a sliver of brightness seeped under the curtains. If she breathed in and out with her mother and father, it would be as if they were all the one person making the blankets rise and fall like the sea. She couldn't keep it up. Soon their breaths were all at odds with one another, as if they didn't belong together at all. Jacqueline thought of her mother's wedding dress in the wardrobe and how it was always cool to touch, smooth and silky, and the colour of cream. That was part of how this room was a playground too, because the dress was the loveliest thing she had ever touched, as if her mother had stepped out of her skin and given it to her to wear. Of course she got into terrible trouble once when, somehow, she pulled it down round her and found herself suffocating, trapped by too much beauty.

'Stop kicking, Jacqueline, or I'll have to ask you to leave,' she was ordered by Imelda, in the middle of her thoughts.

'I can't go back to my bed ever,' Jacqueline said.

'In that case, you'll have to sleep in an outhouse. Can we have some quiet here?' Teddy piped up. He was hotter than a fire, warmer than the steam-puffing cooker in the big kitchen, and Jacqueline pulled away from him. She had to close her eyes tight and stop moving. Soon her brothers and sister would sense she was here, and want to join in the fun. Shortly afterwards, they would all have to leave, and she would be forced back to her own room. At least, she would have had some time with Mammy and Daddy, like a secret memory she could recall later. However nice it was, though, it wouldn't get rid of the lurking lobster.

Chapter Five

The thing Jacqueline liked best about her father was how high and commanding he was, like a tree she had an instinct to climb, to be in his arms. She found herself retreating into silence, though, the way a flower closes up as night falls, when a bad mood made him storm and fret. One of the worst times he was annoyed like this was on one occasion concerning her pony Blackie. Jacqueline had to admit to herself that his outburst was all her own fault. She, as well as Blackie, had let Daddy down, because she couldn't be the perfect rider Teddy expected her to be. After all, her father could sit on a snorting animal and even pull it back to earth when it reared those big hooves liked saucers into the sky. She couldn't even get her pony to leave the stable.

Blackie had been a present to Jacqueline for her fourth birthday. Even though her father said the diminutive creature was a perfect size for a little girl, and very docile, she thought she was too far away from the ground when she was lifted onto his back. Blackie was her enemy too, determined to create mischief and only pretending to behave. She could see this, glimmering in his crafty eyes. Blackie lived in a stables at the back of the hotel. He often had the company of other horses that were the colour of liquid toffee and swished about on long legs and swung tails in the air that were like glistening threads, but he was never one of them. She imagined that, seated on one of those coppery beauties, she would be their charge and be ferried about without effort, as if her mount had wings. Instead she had sullen Blackie.

Her father's disappointment with her relationship with Blackie went back to the day Teddy had abandoned his efforts to give Jacqueline her first riding lesson. It was before Kitty told her she was planning to leave, and they could still be pals together. Jacqueline had been cajoled to sit on her knee on a bench out the back, promising her a sweet, but the sound of her father's voice, like deep bells coming in from farther down the yard, summoning her to him, were far more compelling, and she wriggled off. At the same time, she spotted Ken Doyle, the new bar-boy. He'd swung out through a side door with a crate for the bottling shed, and stopped to talk to Kitty. It was embarrassing to be seen being treated like a baby, and she raced forward.

On her way out to her father, Jacqueline passed by a number of curiosities she would have liked to delay to inspect, if she had had the time. The open door to the coffin-making loft was one of them. As well as running a hotel and doing other things, like having a butcher's stall, Teddy had an undertaking business. If Jacqueline could have read, she would have the seen the words *T. T. Clancy Undertaker* in powerful black lettering on each of a neat pile of cards stacked on a shelf close to a hall-stand in the lobby of the Avalon Hotel, but they were a bit high up for her to retrieve, or even attempt to do so. Gazing up at the entry to the loft, Jacqueline recalled her impression of these doors before, as sucking in light. It was because once, although she was forbidden, she had been drawn through them, to that airy space inside.

Despite her need to hurry, Jacqueline put a foot on the first loft step. On her previous occasion here, she had had an urge to climb a pile of thick lengths of honey-coloured wood piled up against a low wall inside. It would be lovely to do so again. The creamy planks had gathered the day-brightness of the trees they once were into themselves: she had seen how they glowed, as if beaming that light out. They emitted a sharp and satisfying smell that said, 'Sit on me,' when she bent close. As soon as she ventured on them, though, they made an alarming groaning sound, and the end of one plank swung out. Two men she knew as Ger and Andy were sawing a long piece of wood and then using a plane on it, so that chips flew about like confetti. They were whistling as if they were at home, and she had swung her arms to their tune.

'We'll need a big one this time for ten-tonne Tess.' Ger paused in his melodious air. He put his saw down and stretched. 'We'll be lucky to get her out the door.'

'The worms will have right feedin' on her. God rest her soul.' Andy nodded. 'She won't be sneaking into the hotel bar for a shot of firewater any more.'

'She'll be lucky so, if she gets into the hot-spot down under,' Ger was winking. 'Give us a quick one, auld Nick, or you'll feel the weight of Bridie's stick.' He waved a thin piece of wood in the air, and Andy picked up another slat, and they began to fence and leap about. Her father was probably afraid that a sliver of the golden wood would fly into her eye and lodge there, and stop her from seeing. It was the reason she wasn't allowed to be in such a jolly place, Jacqueline decided.

Reluctantly taking her foot from the loft steps, Jacqueline skipped on towards the stables. By the time she reached them, Blackie was out in the yard, and when she closed the stable half-door — because Teddy said he didn't want the lazy good-for-nothing to have the opportunity to go back in there rather than do what he was bought for — she got a musty smell. It was straw and horse-wee and dung all mixed up in one, she knew, and wrinkled her nose. Still, there was an eerie sensation lingering in her mind, she had got when she'd looked into the pony's home. There had been a sense that although the small mare had vacated the stable, she was somehow still there. The walls emanated a faint warmth, and the straw had her shape where she'd slept. She had left the invisible part of herself to come back to later, Jacqueline decided.

A spider that clung to a web, like a circus girl who had fallen into a safety net, afforded Jacqueline more distraction. She raised the shadow of a twig over its head.

'Come on dear. We haven't all day. I have to see a man about a dog,' her father said cheerfully. He lifted her up in the air and deposited her on the saddle he'd strapped onto Blackie's back, as if she was no weight at all. It was hard and uncomfortable, and when she moved her legs at either side, her skin began to itch. Soon she knew there would be red patches.

'It hurts. Mammy said I wasn't to get up on the pony unless I had my jodhpurs on, or else I'd get a rash,' she said.

'Your mother knows everything. One of these days she'll find the power to make us live forever,' Teddy replied cheerfully. He hit the pony on the rump and Blackie shifted sideways. Jacqueline jerked at the reins and Blackie turned its head and glared up at her with one devil eye. It shuffled forward.

'There's a phone-call for you inside, boss,' Ken hollered from the gate of the hotel back garden, and Jacqueline reddened at his presence.

'Don't budge. I'll be back in a minute. I'll make a horse-woman of you yet.' Teddy ran off, leaving her high and dry, for Ken to comment on, with Kitty, later.

Blackie is my enemy, Jacqueline thought when, although not allowed to, she sucked her thumb in bed that evening. She could tell nobody she was being made to do what she didn't want to. Her sister tossed in the other bed and began to snore. The spirit of Blackie had been nicer; the part of her she'd left behind in the stable. It was like the warm part in the bed when all the children were tucked in with Mammy, and her father had to get up. A scarlet toy fire-engine that Tim, Susanna's twin brother, had been playing with, poked out from under the bed. She could be a heroine instead of a good horse-woman, and save everybody if the hotel went on fire, like the house across the road. That would make Teddy proud of her, she thought.

Chapter Six

If Jacqueline and Blackie were having a hard time hitting it off, she knew she could trust Floppy, her dog, with her life, the beleaguered girl decided. The dog's real name was 'Rufus', but although her parents didn't realise that the animal had no sense about it of being a Rufus from the day it was first given to her, they continued to call it by that unsuitable name. Jacqueline herself called her dog 'Floppy', because it had long ears that made her laugh when they flapped about.

Jacqueline remembered the first time she saw the puppy. It was in the yard of her father's old home, Templederry Castle. They arrived at the castle haggard first, before visiting the old farmhouse and its new owner, Pauline Fitzmaurice, because Teddy knew where the litter was, snug and cozy on a bundle of straw in one of the old sheds. Jacqueline had to edge past him to gaze down. 'Pick out the one you like,' Teddy suggested from the shed door. The pups all seemed to belong in a bunch, because they were snuggled up to one another as if they were stuck together with glue. When she prised Floppy away and put him standing on his own, he shivered. She stepped back from him and called him, but he didn't come running, like in the stories Teddy read to her. Then she didn't know whether the puppy wanted to be her friend or not. He peed on her arm when she picked him up, and the wet got rubbed back into his silken hair and made it thin and stringy. After that, he licked her face as if she was a lollipop, which meant they were going to stay together forever and be best friends.

'She can have the whole bloody lot. I've no use for them,' Pauline Fitzmaurice laughed with the same snorting sound a horse makes when Teddy knocked on the front door later and a happy Jacqueline thrust the puppy she'd picked out forward, making Pauline grunt. The house where Teddy used to live went so far up a winding stairs when you were inside, Jacqueline was afraid that, if she climbed to the topmost room, she might have gone too far up to be able to come down, or even too far to be capable of finding her way back. With the help of her puppy, though, it would be different. Jacqueline eyed the stairs at the same time, standing on tiptoe.

'You're a hoot, Pauline. Thanks anyway. One pup will be hard enough to manage,' Teddy said, and Jacqueline pulled her pet close. Teddy wasn't to know she would, if she could, take all the pups, because she had bent down and hugged the others when she'd separated out Floppy, when they were in the shed. She'd promised as well to be back to say hello to them in case they were lonely for their tiny brother. It was impossible to stand still, and since the stairs offered an escape, she gripped Floppy and began to climb. Rounding onto the first landing, leaving the others behind, Jacqueline imagined that the pup was watching everything. As soon as he met his brothers and sisters again, he would talk to them in doggy language about what he had seen. Reaching the second flight of stairs, she almost turned back. She thought about Blackie, always reluctant to leave her stable. She and Floppy understood each other, but Blackie never showed he cared. One day, though, she would be the boss of the pony, because in his pony-head, he would suddenly realise that all she really wanted to do was please Teddy.

Returning to the hotel in the car from Templederry, Floppy had started to whimper. 'Something is wrong with Rufus. He won't stop crying. I think he's lonely and wants to go home,' she said from the back seat. Tom, who was sitting in the front with Teddy, began to titter. He said that was because she was a girl, and all girls are cry-babies. Jacqueline knew he didn't mean it, and that he just wanted to stop a row starting, in case Teddy got annoyed with her for complaining.

'We can let her out here and let her make her own way home, if you like. Dogs have an unerring sense of direction. Would you like that, Jacqueline?' her father joked instead. His head darted around to look at her, and his eyes were wild, with dark spots.

'He'd get killed. Anyway, he's mine and nobody else's,' Jacqueline declared. She had a sensation then of being torn from her own brothers and sisters and her mother, as though some invisible hand had cupped her round and lifted her out.

Some time after that, in a funny way it was Floppy, and not Blackie, her pony, who got her into trouble. It was ages after getting Floppy, and Teddy's sister, Auntie Mina, had come to live with them. Jacqueline hadn't been good, and had jumped off Blackie in the middle of a lesson. It was that further point in time too, when she really would have wished to do something to please Teddy, because he didn't look very well, but instead her dog had come barking at the pony's heels. Teddy's face had turned a shade of purple. She knew she was in serious trouble because her Auntie Mina, lifting her off Blackie, had told her she was not to bother her father, because Teddy's life hung by a thread. What her aunt really meant was, it would be Jacqueline's fault if her father died.

The last thing Jacqueline had on her mind in the car now, was the possibility of somebody coming to live with them. Lifting Floppy to her face, the pup bit her finger. She saw the pincer-marks of a lobster before she could put him down.

Chapter Seven

Jacqueline was five in September 1954, and that month she started school. Sister Clements, the nun who was in charge of her class, loved her. Jacqueline loved Sister Clements too. She wore all black because she was a nun, but Jacqueline could see her sandaled feet protruding underneath, with toes that had big bumps on them, and she knew that Sister Clements was just a person in disguise. Sometimes her long black dress had a coat of white powder shaken on it. Jacqueline realised it was chalk-dust, and often this new schoolgirl thought of her teacher as somebody who had had flour shaken all over her, like the big table in the hotel kitchen during bread-making. That made her love Sister Clements even more. It showed she could be given out to as well as any child for making a mess of herself, and that meant she was as good as being one of them. Jacqueline liked her first days at school straight away, because Sister Clements told her class that they were there to play, most of the time. Sister Clements was old, but she was going to teach for a long time more, please God, she announced in the first week, and Jacqueline was glad, because the nun gave hugs and sometimes had sweets for the children, and said they must be a secret between her and them. They played with sand in a long wooden box and they built houses with toy blocks. Sometimes they ran around the floor and Sister Clements laughed.

In the mornings in the hotel, Teddy and Imelda fussed about so much, to make sure their daughter got to school on time, that Jacqueline wanted to put her hands to her ears. It wasn't her fault that breakfast took so long to swallow down. Most of the time she didn't feel like eating it at all, as if there was a plate of stones on the table, not toast. At this juncture, her parents had to decide which one of them was free to bring her to the school gates, where all the children streamed towards the school buildings, blocking her way, and pushing and calling. In the end it nearly always fell to Teddy, and he would raise her in the air and throw her towards the ceiling, saying, 'Come on, sport. Time to put the reins on. Maybe you can have a day off this week, if you're a good girl.' And Imelda would say in answer, 'Don't be giving the girl ideas about free days. We don't want another dum-dum like her Daddy on our hands,' and kiss him on the cheek and say, 'Sorry, dear,' and laugh. Teddy was right, though, because it wasn't nice to have to be in one room and not know what a grown-up was going to order you to do, for hours on end. Everybody at the hotel said she was spoilt and always got her own way. In school, nobody knew how important she was, at all. After a while, Jacqueline realised that however hard it was to be in school, especially when a nun with a face that looked carved out of a stone came to take over from Sister Clements, sooner or later she would get home. There would be Imelda with soft lips curving up, in a welcome-back smile.

Chapter Eight

One day Jacqueline told Kitty to get out of her way when Kitty blocked her from going on the stairs because it was her bedtime and she wasn't allowed out. Jacqueline said she hated her and that Kitty couldn't tell her how to behave, because the hotel was her Daddy's, and that meant she could do whatever she liked. Then Kitty said she hoped she would never have a child as bold as Jacqueline, and that she was very spoilt, but she let her race past. Jacqueline knew that Kitty was the one who was wrong, because she wasn't a bad girl, just somebody who enjoyed very much doing what she liked. There was no proper reason why she shouldn't be allowed to do it.

'You can't be going out on the street at all hours. The bogey-man will get you,' Kitty had shouted after her. When Jacqueline looked back at her from the door of the hotel, she decided that Kitty looked like a doll with a white face she could stand up to as much as she liked, because dolls can't fight back. Even so, she only went down as far as Walsh's shop window when she did go out onto the street, because something might emerge from a doorway to prevent her getting home, and there were already too many dark alcoves between the hotel and the shop. She didn't know what it could be, but the shadows in doorways were thick and deep. A tall thin creature with long arms could be pressed into such grayness, and when it reached out to grab her in, she would be too frightened to fight back.

Although she was only five, Jacqueline was sure she already knew what things suited her to be a part of, and what didn't. She hated being told what to do. For instance, she didn't like having to hold the handle of the pram when Nurse was bringing her twin brother and sister, Tim and Susanna, out for a walk. She also knew that if she said 'No,' often enough, Nurse would give up. 'We must dress the two girls the same,' Imelda said one day, and had mustard-coloured coats with brown velvet collars made by a dressmaker for Susanna and herself. Right from the start, when she was being fitted, and felt the roughness of the dark yellow tweed against her skin, Jacqueline complained about being imposed upon. She had to do what her mother told her, of course. I'm not just something to be dressed up and made look pretty, she stormed inside. Just to show what she meant, when her sister held her little hand up to walk with her, she pushed it away.

Jacqueline loved her world of the town. It had vast boundaries, the full extent of which she had yet to explore. Of course Teddy knew every inch of it, and so it would always be safe to wander round in. She could have adventures and make up games, but best of all she would always be free. Jacqueline was not quite sure she could describe what 'free' meant in words, but a bird wouldn't be able to explain the beauty of being able to dart about hither and thither in the air, wherever the fancy took it, either.

'What does the bogeyman look like?' she said to her father one evening when Imelda had shoved Teddy gently in the door of her bedroom, saying that he shouldn't be so busy that he wouldn't kiss his daughters goodnight. Jacqueline clung to his hand to stop him from getting away.

'He's got big teeth. He lives under the stairs and he eats up little girls who don't behave themselves and go to sleep when they're told,' Teddy laughed.

Later on, Jacqueline wondered was it because she didn't listen to Kitty — something her father would have been annoyed about — that not a long time after she had asked that question, Teddy didn't laugh much at all.

Chapter Nine

The smell of Teddy's butcher's stall sometimes became a large invisible lump in Jacqueline's throat and made her want to get sick. It was a smell that, once you stepped inside the shop, became part of the air you breathed. Even when she left, it seemed to linger, as if she was surrounded by its leftover trail. The butcher's stall was next door to the hotel. It had its own glass door, usually ajar, and shining plate-glass windows. If she stood on tiptoe, she could usually peer through the windows. Inside there was a counter before which people stood, and behind the counter, as much as the shine of the windows permitted, she could see a chopping table that was really four legs and a block of wood that no cup or saucer would ever balance on, it was worn into such a hollow in the middle.

Barely discernible as well, so caught up in their own world that she might as well not exist, the figures of Teddy and Peader, his right-hand man, as he called him, danced, or stood about. The window held its own trophies, because hanging from hooks to create the sense of a curtain coming halfway down the pane, a line of marbled meat sides met her gaze. She knew that, if she touched them, they would be cold and lifeless.

Jacqueline was forbidden to go into the shop. 'It's no place to have children running around. There are too many sharp knives about. It would only take a split-second for a finger to be sliced off, or a hook to go into somebody's arm,' her father had complained on a day when Imelda had to temporarily leave her in his care. 'It's hard enough to keep everything ship-shape without adding distractions,' he grumbled on.

'Just for once. I could leave her with Nurse, but the twins are kicking up. Besides, there's nobody as good as her Daddy to keep an eye on a little girl. She'll be perfectly safe,' Imelda had wheedled. Hoisted beyond the barrier of the counter, like a sailor coming on board, Jacqueline stood uncertainly on the sawdust-covered floor. She would have to be ready to dodge at any moment, because pointed blades, like swords, were flashing. Sometimes a cleaver was raised high in the air, and came swiftly, heavily down. Hooks were emptied of those suffering carcasses, and filled again.

'I'm Berlington Bertie, I rise at ten thirty, I walk down the Strand with my gloves in my hand,' her father sang. Sometimes Teddy's face puckered in thought when he looked at her, as if he had forgotten that she was there. When she trailed after him to the cold-room and a blast of icy air met her as the door swung open, he invited her inside.

'Such is life, here one day, gone the next, but these unfortunates keep the wolf from the door all the same,' he said, hoisting a carcass down from a steel rail. The interior was dim. When Teddy moved into it, the hanging bodies hid him. She shivered.

'Hurry up, Daddy. I'm getting cold,' she called weakly. He had disappeared. If she left and called Peadar, the door might swing closed. Those upside-down bodies were more like the real thing than the half-ones in the stall, because they hung from their legs and had heads.

'I'm Berlington Bert, I haven't a shirt, but my people are well off, you know,' her father sang from deep in the bowels of the cold-room, submerged in the depths, as if his ship had really gone down and it was his ghost that rang out the merry tune.

'Daddy, I can't see you. I want to do a wee-wee,' Jacqueline called out. Her breath created a little fog in the air, which Teddy would surely notice.

'I'll close the door of the cold-room for you, boss,' she heard Peadar call out, and felt warmth seep from her body, as if she had been forced to remain inside, forever.

As well as the butcher's stall, Jacqueline didn't like car journeys too much. Being in the back of the car when Teddy was driving made her feel as if she was too full of food, as if it was churning about inside. Then her mouth would fill up with spit and she would want to get sick She could sit in state like a princess, perched up on the seat when Imelda was driving though, and be perfectly all right.

Imelda said it was because Teddy was a bad driver. He drove fast and put his foot on the brake too much, making his daughter jerk forward. 'There's no point in dilly-dallying. A car journey is to get from A to B, not to admire the scenery,' Teddy would say. Then he would put on a funny face, as if he had eaten a sour orange, making her mother smile. The pot-bellied appearance of a cow stepping out from a gateway to obstruct their passage, or a dog barking at the car, would cause her to laugh also, as if the world was a big comedy show. That was when Jacqueline, from her back seat, saw Teddy grip the steering wheel and murmur, 'Love you always,' and lean across and kiss her mother on the lips, so that the forgotten car headed for a ditch.

When Imelda was driving, she sang in the car as they sailed along, and her words, and the melody, floated in the air over Jacqueline's head, as though sound was a clear wave. In the back seat, washed over by song, Jacqueline saw how Imelda's hair, lifted out in a breeze blowing in, became mermaid locks. The family car had another use, in her life, because she could play hide-and-go-seek with Tom, crouching down in the boot, snuggling up in the semi-darkness as if she could stay that way forever.

The night, shortly after Auntie Mina had arrived, Teddy had stood in darkness in her bedroom doorway and said he was cursed because Imelda was gone and it was his own fault; too many children had sucked her dry, it was impossible to lie still, like she did with Tom in the murky boot. As if it was meant to be, she herself had suddenly woken up and seen Teddy. To help her go back to sleep, she would think of something good, and started to replay her fourth birthday, now so long ago, she'd decided. The celebration had taken place in the hotel dining room, the big one with all the tables and chairs, and it had been the best day in her life, until the trouble started. White cloths like sheets were spread along the tables, and bowls and plates of colourful food made the place look like heaven. There was the beginning of the party she didn't like, because they had to eat sandwiches she thought tasted as dry as paper in her mouth. But then they had blancmange that slithered satisfyingly down your throat, and milky melting ice cream.

'Nothing is too much for my little girl,' Imelda had boasted, and invited half the town's children. In the beginning, Bartholomew, the hotel waiter, had served them at the tables. All the children had climbed onto seats, to be able to reach for the food spread along the tables brought together in neat rows, looking like the boards that stretched whitely in the undertaker's shop.

Tom said it was all the fault of the gangs in the town when the disturbance began, but Jacqueline saw him throw the first bun. In no time, it seemed, groups of children were barricaded under the tables and Teddy had to be called to restore order. The tablecloths had been pulled down over the edges of the tables to create hiding places for the different factions, and food was pelted out by lifting up the corners and taking aim. Jacqueline heard calls and cries of laughter fill the air. Bodies of children she didn't know darted about until somebody shouted, 'Got you in the back, pal,' and they dropped dead. Her hair was pulled, and she grabbed somebody

31

back, and they rolled about. Tom said this was real fun, that it wasn't a sissy's party, and she had to agree. It was a thrill to be part of a bigger-boys' game.

Teddy's face was white when he stood in her doorway that night shortly after Mina arrived, like somebody from a cold-room. At the same time, she'd heard Imelda's voice calling. It seemed to be a voice from a dream. Somebody put a light on in the passageway outside. It shone above Teddy's head like the star of Bethlehem on their Christmas crib.

Chapter Ten

It was the morning when Jacqueline was to be present at the setting out from Tooradulla, of her first foxhound hunt. A cloud of unease had gathered inside her, because if Tom was already dressed and ready to go, Jacqueline was sure she wouldn't be able to get Blackie out onto the street. That was, until Imelda explained that she would stay alongside them and make certain the sulky thing behaved. If it tried to be headstrong and turn back, that was good, Jacqueline decided, because her mother would note the bad habit and put manners on Blackie. On the other hand, as soon as they reached the starting-point at the crossroads where the hunt was to begin, the pony would have become used to the routine, and the fact that Jacqueline didn't know how to ride would be forgotten about.

Early that morning, when Imelda came into the bedroom, especially to dress her in her hunting outfit, the little girl didn't like what she had to put on. Her mother's presence was fortunate in one way, because the lobster was back, scratching on the wardrobe door to get out. Maybe her old pals Betty and Lou would get it to stop. Jacqueline loved her friends, just as much as anyone in her life.

'Introduce me to your invisible friends,' Mamma had said about them once. But there was a hurry to get dressed now, and this was no time to talk about them.

Toys lay scattered, and Imelda cleared a space so that she could kneel down. Jacqueline's new kitchen set she'd got as a present, with a press and sink and taps, and a table and chairs for her friends Betty and Lou to sit at, was calling out to be played with. Expressive pleading eyes her mother didn't seem to see, gazed and waited for everything to begin, and she was being forced to shut her pals off. Milky-white light from the window came into the bedroom, highlighting a doll's house. When Jacqueline looked towards it, her friends Lou and Betty had moved to there. They were ignoring her, climbing the stairs of her playhouse, as good as a real building, and then arriving in a bedroom, sticking their heads out a window and laughing and chatting, as if it was the happiest thing in the world to be beginning a day in your own place.

'You'll be the smartest and best-dressed in the hunt today. Now stand still while I put these on,' Imelda enthused. Her new jodhpurs were being held out towards Jacqueline, and she leaned into her mother and put one foot in. A sweet smell came from Imelda. It was like the scent when bending down to a rose in the hotel garden, but stronger, more like being in a room of roses, Jacqueline decided. She sniffled, and a trickle of thin mucus emerged from her nose.

'*Singing willow, tit willow, tit willow,*' her mother trilled, as if she was a bird, and her fingers flew about, buttoning Jacqueline in. 'Cheer up, shoulders back, and wave at the world. Here's a treat for sore eyes,' she said gaily, and spun Jacqueline around. She was lifted and brought to a mirror in the bedroom, and made to look in. The child that was her gazed back and squirmed.

'Give me a kiss and say, thank you, Mammy,' Imelda said, and made a funny bow.

'I don't want to wear a hard-hat. My jacket is itchy and I can't walk because my knees can't bend.' Jacqueline surveyed herself again. A noise came from Betty and Lou's big airy house in the sun-patch. The pair were shifting a bed about, deciding where it should be placed.

'This can be your bedroom from now on, Lou,' Betty declared. 'There's enough room for you and Floppy, and you can keep as many toys as you want to. You can all sleep in the bed together.'

'And can we have ice cream for breakfast?' Lou asked. Jacqueline saw Betty put her hands together and frown, as if to say, 'no'.

'Of course,' she said then, promptly. 'But not Floppy. He'd prefer a bone.'

'You'll be the death of me yet. Why can't you be a good dear for Mammy, just for one day. About to join in their conversation, Jacqueline heard her mother sigh. 'Teddy and I love you very much, remember. Perhaps that might make you behave.' She stood beside the girl in the mirror, and Jacqueline took them in.

'When I grow up, you won't be dead, like you said, and I'll invite you to come and live in my house. If you like lobster, I can cook it.' Jacqueline felt hot tears coming, because just this moment the red creature had jumped from the opened wardrobe and scurried under the bed. She noted too how Betty was staring out her window with binoculars like Teddydow with binoculars like Teddy's, only these were small toy ones.

'You're right, nobody is going to die in this house,' Imelda laughed. This time, Teddy arrived at the door in a flurry of movement and swept Jacqueline up on his shoulders, making her bend her head to get back out, as though she'd suddenly grown tall and it was the hotel that was a doll's house, not the one on the floor.

Andy, who worked in the undertaker's, led Blackie forward with Jacqueline perched on her back, when it was time to go. They were heading for where the hunt was gathering, in the centre of the town. She was deposited on the edges. Any minute now, Blackie could turn round and go back to the stables, but the pony seemed to be rooted to the spot. Horses towered round Jacqueline, like giants, and tossed their heads and snorted little beads of airborne clear liquid. They pawed at the ground and bared big teeth, or called out triumphantly. On top of their shifting backs, black-coated figures rested; not see-through and insubstantial like Betty and Lou, but more like Tom's tin soldiers, who could rise to deeds of daring and courage and make their mounts always comply. Soon she saw that Blackie was swept up by the contagion, as though she'd forgotten that Jacqueline couldn't ride. In the middle of the pack, her father's scarlet-coated figure cried out imperious commands. A horn was blown, like announcing a death sentence, and the pack moved forward. Although Blackie was the smallest horse there, the ground was still far below, Jacqueline decided as she stepped along, keeping abreast of the other clattering animals. Imelda seemed to have forgotten that she was only a child, and that Blackie might suddenly discover its true nature and take off with the other horses, because her mother had disappeared into the throng.

The hunt reached a crossroads at the outskirts of Tooradulla. Nothing was familiar now, Jacqueline decided. This was not a child's game, and yet the gauntlet had been thrown down. She had to prove she could be brave. Green fields and forbidding-looking hedges awaited the fray. Teddy approached, wheeling round her. His whip cracked in the air like a circus-master's. 'Remember what I told you. Keep the reins loose and sit back into your seat,' he boomed, and his eyes flashed.

'I don't want to go on the hunt any further. I'm scared,' Jacqueline found herself saying. She was a failure and she knew it, and all around her a hush seemed to develop and show up her words. Teddy flung an annoyed hand in the air. Tom, whom she now saw had been riding alongside Imelda, brought his obedient mount alongside Blackie, and leaned across to take her rein.

'Jacqueline wants to go home. Don't be mad at her, Daddy, she's only a little girl,' he said bravely, but Jacqueline wished he had stayed away. Despite everything, her courage might have surfaced at the last minute, and she pouted.

'There'll be no gallop for you today. It looks as if it's going to rain anyway. Besides, you've cut a great dash. Better luck the next time,' Imelda said, appearing beside her like a saving angel, but Teddy had other ideas.

'The girl is spoiled. It's only a field to start with, and then Andy will bring her back. She'll be good for nothing because you keep giving in to her. Make her stay. Even if she does fall off, she'll be near the ground,' he stormed. Horses milled. The pack of foxhounds, which had streamed out in front, set up a continuous yapping. The horn blared, and Teddy's big chestnut sidestepped.

'Don't leave, Imelda. You know how you love the chase. It's your only opportunity for God-knows-how-long.' He bent towards Jacqueline's mother and patted her tummy.

'None of this gloom and doom about the end of my hunting days,' she said, pushing him off, and laughing. 'Such nonsense won't bag a fox's tail. Besides, I'm not ready to hang up my spurs yet.' Her friendly horse nodded in agreement. Teddy doffed his cap and clattered away.

'I'm sorry, Mammy,' Jacqueline said as they turned for home. Even so, for a few minutes she'd have Imelda for herself.

Betty and Lou had pulled the blinds down when she next visited her bedroom. She crept in, hoping they hadn't missed her. They must have travelled up the bedposts of her single bed, because they were sitting on her pillow. 'I think it's time to cook dinner. After that, we can go for a drive and have a picnic by the lake,' Betty said. She slid down the pillow, laughing, and then climbed back up it, and Lou did the same.

'I'll drive the car, and if we see any hunt or horses, we'll wait until they've passed, and wave,' Lou said. She built a swing out of nothing on the pillow and began to kick vigorously up and down, so that Jacqueline noted a wind lift her skirt and heard her laugh.

'We'll all eat and go to the lake together,' she said. 'Dinner is strawberry jelly and cream,' Jacqueline declared, and soon began to feel better. When they met the hunt on the way to their picnic, it would be small, like a thin inconsequential stream of black passing before their bright car, she knew.

The thought of the jelly reminded her of Teddy's scarlet coat. Should she have to wear a coat as heavy as that, she'd be too tired to eat anything.

If it was thrown on her shoulders, there was always Imelda about, to remove the stone-weight.

Chapter Eleven

Summer was in full swing, and Jacqueline and her brothers and sisters were being brought on holidays to one of the Aran Islands. Nurse Dell was coming with them. Teddy and Imelda would appear towards the end of their stay, and so Jacqueline felt quite alone, the way Heidi in her story-book must have done, when she moved from her neat home cocooned in a Swiss valley, as cosy as an underground warren, to a cross grandfather's shack that clung to a mountainside, though bathed in clear blue light.

'I promise I'll join you in a few days. Really the hotel is very busy at the moment, otherwise nothing would keep us away from Inis Oirr. I can hear the creamy sands calling,' Jacqueline had heard her mother declare to Nurse Dell before she left. They had been bundled onto a train. Teddy had filled up a carriage with books and cases, cramming seats to the top. They had had a feast on the train to Galway; Jacqueline, despite her fastidiousness about food, had been forced to eat because she was hungry. Outside, scenes of pop-up houses and mildly surprised cows flitted past the carriage windows, and soon the ship that would carry them across the water came into view, embedded in licking waves but big enough to run around on when they'd get on board, ready to swing out to sea.

'They were in charge because they were explorers,' Tom announced, the minute they stepped onto the deck. 'Being on board meant that they were cut off from the Old World to seek new lands.'

The first thing that Jacqueline noticed when they moved away from people and cars standing on the quayside, growing as small as the toys she played with, was that the tap-tapping sound of waves as they played against the high curved sides of their ocean-carriage, was gone. Now the creaking craft was the weaker thing, trusting the sea, but surrounded as far as the eye could see by huge and glossy mermaid-filled waves.

Jacqueline didn't mind saying goodbye to the laughing creatures of the sea when their ship slipped into harbour, far away now from that sturdy stone-wall of the city pier they had left behind, because their new adventure was only beginning. She announced this to Tom, since a rope from the boat had been tied to an enormous peg on this new quay. Men had jumped off and were now reaching towards the children, to swing them from the deck.

'Mammy put me in charge. You're to do everything Nurse Dell tells you, otherwise I've to report back. It doesn't matter if we do daring things together, so long as you're with me,' Tom gasped, then a smell of fish and salt in the wind trapped her, and she was in mid-air. She saw the gap between the ship's side and the grey pier widen, enough to let a whale's eye wink hello to her from the sea underneath, and she had landed.

A tree bent by the wind guarded her holiday house when they arrived, and an emerald field sloped down towards the shore. 'You have to eat everything you're told, and drink warm milk straight from the cow, when you have a meal here. It doesn't matter whether you like it or not. It's the same for everyone,' her cousin Róisín declared. Róisín had hair as straggly as Blackie's mane, and her eyes were piercing like a witch's. When Jacqueline was at home, she didn't eat a lot of things, and although Mamma gave out to her, she never made her do anything like this, and Jacqueline could feel tears rising to her eyes.

'Holidays are different. You're only able to tell me what to do because I'm in your place. I'm not going to be left here alone forever,' she said back. At the same time, there was a clap of thunder and the tree bent down before the kitchen window, as if it would push inside.

Jacqueline and Róisín and her other cousin, Coleman, went down to the harbour, to be there when Teddy and Imelda were due in, a few days later. In the beginning, she thought that the ship that was pointed out as a dot on the horizon was really a rock, or that whale whose giant eye had invited her to play when she had been hoisted onto dry land on her arrival. There was great excitement as the ship got nearer and she saw she'd been wrong.

On the pier, her cousins acted as if they owned the place, playing tag with their dog Bran, and only remembering at the last minute to ask Jacqueline to join in. When she found Coleman crouched behind a pile of fishing baskets for lobsters, he pulled her near and put his finger to his lips to tell her to be quiet. A salty smell came from the baskets, and although she fought against the hard press of his fingers digging into her skin like claws, and squirmed away from his hand pressed on her mouth to keep it closed, she thrilled at her own strength. His thick eyelashes were as plentiful as straw on the edge of a thatched roof, and then the shadow of the ship swept over the quay, and Imelda emerged from its depths.

'Mammy won't know I'm here if you don't let me go,' Jacqueline said, giving an almighty last push to wriggle from her cousin's grasp. Lucky Imelda had come to the rescue, she thought, because Coleman was just about to win out, and she raced away.

'Come to Mamma, darling,' Imelda called out when she stepped from the ship onto the quayside, and Jacqueline leaped into her arms. Next time she'd choose to stay with Coleman, Jacqueline thought, hugging her mother tight. Sooner or later, she'd be able to beat him in a fight.

'I hate this island. I want to go home with you, Mammy. Don't ever leave me on my own again,' she found herself wailing. A fierce gust of wind tore her from Imelda's arms, and then Bran came barking between them.

'No more whimpering. I thought you'd be glad to see me,' her mother scolded. Some weeks after that, in different circumstances, when the scene returned to her mind in full force, Jacqueline was sorry she hadn't agreed. Out of the corner of her eye, she saw a lobster had escaped, and had paused beside the basket to capture her in a beady gaze.

Chapter Twelve

Mamma was missing for some time before Jacqueline found herself asking where she was. Although they were back from their holidays for what seemed ages, some sand had become deposited at the bottom of her wardrobe, and she wanted to show her. She found it there when she was emptying the hidden depths, to find a missing chair from her doll's-house dining-room set. Suddenly she was back on her island holiday. The splash of green where the house stood stretched before her, dipping towards distant waves. Only a thin line of sea had been visible from her window, but Jacqueline knew when she got nearer that it would be powerful and calling out, as gay-looking as a woman who wants you to leap into her arms to play.

'Isn't it wonderful? And look how it takes its ease in fine weather, pale as the face of the moon,' Imelda had exclaimed when she and Jacqueline had made their way down to the shore for a picnic. Far away from them, a collection of horses with riders like dots had set out to cross a limitless smooth beach, like soundless spidery things scurrying in a line. For a moment Jacqueline imagined herself on one of them, as if the unreality of their appearance suggested they flew on wings.

'I'm going to stay here all day and build sandcastles,' she said to her mother.

'Dig a hole deep enough to bury yourself in, and I'll cover you with sand. The others will think the rest of your body has been cut off, that you're only a head,' her mother laughed, and they began to excavate a hole in a frenzy of jerky movements. Flurries of sand flew about them like gritty rain, and Jacqueline was sure they were getting nearer to the centre of the earth.

Kitty was the first person Jacqueline met when she set out to find her mother, to show her the sand. The maid hadn't gone to Dublin yet, because she'd spent money she shouldn't have on make-up and cigarettes, she'd explained to Jacqueline. Even so, the little girl had seen a suitcase on top of an old press in the back-kitchen, that had never been there before.

Jacqueline had rubbed her fingers in the gritty particles of sand to get the feel of it, and patches still clung to her warm palms. 'I want to tell Mammy about something I found,' she said, opening her hands for Kitty to see. 'She loves the sea and she likes to hear anything about it. Once she told me a story about a kingdom of fishes under the waves. It is a place where there are palaces made of coral, with cockles for doors and seaweed gardens. The story is about a girl called Shelly who used to peep at humans and then fell in love with a boy named "Art", and she had to find a way to join him.' Jacqueline rambled on. She had to keep talking because Kitty's cheeks burned red, as if somebody had given her slaps.

'Your Auntie Mina is coming to mind you in a few days. It's a big surprise, because your mother has gone away on holidays. If Mina Clancy is looking after the hotel, we'll all have to look out. I can't stay chatting idly. There's work to be done.' Kitty rushed her words together. She sidled away. It was fortunate for Jacqueline — because she didn't know what to say next — that she caught sight of Betty and Lou just then. They had arrived beside Kitty's feet in their red car. It was one of Tom's cars without a roof, and they had two pieces of luggage thrown onto the back seat.

'Hop in there, Jacqueline,' they chorused.

'We're off to the beach to build sandcastles,' Lou explained. 'We're taking a boat, and if we see a magical land where a pathway winds up to a castle on a high hill, we'll stop off. Teddy is probably there with his binoculars peering out a window. We heard him say yesterday that Imelda had been stolen from him, and that he couldn't live without her.

Jacqueline couldn't answer Betty and Lou straight away, because Kitty had started to stroke her hair. Any minute now she would yank it painfully, the way she had before.

Chapter Thirteen

Nurse Dell usually spent her time taking care of the twins, wheeling them along in their big pram, but today she was going to look after her, Jacqueline found out, the morning after she'd discovered the sand. A grey light flooded the bedroom. Yesterday she didn't have to go to school, and now, even better, she was going to get special treats all day long. Although Jacqueline truly loved the hotel, she would welcome a change. All the day before, she and Tom had been left to mind themselves. In the afternoon, Tom took over. She felt quite grown up all the same, because he said she could play with him and his friends. Recently, at the back of the hotel, Teddy had constructed a maze of interlinking wooden pens for his new cattle mart. Tom had invented a game involving them, but because he knew it so well, it was difficult for her to join in. He and his friends took over the pens and scampered on and between the beams with practised ease. Soon they managed to be everywhere, and she found she couldn't keep up.

A smell of cow-dung clung to everything. Magically, the boys seemed to avoid the pats of brown left here and there, and laughed when she complained. She swung onto one of the crossbars and watched, waiting for her cue to enter the chase. But it wasn't enough. They were like bees buzzing about in a rehearsed way in a hive, and they said it was because she was a girl that she was so clumsy and awkward. Even Tom, who was the most graceful of them all, slipping through and over the rough bars like an eel, couldn't take her seriously. She cried and said she would tell Imelda, but Imelda wasn't to be found.

Jacqueline knew that going to Nurse Dell's house was going to be good, because looking across the street during breakfast, it was reminding her of ice cream. The sun had splashed creamy light over that side of the town, and made it look like a row of stuck-to-gether different-shaped yellow ices. The hotel, on the other hand, was sunk in shades of sombre grey. Any minute now, Imelda would appear, because she was playing a game with her, and hiding in one of the hotel rooms.

'I want to say goodbye to Mamma,' she said, pulling away from Nurse Dell, who was fluttering about in the hotel lobby, before they left.

'You won't be able to find Mrs Clancy. She's taken a few days off. Your Daddy told everyone,' Nurse Dell announced. She grabbed Jacqueline's hand back, but the movement had caused a beret perched on the side of her head to slip, and she paused to fix it.

'I want to talk to Daddy.' Jacqueline got to the stairs. Even so, her mind, in secret, was being beset by another thought. She had a feeling that if she searched for Imelda too hard — because unlike Tom and his friends, her mother was playing some sort of adult game she didn't understand — she would find out something that was too hard to take. It was probably true that Imelda had left the hotel for a few days, maybe to go back to the island for a quick visit. It could have been because she needed a break from the children, as she often said. It might also have been because she herself had become impossible to handle; words Kitty sometimes used. Mamma's absence felt like something like a danger sign had been stuck up before her, which said, *Stay away. Keep out.* She knew that if she probed the existence of her mother's absence, there was something about it that would make her cry. Thinking all this now, standing beside Nurse Dell, and about to depart from where Imelda hid, abandoning her to the darkness that was taking over the hotel, like something lurking there with grey jaws and big fangs, Jacqueline had an urge to cry. It was just as well that Betty and Lou put in an appearance right then. Betty took her hand. 'You're my beautiful girl. Amn't I the lucky one to have you in my life? One day you'll make me proud,' she said. There was laughter in her voice, and her eyes beamed like twin suns. 'Don't get upset if I go away for a few days,' she added, and Jacqueline remembered where she'd heard those words before. They were exactly what Imelda had said to her, not so many days previously.

'Is there anybody for a picnic? We'll have iced buns and lemonade, and toffee as sweet as treacle,' Lou called out, before Betty could continue, changing the subject completely. She was sitting in her open-topped car. Her hair was exactly like Imelda's when Jacqueline would sit in the seat, behind her. It had that wispy look of feathery grass lifted by the wind.

'It's too early for a picnic. If I stay in the hotel for a few minutes, I'll be able to speak to Imelda before she goes away forever,' Jacqueline found herself saying. It was too late to stop the game now, though, because Lou had sat into the car and was blowing the horn.

'After the picnic, we'll climb trees and play with our dolls. They'll be good girls and do what they're told, or else we'll give them a slap and make them go to bed early,' she declared. She should run to the red car because Jacqueline heard a cracking sound behind her. The hotel was tearing down through the middle and the monster with grey fangs was coming out. If she went, it was all up to Teddy to stop an attack. The beast towered over her and she clung to a coat-rack.

Chapter Fourteen

Jacqueline had never been in a house at the other side of the street before. 'We'll have high tea and sandwiches and lovely cold milk. You can drink from a glass with a straw.' Nurse Dell lifted Jacqueline's mustard-coloured coat from the hall-stand, ready to leave at last. Jacqueline had often heard Nurse Dell's cross voice, like when she rocked the twins in the pram so hard to get them to sleep, she thought the earth itself would shake, but this time she was the same as somebody who had been awarded a prize, it looked to Jacqueline, because her eyes twinkled. 'You can meet my mother, Josie. I'm always talking about you and your brothers and sisters. This will be a special treat.' Nurse Dell buttoned up tight that tailored coat she so disliked, and squeezed her hand. Voices drifted in from the street. Looking out, Jacqueline saw somebody bless themselves, as if they were passing a church.

'I need to kiss Mamma goodbye before I go,' Jacqueline said, making a final determined effort to stay. A cold wind blew in the hotel door, a wind which had not been there before, and she experienced an ache in the pit of her tummy Imelda would make better. Her toes were hurting her too, which meant that her feet were getting too big for her shoes; and she had an urge to dress up in Mamma's jewellery and put on high heels and see her mother laugh when she paraded around like a miniature beauty queen. 'I want to play with my toys. They might get lonely.'

'I have my old toys you can play with. There are building blocks and snakes and ladders and a big doll I call "Diana". One of her eyes won't close, but she was my dearest friend once.' Nurse Dell bent suddenly and hugged the girl beside her. It really was better to go, Jacqueline began to think, because beyond them, Betty and Lou had set up their picnic. They were on a hill. Trees swayed at their backs, like mops propped against a powder-blue sky. Ladybirds flew about, and there was a path leading down to a well. Lou ran down first, to dip her face towards the cool water and have a drink, and Betty followed. Jacqueline could see the mirror-well they gazed into. Tiny insects and other living things scurried under the surface, but Imelda's face looked up, clear as day.

'I'm ready to leave now. There's nothing wrong with going away for a little while. Only a baby, or a tiny puppy who has to leave their Mammy, gets scared,' Jacqueline said, trembling. She opened the button of the mustard coat and took a deep breath.

'I've found a swing under the trees. Come and see Betty. You can push me, or we'll sit on it together,' she heard Lou call out. She'd run up the path from the well, picking flowers to lay in the centre of the picnic rug, on the way. It was impossible not to join in, the girl decided, even if it meant a long climb up the hill where the two girls played, and leaving Imelda behind.

'We can stay in the hotel for five more minutes only, but then we'll really have to go.' Nurse Dell must have noticed how Jacqueline was shaking, and she took a compact from her bag and dabbed some powder on her nose, ignoring the mirror and looking around. *Two little dickie-birds sitting on a wall. One named Peter, the other named Paul. Fly away, Peter. Fly away, Paul. Come back, Peter. Come back, Paul,'* she chuckled, and Kitty, who had come into the lobby, put a finger to her lips.

'How can you laugh at a time like this? We should be down on our knees praying for the poor woman's soul, may she rest in peace. Look at the pain and grief she left behind. The boss will never be the same again,' she murmured.

In the picnic area, where the pathway led down to the wall, Jacqueline saw that rain had started to fall. One drop immediately fell on Jacqueline's face, but she smiled on. The sound of a church bell came through the hotel door, and this time people in black hurried past.

'Say what you will; I have a small girl to look after. She's everybody's care now,' Nurse Dell remarked. 'Tally-ho, fox away,' she said, pretending to be a horse. She swung Jacqueline onto the counter of the reception desk, to give her a piggy-back out.

'Maybe Mamma fell off her horse and got stuck in a well, and we can go and find her. Come on then, she won't wait all day,' Jacqueline said.

Nurse Dell's house had a shop downstairs, which meant the kitchen was upstairs, Jacqueline concluded, as soon as they arrived at the house at the other side of the street. In a way, it was a bit like the hotel. She would have much preferred to choose her own adventures and be boss of all she surveyed, but at least, walking up the stairs, she quickly became the centre of attention. There was only her, not the twins or Tom, to be fussed over, and Nurse Dell's mother said she was proud as Punch to have such a visitor. Lou and Betty, who had driven back from the picnic and followed her into the sun-drenched kitchen, immediately made themselves at home. Lou seemed to think she was going to be living in Nurse Dell's permanently An orchard had appeared for her under the kitchen table. It spread as far as the eye could see. There was even a basket of washing, to be hung on a clothes line strung between the trees.

'Don't be lazy. Pick some apples for a tart,' she said to Lou, when her friend stepped from view for a moment, and then could be seen reclining on a deckchair. Jacqueline caught her out when she slipped off her own hard chair pulled into the table, to join the fun. Birds glided like tiny aeroplanes above the ice-cream-cone trees as she looked on, and Betty was throwing stones into a sparkling stream.

'I can't come into the orchard at the moment. Imelda is missing, and I have to watch out for her and be brave,' she explained.

'Don't get lost down there. Come up and join us,' a voice called above Jacqueline's head. 'If you don't want to eat your sandwiches, we understand. This is an exceptional time, and we have to make allowances for a child with troubles.' Nurse Dell drew her up onto her knee. Across from them, Josie smiled. She had horse's teeth, Jacqueline decided, or maybe she was a witch with a wicked plan to keep her prisoner on the other side of the street forever.

'I can hear Imelda calling. I've stayed here long enough, and I'm getting homesick,' she lied. Moments later, a baby cried in the room beside them.

'I'm coming William. You poor motherless baba,' Josie hurried away.

Chapter Fifteen

The following morning, Jacqueline couldn't find her doll Babette, which she'd got from Santa at Christmas. It had pink cheeks, and its face felt like rubber. Unlike Nurse Dell's doll, whose eyes opened and closed, Babette was stupid. She just stared all day through glass eyes that couldn't see, but up to now she'd always been there, like her reliable friends, Betty and Lou. Babette could be counted upon to be put sitting up in a game and be told what to do. Unless she cried, and then Jacqueline had to wipe those silly eyes and ask what was the matter.

The discovery about Babette being missing had been made when Jacqueline went into the hotel breakfast-room quite early, the day after her visit to Nurse Dell. The twins' play-pen was full of toys. Tom's train-set was on the floor, because he had placed it on the sheepskin rug that spread out in front of the gramophone, where Mamma often played the records she liked. Some of the train carriages had caught in the soft tendrils of wool and toppled over. Shortly now, Jacqueline knew, Betty and Lou would come and have a chat with the train-driver. They would stare along the track at the upturned carriages and shake their heads and exclaim.

Normally the room was busy. Kitty would tell her to keep out of the way while she tidied up, and soon a smell of polish would take over, drenching the air as if clumps of lavender flowers the same as on the tin, were being waved in her face. She must be up early because through the window somebody could be heard distinctly, whistling, and voices that began to talk below seemed to boom, as thought they were the first people to have been swept into the town, deposited by the tide of a new day.

'I'm coming to find you, Babette. You've probably run away and now you're lost,' she called out. She knew that Betty or Lou would be listening. Together they would explore the sleeping hotel. Kitty might find her during her search and put her back in bed and tell her a story. Jacqueline hoped so. Either that, or when she got back to the room her mother would have breakfast ready and they would all sit down at the table together. She would tell Mamma a funny tale and make her laugh.

It was because she was up so early and now had skipped down to the hotel door to peep out, that Jacqueline was the first person to see the circus trucks go past. They made a rumbling sound; just as she watched, the cavalcade halted in front of her. A lion in a cage was prowling forwards and back. Any minute now, it could escape out and run up and down the main street of the town. It would be huge and magnificent, and flay its tail about and roar. She imagined a wrinkling nose sprouting whiskers, and how it would grin at her.

'Go away, this day. I don't want it to happen. God take this bitter chalice from me. My pain is too great.' A moan from Teddy penetrated the quiet lobby. His voice had drifted over the banisters of the hotel stairs from a concealed landing.

'Boss, come back. This is helping nobody,' Peadar from the butcher's stall called out next, and the two figures came into sight. Teddy was on his way down the flight of steps that led from the bedrooms, and Peadar was attempting to move in front of him to prevent him from going any further.

'Imelda, how could you do this to me?' Teddy's question resounded. A roar trembled in the air, and Jacqueline saw that the lion had escaped and bounded into the hotel.

'Watch out, Daddy,' she called, but there was no more time to warn her father. The lion was twisting between Peadar and Teddy, and her father was pointing at her, as if he felt no danger.

'You've broken my heart, all of you.' His voice grew hoarse. 'It's because of you children that all this happened.'

'You're not in your right mind. You don't know what you're saying, Boss. Now come into the bar with me,' Peadar said, leading Teddy past her. She hadn't realised that he'd been bitten by the lion: he was limping, and his shoulders drooped. Such a terrible thing as a lion's bite had never happened to her, and she began to cry out with fright, as if she had felt the lion's hot breath on her face too.

'Your father is not well. He's had a bit of a shock and it shook him up.' Peadar reappeared by her side next. At the same time, the lion sat on the hotel mat, at the entrance. He stretched his head back and yawned, as if the effort to escape had made it tired. He licked his paws and relaxed, shaking his shaggy mane.

'Daddy shouted at me. I want my Mammy,' Jacqueline sobbed. The lion looked back at her and blinked, as if it understood, but maybe it had leaped on her mother too. The thought made her cry afresh. Peadar crouched down, so that he was at her height. He took a handkerchief from his pocket and wiped her eyes.

'Don't worry. You'll be seeing Imelda tomorrow or the day after,' he soothed. 'Now wipe those tears away. Teddy would like to see his little daughter happy, not sad. That's how you'll please him most.' He fished a coin from his pocket. 'Look what Peadar found for Jacqueline. From now on, things will get better, I promise you. Teddy won't be so upset, and if you see him worried, you can be Daddy's little helper and put on a smile.' The money flashed like a trick coin. When she looked at the door again, the lion was gone.

Peadar's eyes were more like Floppy than a prowling cat, and she let him take her hand.

'Everything is lost today. I can't find Babette, as well as Mamma,' she said, and waited to hear his reply. In the meantime, the circus trucks had started on their way again, each one more colourful than the last. She would use her money from Peadar to go and see it. Kitty would bring her, and they'd have ice cream. Instead of the lion, a man with a black hat darkened the doorway. He had a notice to pin on the door about the day's arrangements, he said, and brandished a hammer and a thin nail in the air. The moment he began to bang the nail in the door to pin a black-rimmed card on, Jacqueline felt it go through her head.

Chapter Sixteen

Jacqueline had almost given up on her quest to find her mother when Kitty's friend Phyllis explained how she would soon see Imelda. After the incident of the lion coming into the hotel and Teddy reacting so badly, Jacqueline had found it hard to settle down. There were plenty of things going on around her, of course, but she was keeping her eyes and ears open for something else. She was on the alert for her mother's voice. It wasn't that Imelda had forgotten about her, she knew; she had the distinct feeling that Imelda was fighting a battle of her own, that perhaps the sight of her daughter might help her win. It wasn't fair of Imelda either, Jacqueline thought, to have disappeared so completely. She should have at least anticipated something was about to happen and have told her not to worry, that she would see her soon.

'I brought you something that came all the way from China. Wait until you see it. You won't believe anything could be so beautiful,' Phyllis had enthused as soon as she arrived at the hotel. 'We're all going to have such a lovely time; you won't feel the hours passing. First of all a party, and look what I have for you: it's just right for a tablecloth.' She shook out a headscarf that had trees and flowers on it. 'It will be the same as if we're down by the lake in the park,' she explained.

Jacqueline gazed at the square of cloth, entranced. It had a cottage painted in the centre, with ivy growing up the outside, and a thatched roof. There was a stream that started halfway across the surface of the scarf, and then plunged behind a rock and disappeared. Apple trees hung heavily laden branches dipping towards the cottage, but most satisfactorily of all, to suit Betty and Lou if they arrived, tucked into one of the tree's rosy branches a tree-house plainly showed, perfect for making their own. It was where she herself could come and visit to play games in, anytime she liked. As if she could read her mind, there and then Phyllis opened her present, and Jacqueline exclaimed with delight. A doll's tea-set, which would be perfect for the tree-house, was revealed. The set was packed in straw, and Phyllis took the cups and saucers out, one by one. She laid them neatly on the headscarf, making a slight tinkling sound. 'Careful now. That's full-up and piping hot,' she said when she put a flower-imprinted tea-pot down. Jacqueline could see a thin line of steam coming from the spout, like pale smoke.

'This is the best day ever. We'll have a big tea party and invite all the people who live on the headscarf to come along: the rabbits and hedgehogs and a fox, as well as Betty and Lou. You'll be a special guest, Phyllis, because you brought the tea-set.' Jacqueline closed her eyes for a moment to imagine it all. The cottage had come alive, and whoever lived in there was singing a song. It was Imelda, of course, waiting for her to run in for a hug.

'Don't sit on the wet grass without putting a rug underneath you,' Imelda called. When she appeared in the doorway, she was just as Jacqueline remembered: the perfume she always wore enticed the little girl over. 'We must pick some roses for the picnic cloth,' Imelda began to say then, until Jacqueline noticed she had started to fade.

'Don't look at me like that. You'd think you were seeing a ghost,' Imelda said with a laugh. At the same time, Jacqueline saw that the cottage behind her mother had started to curl up at the edges, licked at by hungry flames.

Chapter Seventeen

The picnic was over. Phyllis had gone downstairs to get herself something to eat, and Jacqueline was suddenly aware of more movement than usual in her part of the hotel, as if old boundaries between where the public roamed, and the family doors beyond which they could not go, had been forgotten about, and the world had invaded. The headscarf had been lifted from the floor by Phyllis. Betty and Lou, who had decided to go back to their own house in Jacqueline's bedroom, because they were expecting visitors and wanted to bake a cake, had been absent for some time, and Jacqueline sat still.

The noise of people everywhere was like being in a hall of magic: Phyllis had left the door open behind her and subdued babble travelled in, until there was sudden silence and then a continuous chanting, like in a church when she went there with Mammy and Daddy; that was, until she got bored and Teddy had to take her away. The reason why it felt magical was because they were part of a game, she decided. It was because the voices might not be real people. They might be ghosts, and the only way she would make them real was to find out where they were hiding away from her, and touch them. At the same time, she saw that Phyllis had left her bag, as well as the scarf, on a chair. The clasp of the bag was open and a mirror gleamed inside. Jacqueline opened the bag wide. She spied some lipstick. There was a photograph of Imelda on the mantelpiece of the breakfast-room, and Jacqueline took the lipstick out and wandered over. Imelda was smiling in the picture; Jacqueline knew she was smiling at her. *Cheer up*, the picture said. *Those people who are making all the noise in my room down the passageway have detained me. Very shortly I'll be able to get away.*

'You've been saying that for a long time now, Imelda,' Jacqueline complained. She had often seen her mother dab on lipstick, and she placed the mirror from the handbag on the breakfast table and peered into it to paint some lipstick on. It was difficult to get the shape right, but she knew how to rub her lips together to make it spread.

'I'm going to the ball to dance with the handsome prince,' she said to Imelda, but her mother never answered back. It might be an idea to get the wedding dress that covered her like a tent, from her parents' wardrobe, but something about the noise of the people, emanating from that room principally she was sure, kept her back. They might capture her too, just like they'd trapped Imelda, and nobody would pay attention to her, even if she screamed.

Jacqueline was dabbing some face-powder from the bag onto her nose when Phyllis arrived back. 'We'll play a game. It's called "Cinderella". You can be one of the ugly sisters and I'll be Cindy in the ashes,' Jacqueline declared. She stretched up on tiptoe, then spread her arms out and bowed. 'In the beginning there were three ugly sisters and their mother, and they lived in a big house,' she began.

'You poor wee mite. It must be great to be able to play a game and forget that nasty world out there,' Phyllis murmured. She placed a tray with food she had carried into the room onto the table and shook her handbag in Jacqueline's direction. 'Any other day, I'd be cross at you for poking your grubby little fingers into what isn't yours. I don't know what your mother would think if she saw you,' she added, and Jacqueline saw her put her hand to her mouth. Phyllis had said too much, the girl was sure of it. Whatever place Imelda was hidden in, Phyllis knew all about it. Tears might soften her heart and make her reveal all, and she began to sob. Phyllis remained stony-faced, and Jacqueline stamped her foot.

'Wherever Mamma is gone away to, I know she'll come back,' she said. She brought anger into her eyes and made it spark out, like she could when she wanted to get her way. Imelda had often warned her not to do that. She was a bad girl, and Imelda was teaching her a lesson by keeping them apart.

Everything came to head about an hour later. Jacqueline had taken Tom's train and tracks from a press by the window to play with, and then, getting tired of the game, had climbed onto the lid of the toy-chest instead, to look out. Floppy had arrived in the room at the same time and was sniffing about. Just as she hugged him, he put his nose in the air and whined, as if he had suddenly remembered his brothers and sisters again, and how he'd missed them.

'*Woof woof,*' Jacqueline yelped. She made the noise to pretend she was a dog, to be able to confuse Floppy and make him feel less alone, but the dog twisted out of her arms and ran over to the door of the room. This time the whine had a pleading sound: the dog wanted to be let out. A clock in the room played a tinkling melody and struck twelve. She counted the beats out loud, to let Phyllis see how good she was at school.

'Floppy is looking for Imelda. She hasn't brought her for a walk in ages.' Jacqueline had a sudden brainwave. They could all go for a walk together. It was never any problem crossing the big wide Main Street with Mamma, and this time she wouldn't pull away from her mother's hand. The dog continued to whine, as if in agreement. Jacqueline stood up on the chest. The last time she'd done this, she'd been as tall as her mother, and had looked into her eyes.

'One of these days you'll pass me out, you're getting so big. You won't have any need for Mamma at all.' Imelda had made her own eyes as round as an owl's. 'My, my. Who could believe my little girl could grow up so quickly?' Nobody could believe it, of course, because it wasn't true, but Jacqueline had noticed that her mother's eyes had glanced over her, and she had also put on her secret smile, the one she wore when she was feeling gayest, like when they were sitting round on rugs in the hotel garden for instance, and a quick burst of sunshine created an air of paradise about their surroundings.

She jumped up and down to make a noise on the chest, and the lid rose a little with her movement, as if it was on a spring. On the second bounce, Phyllis caught her in her arms. 'Stop, or your mother will kill me for letting you break up the furniture. I mean, she would have complained,' she said, and her face grew red. Jacqueline had an instinct to stay in those strong arms, even if they were crushing her too tight, because she felt as if she was falling. Nobody had told her that missing Imelda would be like standing on something too high up, like the tip of the hill where Betty and Lou had their picnic, and getting dizzy looking down. Over at the door, Floppy had managed to prise it open and was gone. Jacqueline snuggled in close.

'When is Imelda coming back? Floppy is looking for her.' She rubbed the centre of her chest, where a pain had started. There had been crows flapping against the window, and a loud sound of voices and cars on the street. A bell rang slowly, like the clanging of Tom's train when she made two carriages crash and the passengers spill out. Jacqueline decided that Betty and Lou couldn't let that happen, because they had come in the open door just now when Floppy had left, and had taken their places on Tom's train for a sightseeing journey.

'Goodbye, Jacqueline. We'll tell you all about our great adventures. We'll be going to the edge of the world and back,' Betty said, waving, before they set off. At the same time, Phyllis took

Jacqueline's hand and lifted it to make it signal down at the street. A line of black cars was passing underneath the hotel window.

'Wave goodbye to Imelda. She's going to heaven for a little while, but don't worry, she'll be back,' she said. Jacqueline saw her own closed fist being dabbed in the air. Running alongside the first biggest car, like the one Andy often drove out of the hotel yard, was Floppy. It was how Jacqueline knew that the dog differed in his opinion to Phyllis, because he was barking so loudly even she could hear. It was as if her pet knew that Imelda needed to be dragged back, before she was forced to leave.

Chapter Eighteen

It was all right for Jacqueline to range about on the main street of Tooraloo, stretching as far as the eye could see, during the daytime, but at night, when darkness closed in overhead like the petals of a dreaming flower and the countryside all about breathed in sleep, it was only possible to say goodnight to her familiar places by pretending; standing at her bedroom widow and viewing a pin-cushion of stars. Since Mamma had gone away, and in the days that followed, she had made a better friend of the town, because she was her own mistress. Nobody was really in charge of her, and she could come and go as she pleased. There was no Imelda to say what could and could not be done — like putting a limit on what tree she wanted to climb, or how far out on a limb of that tree she could go. Instead, she was like that trapeze girl in a circus, sky-high and kicking her feet gaily as she swung up and down, able to rise up as far as she liked, with nothing but air between her and the distant ground.

Moss Leahy's grocery shop was always her first port of call in her newfound freedom. The interior of the shop smelt like the inside of a recently emptied loose-tea chest, mixed up with pipe-tobacco smoke. Moss himself was tall, with a humpty-dumpty look, making him appear as wide as he was high. He was not just a shopkeeper, but a genie in charge of mysterious stores, waiting for little fingers to investigate. Moss was Jacqueline's godfather: he had stood for her at baptism. Gifts of money resulting in this, was how he became her secret ally in the tasks she undertook and visits she made, to fill out the hours for the excursions that would follow. Taking charge of her own day had only happened recently. It came about when she kicked up a fuss with Teddy, shortly after the day in Nurse Dell's, about going to school. Teddy replied that she was an impossible child, and he was giving up on her. 'Look after her,' he said, turning to Nurse Dell. 'There's only a few weeks left until she gets her holidays anyway.' Teddy's face had collapsed. It was as if he had ducked too long underwater, Jacqueline decided, because he made short shallow gasps for air, and his eyes stared ahead without really seeing, as if they had been blinded under the waves, and being immersed had tinged his skin white.

'I hate school. You have to sit in the same place all day, and our new teacher Sister Pascal raps you on the knuckles if you can't do sums. It's too hard to keep up, and I can't see the board properly from where I'm sitting,' she'd complained. She didn't remark that when she was with all the other children in the class, she felt different, and that it was lovely not to feel poles apart. That was the way it was when she wandered about on her own. Being adrift alone was better in a surprising way too, because being just one of the crowd meant that Imelda having gone away didn't matter as much. She didn't remark on these matters aloud, either, because it would distract from the real truth. People might put it at the back of their minds that she was suffering, and then forget it. They might not continuously recall that what was happening should not be allowed to go on.

Jacqueline knew that the town she was getting so well acquainted with had a vast hinterland, and hoped that, as she grew older, more of it might reveal itself, like a map that was being rolled out further and further. Tom, in his Cowboys and Indians game, when the town was a prairie and the bikes he and his friends rattled about on were trusty steeds, often galloped into those mountain ranges that were the sprawl of outlying streets. Presently, her games were different. Usually Betty and Lou went with her when she set out to make her social calls. They enjoyed it because, somehow, they seemed to know a lot of people, like the train-driver of Tom's engine they hailed as Mister Cat's-whiskers, usually to be found leaning like a loafer against a town-hall wall, deep in conversation with his friends, and then throwing back his head and laughing. There was also Mister Pig, who ran a fish-and-vegetable stall, and about whom Betty and Lou complained because he overcharged, and sometimes slipped them a wrinkled cabbage or a lobster that grabbed at their fingers and clung on like a vice.

There were many more characters crowding out the town's main street, really more a square because it was so wide, so that Jacqueline wondered how she and the girls made any progress in their travels at all. Greeting and chatting with so many often left very little time to do her own errands, such as visiting Moss. 'Here comes my little princess. Let's see what we have for her today,' Moss would greet her when at last she'd pay that call. She might find him delving into a deep box to take out the deliveries inside.

It was a box for burying a body in, under the ground, Betty or Lou would explain, but Jacqueline always disagreed. Instead, if he wanted to be in a box like that, he would chose to step inside one of those with the purple lining pressed against the sides she had seen in the loft where Andy and Ger worked, and use it as a bed to fall asleep on. She was sure Imelda would never make such a choice. She knew this, even if she had heard Kitty whisper to Phyllis that Imelda had looked as if she would wake up at any minute, she looked so life-like, before the lid was nailed on the coffin.

Sometimes when Jacqueline paid her visit to Moss, he would try to get her to laugh. When he was giving her money, for instance, his hand had to go very deep inside his pocket before he found out what he was looking for. He might stick a finger out from inside the material of the trousers and chuckle, but sooner or later a coin would emerge. 'This is a secret between you and me. Somebody has to look after you and give you treats, especially at this time,' he was sure to add. 'A kiss for Uncle Moss' usually came next, and then Jacqueline felt like running away. After that, Moss would just smile and say that it was not his lucky day, and the coin would be clutched in her palm and she and Betty and Lou could escape. Even before she got out the door of Leahy's, she knew Walsh's ice-cream shop was her next port of call. While Betty and Lou went to a hairdresser to have their shining curls styled, she would go inside.

'A penny wafer,' Jacqueline normally said, because that was the coin Moss Leahy usually proffered her, but sometimes she might be lucky and be able to order a thicker wedge of creamy whiteness to tingle on the tongue, better than Betty or Lou ever made.

'I believe your days of freedom are coming to an end. Poor Teddy can't help it, but this is no way to bring up a child,' Pat Walsh had said to her the last time she was in his place. It was because she had dropped the ice cream on the shop floor and wouldn't stop crying until he cut her another one.

'Nobody but Mammy can tell me what to do,' she had gulped back, between her tears. Betty and Lou arrived in at that moment, shaking out their hair and exclaiming to each other about how well they looked, and overheard her.

'Ask Teddy to bring Imelda back, and that you'll do everything she asks. You'll never be a bold girl again,' Betty said.

Chapter Nineteen

The inside of Kitty's cupboard in the small kitchen was dark, and Jacqueline left the door ajar while she searched. She was sure Floppy had hidden her latest doll, Lisa, which she had been given as a present by Phyllis, a few weeks after Phyllis had minded her. Lisa was made of cloth and had painted-on eyes rather than glass ones, and had instantly became a firm favourite with Betty and Lou, who insisted that she be brought along and included in the company whenever they all met. Sometimes they had asked her to sing, the way Imelda would if her mother had joined in their game; as though Imelda was as real as she had ever been. Betty and Lou would stand on either side of Lisa, and she would take their hands, and their new playmate would swing in the air dizzily and laugh, soaring into the blue sky as if there was no tomorrow. Floppy was as large and awkward as an elephant, the way he always barged into their game. When she placed Lisa on a chair, he would snatch at her with his teeth and bound away. Spit would fly from the side of his mouth. Although his tail wagged, Jacqueline sensed that Lisa, already wet and covered in bite-marks, was going to be pushed into some unknown dark place, to disappear forever.

'That's a present for being such a good girl when I looked after you. You won't forget me when Kitty and I go to Dublin, will you?

Maybe someday, when you're bigger, we'll meet in a café there and have a cup of tea. You'll understand everything better then. I'd like that,' Phyllis had said when she gave her the doll. Soon Kitty joined them, and this time, when she brushed Jacqueline's hair, she kissed her on the top of the head, as if she really liked her.

The cupboard was walk-in, and Jacqueline pushed past a mop and bucket and ducked under a low shelf to go further. She heard voices outside. It was only when she heard her own name mentioned that she stopped to listen. She imagined Kitty and Phyllis closing the back-kitchen door to talk, not knowing that she was there. She would jump out on them in a minute, and surprise them. Kitty sounded breathless. She probably had her back to the door, and Phyllis would look up from taking her coat off, because really she had come in for a cup of tea and to gossip, Jacqueline decided.

'There was no need to rush to tell me whatever you know. I could have waited,' Phyllis said, but Jacqueline heard excitement in her voice. Phyllis had a way of screwing up her face if she was curious, and of rubbing her hands together, and that was how Jacqueline imagined her now.

'I'm sorry for keeping you waiting to let you know, honestly, Phyllis. You wouldn't believe what has happened.' Kitty's voice rose up to a high pitch, and Jacqueline was about to shout out, 'Boo! Look who's here,' and come out there and then, but the next words stopped her. 'There'll be no more snacks in the afternoon, or free meals from now on,' she said, 'though it's probably time Jacqueline is taken in hand, before she has us all at her mercy.' She laughed as if she really believed the little girl was a tyrant, and her hidden listener sniffled. As soon as they found her, they would realise she had heard everything, and then they'd be sorry, because she'd tell Teddy, and they'd lose their jobs. 'Mina, the boss's sister is on her way. Mr Clancy had a letter from her just now to say she'd be here next week. I know, because I have to clean out the spare room for her,' Kitty announced importantly.

'I believe she's the head housekeeper with the Holy Ghost Fathers in County Cavan. There'll be no more chats between you and I, so,' Phyllis sighed.

Beyond her in the cupboard, Jacqueline suddenly saw Lisa the rag-doll. Betty and Lou wouldn't like the way she lay, because her face was pushed into the ground. At the same time, Kitty must have seen the press door open, because Jacqueline was plunged into darkness, and she heard the bolt close. 'I'm in here. Don't bury me alive. Lisa will die,' she called out loudly.

Chapter Twenty

Auntie Mina liked to bend over you and kiss you on the cheek. 'Lovely girl. I'm not surprised Daddy is so fond of you,' she would murmur to Jacqueline. She had freckles and pale skin, with just a faint blush of pink in her cheeks. Her eyes were the same colour as a thrush egg, with a similar pattern of dots, and her hair was as thick and russet-tinged as neat thatch. That was unless a charming curl escaped — which it did, however much she pinned the tresses back — and bounced happily when she walked. 'She was going to be Teddy's new helpmate, to relieve the burden of his cares. Teddy needed to make a fresh start in his life, and she would help him do it. She would make those old blues go away,' she announced brightly on the morning she arrived. At the same time, as if to prove her words about the importance of being positive and every day seeing the sunshine the world had to offer, she laughed. Her chuckles were like the sound of a gurgling stream, Jacqueline decided, because they cascaded out and refreshed the air around her.

Jacqueline had been playing house with the twins when Auntie Mina stepped into the breakfast-room for the first time. She had turned over the two armchairs to make a space inside — something the twins liked, because no matter how much she admonished the pair to sit still, they insisted on crawling in and out between them.

Betty and Lou were there in a supervisory capacity. Betty was positioned rather like an umpire, on the bottom rim, now in the air, of the upturned couch.

'Faster. Better luck the next time.' She waved the umpire's flag in the air. Tom had joined in their play a short while before. Instead of playing mothers and babies, he had invented his own game. He would scramble onto the tip of the upturned couch, then leap off onto a cushion. After that, he would race round the room and come at the jump from the other side. Lou had pressed her hands over Suzanna's eyes, as if she was a doll, making her twist her head away and cry, and Tim was feeding Floppy with sweets that Jacqueline had put in front of him, explaining that he must eat up his dinner before Mammy came in to tuck him up in bed, when Mina stepped through the doorway.

'What a happy scene.' Her words were a murmur. 'Isn't it wonderful to be a child, to be so resilient? And so many hidden feelings and fears can be aired through play.' She nodded as the children looked up. This time was the occasion when she gave Jacqueline that first sweet-smelling kiss on the cheek. She had knelt on the ground and spread her arms out, so that Jacqueline could run into them. 'We're going to be the best of friends, Jackie. From now on, you can trust me with all your secrets,' she whispered. It was a pity that at the same time, Jacqueline found that her own mischievous fingers had twisted one of Auntie Mina's hairpins loose. Rebellious strands flared out, as if determined to be free.

Chapter Twenty-one

There was an air of brightness and dappled shade, as though a summer garden had come indoors, when Jacqueline gazed down into the hotel lobby. The sight caused her to pause in her headlong gallop out of the hotel. Fern fronds arched outwards, and newly opened lilies seemed to emit hidden music from trumpet-shaped blooms. Auntie Mina had placed them there, she knew. It was one of the many touches the hotel had benefited from since she had taken over the running of it. There was a sense of order everywhere. Anybody who worked in the kitchens looked less jolly than when Mamma used to preside over them, Jacqueline decided. There was still laughter, and titbits being passed out to her secretly, with a wink and a quick hug, but no song notes crisscrossed, floating in the air like clothes flapping in a breeze. And a red lobster never returned; like a circus act snapping a wet mouth and making angry darts across the big table, as if he might eat you up as soon as he got to you on those thin, stalk-like legs. In truth, Jacqueline could remember Imelda's laughter when she thought of the lobster, as if the walls of the hotel kitchen had taken in her mother's bell-like peals that time they first happened, and now had let some leak out.

'A fresh coat of paint in the dining-room, and new curtains, will work wonders. Then we will spring-clean the bedrooms. Teddy has to be made take an interest in this place again.' She heard Auntie Mina's voice as she paused at the flowers. It came from the guests' waiting-room, adjacent to the lobby. Instead of using clips, this time her aunt's hair was enclosed in a net, Jacqueline saw, as she approached. Next, a cheerful glance was cast in her direction.

'Don't forget, Jackie, we have school lessons in the break-fast-room today. We can't have a little girl growing up like the proverbial lily, beautiful but with no means to look after herself. This is not the time to let ourselves down.' Her hands fluttered open, and she began to fuss at the outer flowers to set some droop-ing stems straight.

'I'm bringing Floppy for a walk. She's been on her own outside for a long time without a friend,' Jacqueline said.

'Then make sure you're back in time.' Auntie Mina smiled and was gone.

Teddy was swinging some meat-carcasses, with Peadar, into a van, when she made her way round to the back door. Beside her, water gurgled noisily from a kitchen pipe, but her father hadn't seen her, and she raised her voice. 'Can I have some money to buy sweets, Daddy? Auntie Mina told me I could.' Jacqueline bit her lip. She hadn't meant to lie, but yesterday Auntie Mina had told her that a little birdie said that Moss Leahy had been behaving in too generous a manner. He had been giving money to Jackie that he didn't have to throw away, because business was bad and he had an old mother to look after. From now on she was to say 'No thank you', politely, if he offered her anything, and if he insisted, she could call Auntie Mina herself. Jacqueline had been amazed that her aunt could understand a bird. She had imagined a robin, sitting on Moss Leahy's shop roof, and then seeing a broken sky-light and flying in. After a while, it would miss the trees, and the sky, and being outdoors, and would perch on a sack of flour to consider how to get out. That was when she must have been spied, because birds love children. She knew the feathered things even bobbed about in the same free-and-easy way as children. Auntie Mina was probably like St Francis, whom Sister Pascal had told them about, and could get birds and bees to speak to her. The silly creatures were a bit dumb and didn't know when not to tell, or give somebody away.

The gurgling water in the drain beside her stopped. It had left soap bubbles on the path, but they burst and went flat.

'You're a charmer, darling,' Teddy said. 'You'll have me broke.' He was going to ignore her request, and Jacqueline hesitated. Her father had been heaving a cardboard box, which had a picture of sausages on the side, into the van to follow the carcasses. The veins on his arms bulged. Maybe they would burst, and blood would go everywhere. Then his body would become transparent, and she would see his heart.

'Teddy is hardly able to bear the weight of his broken heart. He must take care of himself better,' Auntie Mina had said recently. There were bits of flesh from the carcasses stuck on Daddy's hands when he fished out a penny.

'That will do you for now,' he said to Jacqueline. It was difficult to stop herself from looking back in case he'd collapsed, when she ran from the spot.

Duffy's sweet-shop was two steps from the street you had to clamber up, to get inside, and Jacqueline felt the money large in her hand. The shop windows were too high to see in from the pavement, but inside, jars of sweets lined a back shelf, as desirable-looking as an array of Aladdin's jewels. For a while now, old Mary Duffy, who owned the shop, had become her friend. The best about that was that she would often put in an extra sweet, over and above the selection Jacqueline had ordered, or add a lollipop to the small paper bag-full. 'Aren't you a great girl, able to shop all by yourself?' she had said recently. 'We're going to be the best of pals from now on. It's not easy for you to find your way in the world now that you have no-one to ask what to do if little troubles come. You can depend on Mary Duffy,' she added, and from then on Jacqueline hugged the secret knowledge to herself. If she needed somebody on her side to tell everyone what a good girl she was, help, in the form of old Mary, wasn't too far away.

She collected Floppy, grabbing him by the collar, at the hotel back gates, to take him to the park. He began to tug her forward. She couldn't let the dog lead her on: she was in charge, and she had to bend down and give him a hug in case he was annoyed or upset that he couldn't get his way. 'Don't worry, we're only going for a little walk, and then I'll get you a bone from Teddy's stall. I'll always love you, even if you don't like to behave,' she whispered. Beyond the archway of the hotel's back-entrance there was a cobbler's shop, and Jacqueline glanced in briefly. Strips of leather hung like flapping curtains at the window's edges, but most mysteriously of all, as though waiting to be claimed at any minute, a giant boot that even Teddy's foot would swim in, was displayed in front. Jacqueline knew it was for a giant, because the cobbler sat in his shop all day in an attitude of waiting, glancing out with sharp eyes, probably making the matching boot and watching for the ogre to arrive. 'Be back in time for lessons,' Auntie Mina had said. Even before her walk began, Jacqueline knew she was going to be late. After getting her sweets, she had to make a detour past Walsh's shop window to gaze at the toys, but in particular to take in every particular of a new doll that had arrived for sale, splendidly attired in a layered lace dress, which would need a lot of money to buy. After that, there would be the impossible-to-resist park interior, with pathways like a maze. Betty and Lou liked this especially, because they said it was where fairy-tales were made. If she went on such a trip, there would definitely be a problem when she returned.

In the last few days, Auntie Mina had said it wasn't a good idea for a small girl to be as headstrong as Jacqueline was. Life was going to change for her, and she needed to be moulded into shape. 'This is especially true for girls who tell lies,' Auntie Mina said then, and her eyes became a cold shade of grey. They were the colour of the cobbler's hammer raised in the air, to make a new shoe fit better.

Chapter Twenty-two

The gateway to Tooraloo park was right in the centre of the town. Crowned by a stone archway, it was recessed from the road. That meant that Jacqueline couldn't view the entrance from her hotel breakfast-room window. Sunshine never penetrated the spot, making it a place you didn't want to linger in when you arrived, but it was no harm to hurry through, because beyond the high boundary wall, golden sunshine had a way of pouring onto grass and gravel paths, to draw eager feet forward. 'The park is not a safe place for small girls to wander in unaccompanied,' Jacqueline had heard Auntie Mina say to Teddy at breakfast recently, and in many ways Jacqueline could see what she meant. The lake was evil, and if she went too near it, waves might grab at her feet and, like that man before, pull her in. It also had big trees that creaked in the breeze, whispering to each other when she would arrive in their midst, as if she was some sort of prey to snatch into a tree bosom and suck the life out of. To make everything all right, though, the park had parts she had yet to explore, as inviting as untrodden snow. It had gravelled trails reaching into a land beyond her town, where the wonders of the world waited to be viewed and sampled. If she got lost, Floppy was there to lead her home. This last thought was sufficient to entice Jacqueline now, despite a fast-beating heart, to cross the road to begin her adventure into the unknown.

Jacqueline had been in this park before, with Betty and Lou, and they hadn't journeyed very far. Their purpose was more to acquaint themselves with how the park looked, to have a sense of familiarity with how it might be done, in case they decided to move into it further, at some time in the future. They had travelled as far as a concrete stand for a disused tennis court, and clambered to the top of the steps to look down. This allowed a view of the lake. It stretched a long way, tipping over a pale horizon. It glinted like the fish Teddy sold on Fridays, or that gleaming cluster of pearls stitched onto Imelda's wedding dress. Stuck in the centre of the lake, a patch of green had an abandoned air. With Betty and Lou on either side, Jacqueline trained her eyes on the water. If the man who had stepped into the lake appeared, they might have to rescue him. Perhaps he had forgotten who he was, and how to get home. 'He's playing with strangers he's met under that watery surface,' Lou explained. 'He's met some children and is dancing in a circle with them, singing *Ring a ring a rosy, we'll all fall down.*

'It's easy to forget who you are when nothing about you is the same, and so much water everywhere stops you being able to think. We should wait and keep looking, and the moment we catch sight of somebody, call out,' Lou chimed in. 'He'll just need to hear a human voice to become who he was and walk towards us.' It would make Jacqueline a heroine; she nodded at the waiting girl.

'I'm getting tired of sitting so still.' Jacqueline had shifted on her hard seat then, as if it was too cold. After a while, she stood up. 'I don't want to disappoint him if he asks me to go in and join him,' she murmured. It wasn't a selfish thing to say but, embarrassed, because she couldn't help after all, she kept her eyes down as they left.

On her walk when she came this time, Jacqueline turned her back on the lake, and Betty and Lou nodded in agreement. Stopping to gaze at flowerbeds, she broke into a skip. Floppy added eager barking, and ran ahead. It was to say he concurred with her good humour, and that nobody could come between them, because, as with the best of friends, they thought alike.

Putting a finger out to collect a raindrop that clung to a park bench, Jacqueline remembered that she had sat there before, with Imelda. That was when she had been a different girl, when a sense of being alive had a way of bubbling up inside of her, like steam from a boiling kettle. She knew she wasn't the same now, because that kind of happy feeling she associated with Imelda didn't flow any more, as though it had got blocked. It would return, she knew, as soon as her mother found her way back home, and she skipped into the forest.

Soon Jacqueline and her friends were deep in the woods. She was in the midst of tall creaking trees, before she paused to look around. High overhead, with their tips joined, and looking like feather dusters, the tops of green trees swayed. At her feet, narrow paths meandered, more like aimless rivulets of water. Up ahead, their own gravelled passageway forked left and right. Jacqueline would have to make a choice. A robin hopped out of the undergrowth, stopping at her feet before flying off. She considered the possibility of exploring where the bird had come from, but venturing off the path for a few paces, a piece of rotten wood squelched under one foot, and a host of insects scrambled out.

Floppy ran into the rough scrub and began to disappear along a narrow trail. The piece of decaying wood must have dropped from a fallen tree, because it straddled their path. It was host to rows of frilly fungi, curving outwards like layers of Chinese roofs. Bending close, she saw a splash of tiny red spots, as if the old tree had bled before dying. She couldn't be right, though, because before her eyes, it had become a house. She saw windows with gleaming glass and kindly brown eyes peering out, and beckoning her inside. She could go and live with the friendly house-owner forever, and forget about Auntie Mina and how she expected her back. At the same time, Floppy returned to her side, wagging his tail. He barked, and the creature of the tree waved a hand inside and smiled. Betty and Lou clapped their hands because now, all through the forest, little people like the tree-dwarf were out and about. They nodded and called, 'Come and join us for afternoon tea.'

Sitting on the old trunk not long afterwards, Betty was the first to yawn. It was only when Floppy barked loudly and, opening her eyes, Jacqueline saw that the air had grown dark, that she realised that all four of them had been there for some time. She and the girls had been asleep. She rubbed her eyes and raised her arms. Looking around, the forest people had disappeared. Brown leaves at her feet had a mucky appearance, and when she stood up, a chill wind crept round her feet. 'Let's go home, Floppy. It must be late, and I'm getting hungry.' Jacqueline shivered. As she approached the park lake, it wrinkled and gurgled, as though it could open a big deep mouth and swallow them up. Ahead, though, the entrance gate swung crookedly open, and they all raced quickly through it. Her own wide-awake street lay spread before her, like a calm river. A car-horn blew at them. She might still be in time for her lessons with Auntie Mina, Jacqueline thought, as she plunged across.

'I got lost in the forest. There were wolves and bears everywhere. Floppy had to fight them off,' Jacqueline boasted some time later. It was the family tea-time, in fact, held shortly after she had returned. Beside her, the twins had been pulled apart because they were making too much noise. Tom had started to build a pyramid with his toast-soldiers, and her fried egg, which she'd left to get cold on the plate, stared like a gluggy eye. Baby William, who had recently been brought to sit at the table, banged on his high-chair with a spoon. Nobody was listening.

'It's useless in there,' Tom raised his voice at last. 'None of my friends like it. The paths are no good for bikes or tricycles because of the little stones. Dick Long went head-over-heels one time into the lake. It was his own fault because he had no brakes.' He nodded like a wise old man.

'Dick Long told me he liked it because he saw deep into the lake and a water creature danced for him and offered to show him her underwater cave,' Jacqueline replied promptly, but her lap was wet. Susanna had lifted a milk jug from the table and it had toppled sideways and spilled on her. She pulled off her drenched dress and threw it at her little sister, and laughed at the comical sight.

'Stop that, Miss Troublemaker. There's no need to make matters worse at this table by attacking your sister. Pick your dress up and leave the room. We need to restore order.' Mina clapped her hands. The sound made baby William cry, and Auntie Mina jumped up. 'This chaos would never have happened if you'd turned up properly for your lesson at four o'clock, Jackie. Instead, you go into the park and boast about your exploits when you come back. This has to stop,' she blazed. 'Your poor mother would turn in her grave if she saw the shambles her family has become.' She shook her finger, and Jacqueline saw her chin tremble, as if she was going to cry. She has a lake of tears inside her that wants to spill out, she thought.

Give Mamma a kiss. She's feeling hot and bothered, but a Jacqueline kiss can cure her, that was what Imelda used to say. The small girl's mind raced. Auntie Mina put her arms out, as if she had read her niece's thoughts.

'Mamma told me there's no such thing as a grave, and I hate eggs,' she announced instead, and pushed her plate away, so that it slithered off the table. The surface of the yellow eye wrinkled, like that swallowing lake.

Chapter Twenty-three

She expected it to be bought at any minute, but day after day, when Jacqueline checked on the doll in Walsh's window, it was still there. She had to have it. The doll was that beautiful, it might have got into Walsh's window by mistake. Sooner or later, somebody would snap it up. *Two and sixpence*, she read the price on the tag beneath it, and sighed. It must be a superior doll to be costing so much. She could give it all the love she had. They would be the best of friends. Because she looked like a doll that could keep secrets, Jacqueline could pour out her heart to her too.

Jacqueline was thinking of the doll and how she would never be able to buy it, when she approached Moss Leahy's shop adjacent to the hotel, on a fair-day morning. Tooradulla was already busy. After her breakfast, from an upstairs landing she had seen cattle make their way in dribs and drabs down the long Main Street. Now they bunched together in front of the town hall. Their hooves made a clattering noise as they milled about, and a choking smell of fresh cow-dung hung in the air. Looking behind her, Teddy had appeared at the hotel entrance. She had helped to write one of the signs the evening before, and he began to stick it onto a window. *Refreshments inside. Tea and Sandwiches,* her sign said. Teddy looked up at the sky when he had finished; she guessed he was checking for rain. Recently he'd talked about the weather a lot. He said it would be a long time before the sun ever shone for him again. He was testing the sky just in case of this; she was certain of it. She must have paused too long outside Moss Leahy's doorway to gaze back at her father, because the shopkeeper was calling her inside. He beamed at her from behind his high counter, and shoved a pencil behind his ear.

'Well, the Lord save us. Look who it is. You came back to see me at last, Jacqueline,' he announced, as if coming in had been her idea. His face grew more serious. He tapped the wood with his fingers and then leaned on them, as if he was about to haul himself up and vault over the barrier between them.

'Hello Moss. How are you keeping?' Jacqueline said. It's nice to be back in your shop again. I missed it. I have to do my lessons for Auntie Mina now, and I don't have much time to come in and say hello,' she spoke in clear tones. Now was the time to tell him she wasn't allowed to take money from him any more, and she thought of the doll. Moss Leahy had eyelids that took a long time to blink, and a face as round as a moon, and he stared, as if he could see inside her head.

'Give me a smile, and we'll be friends again. Your father and I go back a long way, and I'm not one to be interfering at this juncture. Your Aunt Mina is a great woman, and she knows what's best for you. Make sure you do what she tells you. We wouldn't want to spoil little girls, even if they sometimes need it, would we?' He took a large coin out of the till. Jacqueline knew it was a half-crown, and he spun it on the counter. 'Heads or tails?' he asked, as if a big gamble his visitor couldn't be blamed for watching, because she didn't know what was happening, was taking place. 'Never mind me. Even if you gave the wrong answer, I'd like to offer you as much as this and more. But you'll have to earn it.' Moss flattened the coin on the worn wood surface.

'I can't. Auntie Mina said the next time I was in your shop I was to buy some soap and bring it to the hotel. She said she was going to wash my mouth out if I told any more lies. That was because I told Daddy she said it was all right to give me a penny,' Jacqueline burst out. Auntie Mina said she wanted to mind her and take care of her, and now she was doing it invisibly, by standing between her and the money Moss hid under his fat fingers.

'Isn't that a good one!' Moss shook his head. He removed the pencil from behind his ear and reached for a notebook. 'Let me see, now. We'll have to do it some other way. Your Auntie Mina can open up an account. I'll give you the soap and I'll put threepence beside it to show how much she owes. The only thing is, you'll have to tell her that Moss Leahy knows why she wants it, and that he said she was a great one for the jokes, and that he never knew she could be so hilarious.' He pushed the stilled coin towards her. 'This is payment for services rendered. I'm very grateful you got me a new customer. Now put it away and don't let me see it again,' he said.

'I want the doll in the window. Auntie Mina said I can buy it and put it away until my birthday,' she lied to the shopkeeper Mr Walsh a short while later. Mr Walsh seemed to hesitate. He looked over her head as if Mina Clancy was in the doorway, like an avenging angel.

It was unfortunate the doll had a hard plastic face when it was eventually handed over. Something so cold-looking was too difficult to like.

Chapter Twenty-four

'From now on we're going to treat you exactly the way we treat an adult. There won't be any baby babble. We won't talk down to you as if you couldn't possibly understand, because I respect the intelligence of children. They can be quite as astute as grownups, as far as I'm concerned, and just as capable of reason,' Auntie Mina declared to Jacqueline. 'You see I'm on your side, Jackie,' she added, addressing her niece by a variation on her name she had used before. It seemed to suggest to Jacqueline that she had already changed into the face she presented herself to the world as, because part of the old her, like her name, had been shorn away.

'That sounds like a good idea. I can wear Imelda's beads and put on her high heels and be a grown-up like her. Everybody says I'm the spitting image of my mother,' Jacqueline piped up. She looked down at her jumper, which she'd marred earlier on with a food-stain. She had finished breakfast and the word 'school' had been mentioned. Auntie Mina had decided it would be a good idea to go back for the last few days of the summer term. She had smiled at her niece when she spoke, and now Jacqueline wet a finger and began to try and rub the stain off. 'Rules and regulations make a child feel safe. They give them a framework to hang on to, especially when the world they knew has been torn apart. School will be good for Jackie. It's something she will recognise as familiar, and that will make it easier for her to go back next year,' Jacqueline remembered her saying to Teddy in a gentle voice the night before, and she began to rub harder. They were in the breakfast-room. She had been put sitting at the table to practise writing letters of the alphabet, and the sound of the other children drifted in from the passageway.

'Do what you think is best, Mina. I'm grateful for your assistance,' Jacqueline seemed to hear her father's reply. She was passing the door of their freshly restored sitting room at the time. Auntie Mina had christened the new room, 'the den'. She had exclaimed with delight when she first spied the snug space, close to the girl's bedroom, and she had pressed the twins, who were trailing after her, to her side.

'What a delightful retreat this will be for your father. From now on, he'll be a free man inside its doors,' she had declared. Any business matters or troubles in his life won't be allowed to enter. I'm sure you all agree: Daddy has to be looked after. We don't want to upset him with long faces and complaints. We're lucky he's with us at all, since everything happened, and you must promise you won't ask him about Imelda. The poor man needs time to recover from his loss, and any fresh reminders of how things were will only serve to upset him greatly. Cross your hearts and hope to die.' She had directed a special glance at Jacqueline, and then picked the twins up and rested one on each hip in a single fluid movement, as if she had been doing it forever. An eager flushed face waited for someone to respond. Auntie Mina's thin, perfectly shaped lips parted then, and that engaging curl dipped onto her forehead, but Jacqueline's attention had been arrested by an item in the room behind her aunt. It was Mamma's gramophone, which had been missing from the breakfast-room since her mother herself had vanished. Cardboard boxes were piled up beside it, with one of Mamma's dresses draped across. It all gave the impression that she had been away but would reappear at any moment. Teddy must be told.

'I'll tell Mammy you're going to make us all tell a lie. She won't like it if you're here when she comes back,' she announced. Auntie Mina shook her head. At the same time, Betty and Lou had made an appearance. They opened the lid of Mamma's gramophone and brought the arm with the needle in it across to start a record playing. Remembered notes filled the air, and soon Imelda had joined in their game and was dancing lightly across the room.

'You're either with me or against me. Try to act the best for your father. From now on, we must do things for his sake. After all, you're young and have the whole of your lives ahead of you.' Auntie Mina shook her head. She turned it slightly, as if she had heard the music too.

'I do believe there's even mice in that room, in its neglected state. They've probably made a nest in the old gramophone. It will be the first thing to go,' she said. Jacqueline saw an instant pleading look in her mother's eyes.

'I want my Mammy back,' she said.

Tom chose this moment to burst back into the breakfast-room. 'Kitty has taken everyone away, and I'm ready for school. Thank you for getting us breakfast,' he said and kissed Auntie Mina on the cheek, as if he was her son.

Chapter Twenty-five

'Every child should learn to swim. Think of the fun they can get from it, and how it would prevent needless loss of life. In the case of this drowning, it would have meant one less family grieving for the absence of a loved one.' Auntie Mina tapped at a picture on the front page of a newspaper, and then let it slip onto a neatly laid table. The family was having lunch in the hotel dining room, downstairs. It was a warm day in Tooradulla. There was a sense of well-being attached to the spacious room, to complement the balmy air outside, and a feeling of time standing still, as though any hurried movement would seem too stark, and contrary, on such a pleasant day. The folded paper lay beside Jacqueline, and she saw a section of the picture of a river, complete with overhanging trees. Beneath the photograph, since she could now read quite a few words, she deciphered the phrase 'washed up'.

The family were seated at one end of the long table, and a white tablecloth gleamed. Teddy was on Jacqueline's other side, and then there was Tom and the twins. They were having their meal in the dining room, Auntie Mina had explained beforehand, because being in such an ordered environment would bring out the best in all of them. 'Being responsive to positive stimuli is innate in every human being, and children are no different,' she had enthused as they trooped into the dining room. It seemed she was right, because so far the twins had sat and eaten up their sandwiches quietly, and Tom had stood and passed slices of bread around from the bread-basket, making Auntie Mina glow with pride. Jacqueline wanted to open out the newspaper further, to see if she could manage to read more, but it wasn't possible. There was a piece of gristle in her mouth from a sausage, and it was making her feel sick. If she didn't spit it out immediately, she would vomit all over the floor. She pushed it to the side of her mouth with her tongue, and dabbed at a trickle of saliva dribbling out.

'The Suir is a treacherous river, especially where that incident happened, but children are always tempted by water. I'm sure the boy had been warned about dangerous currents, and how you can never trust even the most innocent-looking river-stretch, and then it was too late,' Teddy intoned. He seemed to be looking at Jacqueline as if he expected a reply, as though at that moment he and she were peering from a river-bank at silent waters surging at their feet.

Swimming is easy. If Floppy can do it, so can anyone, Jacqueline wanted to say, remembering her dog paddling with ease when he crossed a swollen stream that appeared after rain sometimes, at the end of the hotel yard, but she couldn't speak. A gush of half-digested food had landed on the dining-room table. It had projected from her mouth in a vigorous stream, and she leaped up in her place, making her chair wobble, and ran.

'Her mother never made a fuss about these matters. It's not material if a child is not perfectly clean, so long as she's happy,' Teddy exclaimed a short while later. He had found Jacqueline sitting on a step of the hotel stairs after her exit, because Auntie Mina had gone to discover her whereabouts, and he'd followed. Auntie Mina's nose had a disgusted wrinkled appearance, and she had started to clean off some food on Jacqueline's front.

'It was the sausage caused problems. I'd really like to introduce the children to a more varied diet. We'll start on eggs benedict next week. The flavours are delicate and it's much more wholesome,' she sighed. Jacqueline had a sensation of white rubbery egg in her mouth, and retched.

'You're making yourself sick now. Think about something pleasant. I'll read some more *Alice in Wonderland* to you tonight. Remember how Alice was in the Hare's House and she began to grow and grow until she was completely squashed in. We'll have to see how she got out.' Auntie Mina laughed suddenly. She sat back on her heels, and even Teddy had to shake his head and smile, because the sound seemed to come from her tummy, flowing out in trills and musical notes.

'I only like having Imelda reading to me. You can give me some sweets to eat if you like, though,' Jacqueline said.

The air stayed hot as toast, and the entire town purred with pleasure as the pleasant summer day continued. 'Work can wait. We might not get weather like this for the rest of the summer. I think a swim is called for. We'll take a trip to Lough Derg and have a much-deserved dip for ourselves,' Teddy declared, some time after lunch was over. He had come to the breakfast-room door, and again his eyes seemed to rest on Jacqueline, stretched on a couch under the window.

'It's a great idea, but leave the twins with me. They'd be a handful near water.' Auntie Mina nodded too, in her direction. Jacqueline knew the afternoon was wearing on, because the sun had swung over from the other side of the town, and she had felt it spread across her. Out in the park, those slanted rays in the shape of eyes would still be maintaining their vigil over the lake, watching patiently as the man who walked in tried to figure out a way to leave, or the mer-people flitted about their business, in their weedy green houses.

'It's going to be great. The last time when we went to the sea, at Tramore, you promised me you'd teach me how to swim, Daddy.' She leaped up and to get rid of the phantom man, let her gaze sweep round the room. It was as if waves had gathered there, and the family were all at the edge of a golden stretch of water, touching it with their toes, ready to plunge forward. Despite that, a shiver set in, as if she could feel the coldness of that park lake.

'That's what I was thinking, dear. As your Auntie Mina reminded us, it's one of the skills every child should be equipped with.' Teddy grinned. He lifted her up and swung her onto his shoulders, as though the past weeks had never happened, as though Imelda was there. It was a pity the swift movement caused Jacqueline to want to get sick again. And it meant she was seeing things in an upside-down way, as if he had left her behind, pressed down under Lough Derg, flat in the distance as a big plate.

'Go on your own Daddy' she whimpered she wriggled from his arms.

Chapter Twenty-six

Auntie Agatha lived in a room at the end of one of the hotel's long corridors. This was at the opposite side of the building to where the family rooms were, and it seemed to Jacqueline that she was going into another country. She was setting out to find her. She had been in Auntie Agatha's room before, on the occasion she had been introduced to her for the first time.

'We must knock quietly. Agatha might be asleep. On the very day she came to board with us in the hotel, she told me she likes a nap in the afternoon,' Auntie Mina had explained on that first visit, but even as she spoke, an alert voice travelled to them through the closed door, and said, 'Come in, Mina.' A stern gaze had been bent on Jacqueline too, when they stepped beyond the red-carpeted passageway into the blue room. Jacqueline had thought of it as that, because looking round the room, there was a sensation of having wended up a mountain, to where the air was scented by larkspur and gold-centered aven blooms. Those were the names of the flowers Aunt Mina had given her, for the ones on the cover of her Heidi book, and they had popped into her mind straight away. The sense of a high-up climb came from the bed as big as a throne Auntie Agatha was supported by. Jacqueline was lifted to press her lips onto old cheeks that dented inward with the pressure of her mouth, like a baked apple. A smell of rose-scented powder tickled her nose also, as if Auntie Agatha had been dusted with a puff all over.

'So this is the girl I've heard so much about. It looks as if we're going to have to get to know each other better, I suppose,' a resigned voice said. 'I shouldn't complain. I'm glad to be able to help Teddy out. This is a nice comfortable room, and there's something indulgent about living in a hotel and being waited on, hand and foot. Ted never had much business sense, and a permanent guest like me can only be a help.' Eyes the same light shade of brown as Floppy's stared into Jacqueline's. 'Perhaps if we become good friends, it will make my life less lonely.' Auntie Agatha smiled. 'I'm really your Daddy's aunt. I've known Teddy since he was a tot in a cot, just like your new brother William is right now,' the elderly woman nodded, and Jacqueline had a picture of her father not being able to walk or talk. It was true what Auntie Agatha had said about baby William. She had got a glimpse of him in the hotel around the time Imelda went away, and then Nurse Dell had taken over. The baby had announced itself suddenly, like in the story of Moses appearing in a basket amongst the bulrushes. She saw a helpless thing shaking tiny fists in the air, as if he too couldn't say how he had suddenly appeared in the friendly place he found himself in; as if he had been expected, and now had arrived.

Jacqueline wasn't quite sure what to say, as her journey's end was reached this time, when she entered the room dominated by a bed with a tall figure like a queen, propped up by leaning into layers of pillows. It didn't matter, though, because Auntie Agatha took charge. 'You may greet me with a kiss, dear,' she said when Jacqueline approached that larger-than-life bedstead. It could be a new kingdom, the visitor decided, and that gave her the excuse to pull herself onto it, with a great effort. A silken quilt, as if she had arrived in heaven and was on a cloud, rippled round her.

'I thought since you've come here to stay, I might bring you all the news.' Jacqueline had an urge to talk, and settled herself in. 'The twins are sick. Susanna has the mumps, and Tim is crying all the time, so Auntie Mina thinks he's getting them off her. She says it's better that he gets it over with, so that she can nurse them both at the same time. Tom got a new bicycle for his birthday. It's to take his mind off any sadness he might be feeling, by letting play help him to forget it all.' She looked into Auntie Agatha's faded eyes and thought again of Floppy. With Floppy by her side, she wasn't afraid of anything. Just as Tom might do it on his bike, she and her pet could discover one day where Imelda had been taken to.

'It's very good of you to think of an old lady.' Auntie Agatha was a bit like Red Riding Hood's Granny, Jacqueline thought, because she had a knitted shawl round her shoulders that would be just perfect for a wolf to snuggle up in, and a long white throat he would take that first bite from.

'If you like, we could play house,' Jacqueline said, 'or maybe shop,' because, while stealing a glance round, she had spied a treasure-trove of goodies on Auntie Agatha's locker. There were apples, and an orange, and pears. The queen of the bed also had a bag of mint sweets, and Jacqueline had the sensation of one in her mouth, making it feel pinched inside from a dry sweetness.

'Certainly. Now I'll be the shopkeeper, and you can come to me.'

'We'll use your hairpins for money,' Jacqueline enthused, because a small pile of them lay beside the pillows. 'Whatever you do, don't let a stranger into the shop. It might be dangerous for all of us,' she announced then, because, unbidden, Auntie Agatha's room had become home. It was as good as the picnic-hill she had visited with Betty, or being lifted up by Teddy and flung in the air.

'I like it here. Can I come and play another time?' she asked Auntie Agatha. 'I'll bring Floppy, and he'll keep the wolf away.'

'I think you and I could both do with becoming good friends. We'll look after one another and go for walks together. I'll go much further if I have a companion to make me step along.' Auntie Agatha placed her two hands on the bedspread, and Jacqueline saw fingers with bones like hills on them, and swollen navy blue veins.

'I have a better idea. Maybe we could make the story go backwards and you won't be eaten by the wolf.' She grasped the frail hand as if they were already on a long journey outside the room. We'll close our eyes and go backwards in time, to before when you came. If you weren't lonely before, you could be the same again. Mamma will be back, and Auntie Mina won't be here.'

'Auntie Mina loves you. She's only here for your own good,' Auntie Agatha said quietly. Jacqueline felt her own hand being squeezed in return, but she knew her new friend was wrong. There really was a wolf in the forest, and she knew who she was, too.

Chapter Twenty-seven

Before Auntie Mina came, and Jacqueline's life changed, when she had wandered about the hotel on her own at will, as though nothing could ever go wrong, one of her places to visit was the hotel bar. The floor had a worn, faded look from too many footsteps. Light had difficulty struggling through barred windows, and cast dusty, ineffectual slants into the bare-looking room. On a fair day, a mass of bodies and the hum of conversation or loud shouts made entry to the bar impossible, but generally during the daytime, just a few men presided in their accustomed places to watch her come in. These were standing at the bar counter, as though attached to it by an invisible hook or taking their ease at a round window table. When she did make her entry, she was exclaimed over, like the child of a palace, or a little wonder to behold. She was begged to sing a song or do a dance, and although she never wanted to — because at the performance something might go wrong, her voice might sound squeaky or her feet stumble — it didn't seem to matter. Best of all, she was always given a penny to buy sweets. At that point, Teddy made efforts get rid of her.

'Children don't belong in bars. Find somewhere else to play. You're under my feet,' he would say, and take a brush and pretend to sweep her out. But Jacqueline felt he didn't mean it, because the men in there loved her, and there was always a smile in Teddy's eyes, as if he was secretly glad she was performing her party-piece.

'I'm not allowed into the bar any more. Auntie Mina says there are sights and sounds in there that are not for children, and she feels I should have more wholesome experiences, so that I grow up tall and straight and true,' Jacqueline reported her aunt's words to her friends Betty and Lou, shortly after Auntie Mina had taken up residence in the hotel. She hesitated about divulging her next piece of information. It concerned Ken, the barman, who seemed to have been working in the bar forever. Jacqueline had only viewed him from the public side of the bar, on the days of her performances, or with Kitty, but now, because of Auntie Mina, she had been forced to stand beside him up close.

He had looked like the handsome hero in her *Sleeping Beauty* story-book. His face had glowed, as if a faint light shone behind it, and she got tongue-tied; she wanted to tell her friends. Auntie Mina had sent her into the bar with special dispensation to enter. She was to fetch a bottle of fizzy Corcoran's orange, because her aunt wanted to make her a drink of flavoured egg-nog. When she stood beside Ken, it seemed as if her whole body tingled, and although she really wanted to run, something else was making her stay.

Jacqueline was in the company of her two friends, because the girls had just arrived in the new house they had bought, on the picnic-hill. A smell of freshness, as if the country air had come inside, met all their noses when they peered in the door. I'm Alice in Wonderland again, Jacqueline thought, when she tried to follow the others, because she was far too big. Instead, she lay down flat and gazed through a window. There was a new baby in the cot upstairs. It was her new baby brother, Jacqueline was aware, and she forgot all about Ken, and telling the other two about him, as she watched. This baby was called 'William' too, of course and they rushed about, looking after it.

'See what you have to do. You have to wash him and feed him and change his nappy,' Lou said.

'Coo, coo, who's a lovely little boy,' Betty chuckled, and bent down and blew a rude kiss into the baby's tummy, and they all laughed. Maybe she could suggest to Auntie Mina that Tom might like an egg-nog, and she could get the orange for him and she could see Ken again, Jacqueline had thought, distractedly. Still she didn't say anything. Ken was to be her new secret, she vowed, even if the way she felt about him should be obvious from her silences and shyness, as if she wore the presence of the clandestine fact openly, pinned on like a broach of jewels in the shape of a heart.

'Jackie, come here quickly. You must see William's first tooth. He'll soon be crawling.' Auntie Mina's voice broke into Jacqueline's reverie. She'd been on her bedroom floor playing with her doll's house, and she went to the door. 'Look at the wonderful gift your Mamma gave us. We must thank the Lord for his goodness and praise him,' Auntie Mina held a bundle aloft, and Lou nudged her.

'Ask when his real mother is coming back,' she said, but didn't get any further, because Ken appeared with a bottle of orange. Surely he had heard her, and she twisted and squirmed, as if she too was on display.

Chapter Twenty-eight

'I've almost enough saved to go to Dublin. I'll give my notice in at the beginning of September, and go by the end of the month,' Kitty declared.

'You've been saying that for the past year, and we all know you're going to marry Ken Doyle,' Phyllis said, laughing. She put her arm round her friend's waist and began to waltz her about. At the same time, Kitty put a foot out to tap the kitchen door closed, and then swooned backwards.

'I am not,' she said. 'And if you're not careful, you'll get us both sacked.' Even so, Jacqueline saw that her eyes shone as bright as stars at night, and she put her hand to her chest and pressed, and pressed it. She winked at Jacqueline.

'Never mind what Phyllis says. You and I will escape to where nobody knows us. We'll dress up in the height of fashion and go to all the ballrooms. During the day we'll eat as much ice cream as we want, and visit the zoo to see the monkeys and lions, like in Duffy's Circus.'

'Auntie Mina says I have to knuckle down to school in September, that girls have as much brains as boys and I have to prove it,' Jacqueline said, pointing to herself. She had been lifted with a swing into Kitty's arms, and rested there happily. She got a whiff of talcum powder and a smell of sweat as she settled in and remembered the carbolic-soap smell of Imelda, the same as a basket of sweet-smelling laundry. There was no point in deciding who she liked best, because Kitty was dropping her down.

'In that case, I don't care. Maybe you're right. Ken will come with me and we'll shack up in a boarding house together and live in sin. Mina Clancy would have the bishop writing a letter to us to repent, if she found out.' Kitty laughed. Strands of blond tresses escaped from under the hair-nets the girls were now obliged to wear, because Jacqueline had moved the net back with her fingers when she was in Kitty's arms.

'Shh. We'd better get on with the work or we really will be given notice. We'll be out begging for money instead of taking the train to Dublin. Phyllis put a finger to her lips. She opened the door gently and peered out. 'Come on, you're supposed to be helping us, lazy girl.' She bent and tickled Jacqueline in her side, and the small child sighed contentedly.

'We make a good team. You're good at putting those bags out. We can hardly keep up with you, Jacqueline,' Kitty nodded.

Their task was to fill individual greaseproof bags, neatly laid on the disused black range, with the hot dripping from the big kitchen. Each one, when filled, weighed one pound, and would later be sold by Peadar in Teddy's butcher's stall. It was Jacqueline's job to open up the bags and lay them in a row while the two others poured in the hot melted fat. Jacqueline hadn't minded being prodded, because she knew what Kitty meant. They were looking after one another by working together, as if there was love in the air, she decided — something Imelda must have experienced too. 'Don't go away, Kitty. Stay until Mammy comes back. She'll let you sleep as long as you like in bed in the mornings, and give you bonbons,' she said, because she knew the older girl liked them, and she reached up and took the servant girl's free hand, when she'd put the pan down.

'What's the meaning of this? I suppose it has some explanation, Jackie?' They all turned to look.

Jacqueline could feel her head go fuzzy, as if something had got inside. Auntie Mina had stepped into the back-kitchen and was waving the doll that Jacqueline had bought with Moss's money, in the air. It made a baby's crying sound when Mina's actions turned it upside down, as if it had been fed up lying in the dark cupboard where Jacqueline had secreted it, and had decided to escape to see the light of day.

'It's not mine. That's the doll Santa gave to Susanna for Christmas, and she hid it in the press and forgot about it,' Jacqueline said, stumbling over a lie.

'Santa didn't bring your sister a doll. I know. Your Daddy told me what she got, in a letter at the time.' Mina shook her head and looked so sad, Jacqueline wanted to kiss her better.

'I mean, he gave it to me and I swapped it with her snakes and ladders,' Jacqueline struggled on.

'The Lord hates a liar. Take that back, Jackie. You'll feel much better. Even a tiny blemish on the soul makes Jesus cry,' Auntie Mina said. In a forgetful way, she lowered the doll towards the melted fat, hotter than the flames of hell.

'You weren't here. Imelda was. I saw Santa myself, putting the doll on Susanna's bed,' Jacqueline blazed.

Chapter Twenty-nine

Large drops of rain remained stationary for a moment on the breakfast-room window of the hotel, like tears of liquid glass, and then slid down. They gave the main street of Tooradulla a distorted appearance, making the road surfaces and cars and people wavy. Jacqueline tapped on the window with her finger to encourage the drops to slide down faster. She wiped off the condensation that had appeared from her breath from the cold surface, as she leaned in close. At the other side of the street, she knew, the park entrance beckoned. Stretching up on tiptoes and glancing across from the highest point of the window she could reach, she thought she saw that dark recess. If she dared travel over there again, Lou and Betty would be waiting. They would have set up a table serving lemonade and buns to sell to anyone who entered, and she would stop at their stall and have a chat. A whimper made her twist on the window-seat to look into the room behind. Floppy had come into the hotel, though recently he had been forbidden to, and was giving her a friendly look. His tail wagged.

'Naughty dog. You should do what you're told. Auntie Mina has no time to look after bold dogs, and I can't go anywhere with you. I'm not allowed into the park,' she said. Only the previous week, she had fallen in there, and come home crying with a grazed knee.

'I know it's good for you to test out your own resources and accept challenges, but your father is not in a position to receive any more shocks. It's better that you stay close to home. It means that, for the moment, the park is going to have to be out of bounds,' Auntie Mina had announced at the time, and Jacqueline shrugged. Her aunt didn't know there were flowers at the rear of the park, close to a distant gate and a deserted road that led back to the town; she had gone there with Imelda once, to pick some for the hotel. They were big and purple, she remembered, and their trumpet shapes had released drops of rain onto her head when her mother had pulled them down, making Imelda laugh. Jacqueline had been on the lookout for the blooms since she had started to go into the park on her own. Perhaps, if she did discover them, Imelda might find her way to those flowers at exactly the same time. It would make Teddy even happier than she would be, if she brought her back.

The park was busier than Jacqueline had ever seen it, when, giving into temptation, she and Floppy had stepped in there. Betty and Lou were in position, as expected. They had organised a queue for their shop treats, and she paused for a moment to help out. Floppy sniffed about them, then sat down patiently. There were three witches in the waiting line of customers, Jacqueline noted, and she spotted a mermaid whose tail had opened out, to allow her legs to emerge. The witches huddled together deep in conversation, and then one of them turned, to give her a keen glance. Perhaps they knew where those magical flowers were that would entice Imelda to come back, she had a sudden thought, but when she put the question to them, they flashed pointed teeth and dark brooding eyes, and laughed. Some elves of the forest had bunched together, almost impossible to distinguish from their surroundings, because their hair was cobweb strands one minute and real the next, and now and then their clothes changed from everyday material to green and brown leaves mixed with the petals of wild flowers. Bringing up the end of the queue, Jacqueline spied Tom's friend, Dick Long. He was seated on his tricycle, and he waved and began to approach. Passing the queue, he rolled over the end of one of the witch's dresses that trailed on the ground, and she raised her hands in the air and exclaimed. Dick Long squinted so that one of his eyes closed, and he gripped the handlebars of the three-wheeler, as if to restrain himself from pedalling off in mid-sentence.

'I'm going to cycle from here to the lake faster than anyone has ever done it. Tom said he could do it in forty seconds, but I'm going to make it in thirty. You can count it, if you like, to prove it to your brother.' He smiled, and two large top teeth seemed to take up all of his mouth. 'Ready, steady, go,' he said, and sped off.

'Wait a minute. Start again,' Jacqueline said. There was no point in leaving the park at this stage: a contest had been set up. Barking madly, Floppy scooted after him.

'It was no good. That dog of yours got in the way. You should keep him on a lead,' Dick Long replied.

'Give me a go. I bet I could do it in a count of forty as well,' Jacqueline said, beaming. She loved being able to pedal madly, rising up from the saddle and crouching forward so the wind whistled past. More than anything, she would be experiencing that thrill Tom had every day, of heading into freedom as his bike spun forward, as though any minute it could become airborne, with the front wheel lifting into space.

'If you like, we can play Cowboys and Indians, and you can be the squaw. We'll build a teepee in a clearing in the forest. I'll go out scouting for adventure on my horse Tonto, and you can cook a meal and mind the children. It's a better game than cycle-racing,' Dick Long said. He leaped off the tricycle and scuffed the ground with one foot.

'You only want to play that because you know I'm faster than you. I'm going right into the middle of the park, deep where nobody has ever been before, to look for treasure,' she said, and started off. Floppy raced ahead. She forgot to wave goodbye to Betty and Lou, because, departing the scene, a threat from Dick Long had reached her.

'I'll tell your brother on you, and he'll tell your aunt where you're going, if you don't play with me. I know you're not allowed in the park, because Tom told me. You're just a sissy girl,' the words blazed.

'Tell who you like, I'm not afraid,' she fired back. A tree nearby bent down alarmingly in the wind.

Chapter Thirty

Jacqueline had reached the point where she knew the purple flow-ers should be. There was the road with the deserted appearance leading back into the town, visible over an uneven wall of mot-tled-looking stones, and gained by walking through what Imelda had called on the day *a charming wicked gate*. Before the gate now, only a shady bower of arching boughs with shining leaves met her gaze. Recently, Auntie Mina had begun to say that she might need glasses, and perhaps that was the problem, because however hard she strained to catch a glimpse of giant-size flowers amidst them, perhaps lurking at the back, behind thicker foliage, there was noth-ing there. Floppy darted about, nose to the ground, looking for an interesting scent-trail to follow, and Jacqueline shook her head, as if in a dream. She had been concentrating so hard on getting to this point that she had lost track of time. She should turn and go home.

Apart from the road beyond the wall; where Jacqueline stood was surrounded by a thick belt of woodland, and she twisted uncertainly. Overhead, trees whispered to one another. On the way to this point, she had passed an old man hobbling along her path. If she met him by walking back the same route, he might bar her way. He could have changed into the King of the Fairies, and when beautiful music drew her into his kingdom, she would forget who she was and wander about in enchanted Tír na nÓg. Although Jacqueline would like to see that kingdom, or even pay a visit — it was a beautiful place where golden fruit dangled from trees and wild deer and rabbits let children pet them — there was the problem that in the land of eternal youth you never grew old, and she didn't want to remain at her age, forever. Mesmerised by the swaying trees, Jacqueline saw the day was drawing in, because shadows had started to lurk. There had been a raucous calling of crows, and now the sky became filled with a swirling mass of black dots, like pieces of shredded paper. She put her hands to her ears to cut out the noise, and then the dog darted out the 'wicked' gate. 'I knew you'd lead me home, Floppy,' Jacqueline murmured, and called, 'Wait for me,' and she clapped her hands and followed.

The road was smooth after the rough surface of the park paths, and Jacqueline had to race to keep up with her pet. Thoughts of Auntie Mina telling her the park was out of bounds came and went. There was no doubt, thanks to Floppy and her own decision to follow his lead, that she was on the right road, but really, she didn't recognise where she was. She saw the name 'Avonbeg Park' on a low wall, and, as if he was talking there beside her, Teddy's voice came into her mind, clear as day. It was evening mealtime in the hotel breakfast-room. 'Keep mine hot. I'm bringing Peadar home to Avonbeg Park first,' her father announced, and then hurried out. Beyond this new wall, Jacqueline observed a row of houses standing back from the street. She opened a gate and walked up a flower-lined path and knocked on a door. She had to use her knuckles to bang, because the brass knocker was too high up, but it opened. A heavy hand descended on her shoulder. At the same time she was brought into a hallway, and one of her own little paws was swallowed up.

'Bill, it's the Clancy girl. She must be lost.' The words travelled over her head. She had been rescued by a woman who had such red cheeks, she must be nice, she thought; Floppy, reading her mind, barked in agreement.

'It's all right. My pup was bringing me home, but it was getting dark, and I wanted to see where Peadar the butcher in Daddy's shop lived, to bring me to the hotel faster. Auntie Mina said I shouldn't be out,' Jacqueline said, in a rush. A light penetrated the gloom ahead, and a tall figure appeared. It was a policeman, she saw by the uniform. When she was lifted up, she caught a smell of tobacco, and wrinkled her nose.

'Better get you back to the hotel so. Teddy Clancy will be up to ninety when she sees you've gone. He has enough troubles, poor man.' The burly policeman secured her in his arms. Floppy whimpered.

'I told you we'd be safe. You brought me to the right place, clever dog,' Jacqueline said happily.

There was no point in telling Auntie Mina her real reason for going into the park, because shortly after the policeman left, she was shackled to the leg of the breakfast-room table, with two of Teddy's ties, knotted together. It would teach her not to do it again and upset the whole hotel, her aunt had nodded wisely. That was the moment Jacqueline decided to run away.

Chapter Thirty-one

Auntie Mina shouldn't punish her, even if she went into the park without permission, because her aunt was wrong. It wasn't possible to get lost when you had a dog to bring you home, Jacqueline brooded. She pushed away the thought that it was disobedient not to do what you're told, and that really the only reason she had been forbidden entry into the park was that Auntie Mina wanted to make sure nothing bad happened to her, and because she didn't want to give Teddy cause for worry. It was a public disgrace, though, to be forced to sit in isolation and be tied up, and worst of all, it painted her as a bad girl in Daddy's eyes. The result could be, he might never love her again.

'If you're old enough to go for a walk on your own, then you're mature enough to understand how I feel, and to take your punishment in the right spirit. I can't ignore that fact that you transgressed the rules. After a time, it will all be forgotten about and we'll be good friends again. Having the fortitude to accept you are wrong and take the consequences, puts you up in my estimation,' Auntie Mina said, patiently.

Jacqueline had been given a chair to sit on during her confinement in Teddy's den and, straining at the ties that bound her, she shifted closer to a window to listen. She had to escape. The sound of her brother Tom and his friends playing in the street below had come up to her. She watched Auntie Mina leave the room in her graceful way, as elegant as those white lilies she always said she loved. 'I'll be back in a half an hour,' the departing figure said, and there was the noise of a key clicking in the sitting-room door behind her, and Jacqueline was alone. She wasn't going to say sorry, no matter what Auntie Mina said, she raged inside.

The small girl rocked her chair to bring her back to the room's fireplace. She was never going to talk to her aunt again; she folded her arms. Apart from the boys calling, silence surged in after Auntie Mina's departure. It washed over the chairs beside the unlit fire and brushed past heavy dark-orange drapes. It lay against the multitude of Japanese houses, climbing in the rows that composed the pattern of Auntie Mina's recently acquired Oriental wallpaper. A woman stood in the doorway of each dwelling, and beyond the woman a farmer bent to pick stalks of rice from a field. There was an identical fat cloud hanging above each house, and a replica bird on the identical roofs. The silence lapped round a shining glass cabinet. This had a set of rose-decorated delft, hiding a row of christening mugs behind. There were names inscribed; one for each member of the family. *Tomas, Jacqueline, Timothy, Susanna and Will.* 'Will for William,' she said aloud and felt less alone.

Since her little brother had left old Josie Dell, to come and live in the hotel, it was obvious to Jacqueline that it was right and proper that he should be about, as though someone like him had been missing all along, to finally compliment the Clancy clan: five children who would act in unison to keep each other safe in the world. The thought prompted a picture of Auntie Mina pressing Will to her breast and humming a tune to him with her eyes closed, as she rocked and rocked him. 'You poor orphan. We must lay down a golden carpet of love before your feet, so that you grow up strong and fearless,' she murmured. Jacqueline had noted how Auntie Mina herself had looked like a warrior queen at that moment, resolute and serene.

'Will thinks you're his Mammy, and he wants to give you a kiss,' Jacqueline had said, without thinking, at the time. It was because she had wanted to hug Auntie Mina and tell her she loved her at that very moment, also. A feeling of remorse seized the tied-up girl, and she felt her cheeks blush.

Despite herself, a giggle came from Jacqueline, making her put a hand to her mouth. Suddenly, all thoughts of Auntie Mina had gone, and she could contemplate escape once more. There had been a quick memory of something else in the glass cabinet, and her laughter had come from a feeling of being tickled. It was a picture of Teddy and Imelda on their wedding day that used to be on the breakfast-room mantelpiece and was now locked away. She closed her eyes. She was in Teddy's arms, and the air rushed past her. She really was back in those arms, because he had tickled her so in such a way that she wanted him to do it again. 'There's no doubt about it. Jacqueline is Daddy's girl,' she heard Imelda say, clear as day, and the still girl had a moment of understanding of Auntie Mina, because now she had the boy-child of her dreams too.

Auntie Mina was back. 'Are you ready to say sorry? It would please Teddy very much to hear how brave his little girl can be.' Her voice came into Jacqueline from behind the locked door, calling sweetly.

Chapter Thirty-two

Sometimes Auntie Mina's eyes had the power of searchlights, as if they could read messages in the skies and uncover hidden thoughts and secrets. Jacqueline hesitated before replying to the weighty words directed at her from outside the door. Auntie Mina was right, because on one occasion recently, Teddy smiled at her like before. It was as though she was part of a dream he had dipped into and was enjoying, which could only happen because she was there. It would be a pity to stop him being able to do that. She had a memory of that special smile of her father's, how it produced a glow on his face, as though somebody had turned on a light behind it. And it made those black eyes of his come alive — she often thought looked as dull as the animal eyes in the dead heads in the butcher's stall. Still her mouth wouldn't form the word 'yes' in reply to her aunt's question about her being sorry for going into the park without permission. She rubbed her legs where the ties bound her, and grimaced with pain.

'The reason I went was because I thought Tom was playing in there, and that he'd let me join in his game and we could come home together,' she said at last. It was a lie, but somehow the very fact that she had brought Tom into her account reassured her that her explanation would stand up. She and Tom always stuck together, and since Imelda had set out on her trip to heaven, it was good to have her brother still as much a part of her life, the same as sunrise in the morning; part of her existence for as long as she could remember.

'Tom was with me for the whole time you were missing. He and I were busy with an impromptu geography class. There is a big world out there, and sooner or later he's going to want to explore it,' Auntie Mina enthused, but there was an edge to her voice, and Jacqueline heard the key turn. To the right of the den door, she saw that Betty and Lou had arrived to take up places in the glass cabinet. By some means, they had been spirited in there without their knowing how, and now Betty had her face pressed up against the glass to peer out. She saw Jacqueline on her chair, and waved. Jacqueline waved back. The motion made her shift and lose her balance, and the chair wobbled. Betty stretched her hands out in a flying exercise, and Lou joined her, and they began to step around the christening cups and the delph sets. 'Whee, whee!' Jacqueline opened her arms out and made her own aeroplane movement.

'Stop that. You really don't care what trouble you cause, do you? I've a good mind to leave you in here all day.' Auntie Mina had marched from the door and was standing over her. Distracted, Jacqueline pushed herself back and fell off the seat. It caused her leg to jerk, and she began to cry.

'I hate you. I want my Mammy back. I'll tell her never to go away again, because it only makes Teddy sad, and because I want her to kiss me better.' She sobbed. A thought took hold: if she was going to be left in here, she would set the room on fire. It wasn't a new idea, because she had already seen a box of matches on the fireplace, ready to be put to the neat bundle of paper and sticks in the grate. If she did set the hotel on fire, she and Teddy and her brothers and sister would live in a forest. They would play with the rabbits and foxes. They'd have a cottage. Imelda would cook, and place a rug on the woodland floor. They could have a picnic outside. When Daddy came home from work, he would swing her in the air and say, 'What's my favourite girl been doing while I was away?' Betty and Lou had found a way out of the glass cabinet, it was good to note, because they were sitting, one on either side on Auntie Mina's shoulders.

'Let's plait the pretty hair,' Lou said, and Betty clapped her hands. Soon strawberry-blond strands and stray curls were flying over and back, and the two girls laughed, peering at Jacqueline from the midst of the shining mass. Auntie Mina put her hands on her head and shook it, so that they fell out.

'That's it. I've had enough. Teddy needs to take charge of his own life and children. I've done my best but I'm not capable of going any further with this. I'm going away, even if it means leaving chaos behind,' she said. Jacqueline didn't intend what happened next. It was the fault of Betty and Lou. Having found themselves knocked on to the ground, they had picked themselves up. They had drawn a trapdoor on the floor and opened it wide. There was a ladder to climb down, and they stepped onto the front rung and invited Jacqueline in. She tugged at the ties that bound her fiercely, and cried out.

'What's going on here? Can a man not come home for his dinner, sore in mind and body, and not have some peace? Why did you tie yourself to the table? Surely there are healthier ways to play, Jacqueline.' Teddy had arrived.

'It's only a pretend game. Auntie Mina said I should be tied up, and I wanted to see what it felt like.' Jacqueline hesitated. It was up to Auntie Mina to tell the truth.

'The little child is a bundle of lies, I'm afraid.' Auntie Mina shook her head. She bent low, and Jacqueline felt her skin expand as if she had been patted all over with cool air, when the ties were opened. That was when Betty and Lou intervened. They caught

Jacqueline's hand and made her grab Auntie Mina by the ankle. The trapdoor was right behind her, as if it had been made for her all along.

'Pull now and make her off balance. She's upset. She needs to get away from here,' they said. Jacqueline did what she was told, and Auntie Mina exclaimed and bent down to rub her own ankle.

'I think it's time you and I had a talk, Teddy. Perhaps we need to put a time-limit on my being here. The children need a proper mother; somebody who can be a wife to you too.' She winced, and Teddy shook his head and called out, 'No. Don't say that. There was always only one woman for me, and now she's gone.' He glanced at Jacqueline directly, as if he needed her support.

'I know where Imelda is. You can depend on me. I'll bring her back, Daddy,' the frightened girl sobbed.

Immediately after that, Auntie Mina linked her brother's arm. 'You're distraught, you poor man,' she said, frowning, and looked down at her niece. 'We must learn to leave the past behind, Jackie dear. All this is torturing your Daddy needlessly. What does the sound of a new Mammy who will look after you feel like? I'm sure it must be lovely.' Her voice was like a soft wind.

At the same time, Betty and Lou called out in alarm. Teddy was about to step into the trapdoor hole and disappear.

Chapter Thirty-three

'It's Miss Clancy, isn't it? You're the hotelier's daughter. Many's the favour the same Teddy Clancy did for me, but you don't know what I'm talking about. You're only a little sprat. Have you nobody to look after you, that you can run around the town?' The man who was leaning against the town-hall wall, and had beckoned Jacqueline over to speak to her, spat on the ground. The spit had arched sideways and she had an urge to see if she could copy the action, because at the last minute particles of spray separated out like a neat waterfall. It would be a good trick she and Tom could practise together. She would leave that until later, though, because the eyes of the man who had addressed her had begun to water alarmingly, and he took a wrinkled handkerchief from his pocket and began to dab at them.

'Curse of God on it, for an affliction,' he said, and twitched his nose.

'Yes, my name is Jacqueline Clancy, and I live in that hotel.' She pointed behind her. 'It's very big inside, and there's lots of furniture. I don't even know all the rooms, there's so many. When Mammy comes home, she's going to have a concert, and all the people in the rooms will come to it and clap. You can come along if you like, too,' she found herself rambling on, because the man with red-rimmed eyes, the same as the devil, had begun to dance on the street.

'*Diddle-ei-di-ei-di-ei,*' he chortled. A pair of dirty boots shuffled, and he took Jacqueline's hand. They were warm, like when Mamma held hers, but these were hard too, and she smelt cigarettes from his breath when he leant down. 'I was at a concert your mother arranged once, and she sang a song herself. If you're half as good as her when you grow up, you'll make her proud.' The dancer stopped abruptly.

'I have to go. Auntie Mina said I'm not to talk to strangers.' Jacqueline took a step back. She would have liked to stay to hear more about Imelda, because the mention of her name had made her want to linger and talk, as though she had come unexpectedly into her mother's presence, but around her, she saw, other men had gathered. They were standing and tipping their hats and nodding, as if she was in the middle of a circus-ring about to take a bow, and Auntie Mina might have spotted her from a hotel window. She was supposed to be on her best behaviour since the incident about the park, and the most she could hope for now was that it would soon all be forgotten about.

'This Mickie Hughes was no stranger to Imelda Clancy, God rest her soul.' Barring her way, the man who smelt of tobacco pointed at himself. 'She was the kindest woman the town ever saw, and the place will never be the same without her. Whatever you do, don't forget you're your mother's daughter. Her nature is in you, ready to spring out. You'll amaze us all soon, and that will be the great day. I wouldn't be surprised if you made a grand singer when you grow up.' He drew a coin from his pocket and placed it in her hand.

'I'm not allowed to take money,' Jacqueline stammered.

'It's bad manners to refuse a gift,' Mickie Hughes chuckled. 'Now go and buy some sweets.' The other men murmured approval. 'Her mother isn't dead while she's around. She's the image of her,' she heard one of them say, as she backed off.

It was a pity that Betty and Lou had decided to sit on the window sill of Mrs Ryan's sweetshop as Jacqueline was passing it by, a few minutes later. She had formed a resolution as she left the men at the town hall that she would hand her pennies to her aunt to put into her saving box, but now it was too late, because the presence of her friends caused her to raise herself on tiptoe to stare through to the sweetshop's interior. The window was slightly open, and Betty had managed to dip in and get a snow-white bon-bon somebody must have left behind on the counter, out to where they sat, and was licking it appreciatively. Lou slid her tongue along it too, from her side.

'Brush your teeth every time you eat sweets, or they'll turn black and fall out, naughty Lou,' Betty laughed, and licked more.

'I'll pretend I'm Auntie Mina and I've lost my voice and can't give out,' Lou said, and acted as if she was choking. Then they both continued to lick, enjoying the feast so much that Jacqueline had to enter the shop. There was another reason why she went in. Mickie Hughes had said she was like Imelda, and chewing something delicious would give her the opportunity to experience the words again, flowing through her with the same pleasurable sensation as sugar melting in the mouth. As she was about to enter, for the second time that day she was accosted by a stranger. This time a young woman in black barred the way.

'No sweets today. The shop is closed for sales. Mammy has died and the wake is on above. If you want to see her laid out, you'll have to join the queue on the stairs,' the woman said, her voice quavering.

She would have to go on. It was either that or run into Auntie Mina's arms for a comforting hug. Jacqueline took a step forward.

Chapter Thirty-four

It was lovely to be out walking with Tom, Jacqueline thought; she could tell him all about the antics of Betty and Lou, and the further adventures they hoped to have together. Tom could talk forever about adventure and escapades, because he was older and could range about the town. He knew the best trees for bows and arrows. He could also be relied upon to have a strip of toy gun-shot paper deep in the bottom of his pocket. When he came to a smooth piece of pavement, he would unroll the paper and hit one of the gunpowder bumps on it, with a stone. This would make a resounding bang, and then there was the pleasure of sniffing the acrid smell of gunpowder released, and of seeing a definite flash where the stone had aimed at. If Jacqueline begged hard enough, he would let her have a go. He would tear a piece of the paper roll with the shot embedded in it, and she would place it carefully on the ground and thump it clumsily. When she did succeed in creating the banging noise, and sniffed the sharp gunpowder smell, for a moment she was out riding neck and neck with her brother, two cowboys chasing down a trail, the sun high overhead, blazing as if to proclaim their glory and freedom-seeking ways.

A wind rustled in leafy branches over Jacqueline's head. The trees were rounded out in an apple shape, or else their bunched-up leaves made them look like fat sheep on top of a stick, she decided. She was looking up at one as they passed, but only briefly, because Tom was in no mood to delay. There was a gang called the O'Toole Boys who lived in a cluster of houses off the avenue they were walking along, and if they were caught out in the open like this, they would be surrounded and set upon. Stones would be thrown, or they would be attacked with sticks, he explained. He had a whistle he always carried with him, to call the members of his own gang, but by the time he blew it and the sound of it reached them, it might be too late.

Wide and long as a runway, the avenue stretched ahead. Sometimes, just in case, the travelling pair ducked behind parked cars or pressed themselves against those spindly trees, but held their course so that a church at the end of the street that poked a needle-thin spire into the clouds came closer, and the railings around the adjacent cemetery approached. They could leap over these, Tom explained, and find a tombstone to crouch behind if the O'Toole Boys arrived. 'The 'fraidy-cats won't go near the graves because they think they'll see a ghost,' he laughed, but then nearly knocked his sister down jumping back, because a dog had poked its head out of the window of a parked car they were passing, and barked.

'Aunt Mina said ghosts are a figment of the imagination.' Jacqueline stumbled over the unfamiliar phrase, and had a sudden recollection of the smell of lavender essence her aunt used, when she had bent down to kiss her the night before. Auntie Mina had laughed too, in that musical way that sounded like running water, and taken her hand and patted it. 'I love you, Auntie Mina.' The words had roamed round in Jacqueline's head, but stayed inside. 'Read me a story before you go, then I'll fall asleep,' she had said instead, and had stared, fascinated, at her aunt's mobile mouth while she read, revealing teeth as white as piano keys, as it widened in a smile.

'I don't believe in spirits and things. They're only people dressed in sheets to scare you,' Tom scoffed, but for a while, as if he didn't believe his own words, he drifted in behind his sister. Nearing the start of the cemetery railings, he ran ahead. He seemed to have forgotten the danger the O'Tooles presented, because he climbed up onto the iron paling to peer over. Jacqueline, who was smaller, found a toe-hole in the wall quickly, and hoisted herself up. Peering into the cemetery, she was confronted by a white figure. It was a statue of a woman with her arms outstretched, and Tom followed her gaze. He gripped the railings with one hand and pointed with the other.

'That's Our Lady. She's Mammy's mother in heaven, and now she's our Mammy too,' he explained. Auntie Mina told me that if ever I feel lonely or want anything, I'm to ask Our Lady, and she'll do her best to get it for me. It's God's will,' he said importantly. 'She probably didn't tell you, because you're so young and wouldn't understand.' The girl beside him had a sudden recollection of Tom and Auntie Mina sitting closely side by side. Their heads were bent together deep in conversation, as if they didn't want anybody else to hear. It was silly to say she was too little, because she understood everything. She knew, for instance, that Tom missed Imelda, just like she did, and that was why he let their aunt's arms encircle him whenever he cried, and hold him tight. She couldn't cry as easily as Tom for Imelda, that was all, and Auntie Mina thought she didn't care. Jacqueline had to give up thinking about it then, because in the distance Teddy had gone through the gates of the cemetery.

'It's Daddy. We're not supposed to be so far away from the hotel. Duck down,' Tom ordered, and made her lie flat on the ground. It was why Jacqueline couldn't see what happened next, but heard Teddy's voice clear as day as he stood near their hidden position.

'Darling Imelda, I've come to you again to ask you a favour.' Teddy's mention of her mother's name made Jacqueline rise, until

Tom pressed her back with the palm of his hand. Her brother was wrong. Right now, Imelda was probably standing beside that white-robed figure. If she didn't call out to her and identify herself, she'd be gone.

'It's only a prayer. He doesn't think Mammy can really hear. We'll have to just listen,' he whispered.

'The pain is impossible. If it wasn't for the children's sake, I'd join you and we'd be reunited as one. I'm sorry for my sins, oh Lord, but this punishment is too much.' Teddy's voice burst out, like a thunderclap, making Jacqueline jerk. Beside her a colony of ants had started to move up the wall, and she put a finger out to stop them. They crawled over her finger, pursuing their steady pace. Maybe she could be friends with these ants, she thought. They could bring her into their land. She'd learn how to talk their language and climb upside-down on walls. The ants had gone over the cemetery boundary, and Jacqueline imagined them marching patiently in line until they reached Teddy's feet. They would make him laugh because they would crawl up his leg and tickle him. She relaxed and smiled. She should have realised that the white lady was talking to Teddy from a world of dreams. The lady would have linked Teddy, ready to take him back with her by now, but about to rise finally to see it all, Jacqueline whimpered. A kick from Tom had distracted her. He put a finger to his lips.

'Mina has been offered a job in America. She'd prefer to stay and mind the children, but I can't live with my sister forever,' the crouching pair heard Teddy say with a sigh. 'Tell me what to do, Imelda,' he pleaded next, and Jacqueline's attention returned to the ants. It had to, because they were crawling over her wrist, as if they were a living chain and would tie her to the spot forever. 'I'm going now, but I'll be back tomorrow. Stay with me and light my way. I have to make a decision soon. Goodbye, my dear,' Teddy said, and began the words of the Hail Mary, which Jacqueline knew, because she had learnt the prayer in school. She saw her father's retreating back when she popped up, and the white lady standing still and silent. Before she could call and alert him to their presence, Tom grabbed at her.

'We're blood brother and sister. We don't tell on each other,' he hissed. 'When Daddy is gone, we'll climb over the railings to take the short way home,' he added bravely. It was while she was clambering over the iron points that Jacqueline tore her dress, and because they had made a pact with one another she couldn't tell on Tom and say where he'd brought her, when they got back to the hotel. As a result, it was impossible to tell Auntie Mina how the dress had been torn. It meant that she was tied to the leg of the table a second time.

Chapter Thirty-five

Jucqueline straightened up after rubbing her toes. It was almost a year since Auntie Mina had come to live with them, and now the sandals she had brought as a gift had grown too small for her. She forgot her discomfort, a moment later, clambering into Teddy's car. It was always special when she was going anywhere on a journey with her father. A shout out to Auntie Mina that he was taking her along for the spin; if he was making deliveries with the butcher's van, or ferrying an animal in the horsebox, or even making a visit in the hearse to discuss some funeral arrangements, she would be in with him like a shot, climbing onto the passenger seat. It was different than being with Imelda when she had been at the wheel. Her mother had barely let her move, making sure she sat back into the seat and didn't distract her during the journey, but Teddy often forget she was there, until a bump on the road the car had bounced over made her jolt forward, and she'd call out. Mostly she would ignore such unpleasant sensations, though, because Teddy was just like his name, and even though he used cross words, she could feel his fondness for her emanating from him. It was the same as leaning into Kitty for a hug, or the funny heat coming off a big tom-cat.

This time when she climbed in, Teddy was going to visit a farm called 'Ballyhass' to pick up some sheep for Peadar to slaughter. Normally they were delivered, but he was doing a favour for a widow tied down with a young family, he explained. 'We're off to see Marion Daly, Mina. This shouldn't take too long. It's only a preliminary meeting, to find out how we both feel. Whatever happens now will decide whether or not the matter will progress further.' His voice had come out to Jacqueline from the back-kitchen door first, and then he and his sister appeared in the yard. There was a blush on her aunt's cheeks, and her eyes were glued to Teddy. She twisted back one of those errant curls into place with a hairpin, and she frowned.

'There's no need for any such a thing as *progress* with Marion, especially if it's on my behalf. We can always work things out here. I'll never let you down. The children are like my family too,' she said.

The front seat of the horsebox had bits of straw stuck to the ground Jacqueline saw as she sat and waited. A fly buzzed about. If Teddy used his hands to push the window down, because that was the only way it worked, he could let the fly out. A grey film of dust patterned the upper regions of the window, but looking through it lower down, the half-moon shape of cleaner glass made by a windscreen wiper that always squeaked, gave plenty of visibility. Jacqueline leaned into the leather seat and breathed lightly. The leather odour the seat emitted, mixed with a smell of old horse manure, was creating a wave of nausea. She wouldn't complain, though, because she was Teddy's girl. She wouldn't have minded if he had chosen Tom to be with him, as he often did, but fortunately he hadn't, and she must be on her best behaviour, excited about what new event might be just around the corner.

'You're going to meet the person who might be your new Mammy today.' Teddy stood at the driver's door. Instead of climbing in, because he had put his hand on the steering wheel to swing up, he frowned. 'Come and see this, Mina. I don't think Jacqueline is well,' he called to his sister.

'Imelda,' Jacqueline said under her breath. She had had to speak aloud, because her mother's face hadn't come to her when he had said the word 'Mammy'. It always had done up to then, but there had been a blank. Her mother must have been annoyed, but Jacqueline didn't understand why until invisible as the wind, she finally did arrive.

You must stop this meeting happening, or else I'll leave forever, Imelda's cross look announced.

'Maybe you should stay with Mina. You've gone quite pale.' Teddy wouldn't give up on his daughter's illness. He had lifted himself into the cab and felt her forehead. Sheep called out from the box behind, as if their rank smell had caused the problem. 'It looks as if you might be coming down with something.' Teddy grimaced, and Jacqueline found herself being prised off her seat, like somebody who was a nuisance, or who stood in her father's way.

'You poor thing, you can't travel round like that. Marion will think we don't know how to look after you,' Mina said. She had arrived at the horsebox too, and she raised her hands to take her niece from Teddy. 'Tom can go instead, and work his charms. After all, this is about first impressions,' she announced, and Jacqueline felt the eager boy brush past.

She would never be able to fulfil Imelda's wishes now. A sharp stone dug into her right foot when she stood on the ground, and her toes, in those cramped sandals, curled in pain.

Chapter Thirty-six

By the time the next opportunity arose for Jacqueline to go for a drive with Teddy, she was over her mysterious illness. They were visiting Donnie Merrigan. Her father trained Donnie's horse, called 'Bright Spark', and Teddy was also going to ride it in the last point-to-point of the season, in a field beyond the cattle-mart pens at the back of the hotel.

That morning, Jacqueline had been in trouble with Auntie Mina, because her aunt had found Jacqueline's wet panties hidden under the bed. Of course, wetting herself wasn't acceptable. Jacqueline knew she was too big a girl now to let such a thing happen. She knew that Kitty, for instance, would mock her if she found out, so she had tucked the offending article out of sight. She had stared at it dumbly when Auntie Mina had stooped to pick it up — revealed because her aunt had pulled out Jacqueline's bed to clean underneath — and had promptly said it wasn't hers. It was another lie, but Auntie Mina hadn't reprimanded her. Instead, she said she was going to put a potty under Jacqueline's bed, and that her niece would have to sit on it for at least a half an hour before going to sleep that evening. Jacqueline had squirmed at the thought of such an imposition. If nothing happened and she didn't do a wee-wee, she might have to stay on it for longer. Susanna was no longer in her cot, and had come to share Jacqueline's room with her, in a grown-up bed placed alongside. She would feel she was being treated in the same way as that little sister, as though she was still three, instead of the big five-year-old she had become. Even Susanna would pretend she'd become the sister who was in charge and call Jacqueline a big baby.

Being chosen to go with Teddy was helping Jacqueline put the morning's events out of her mind. Sitting beside her father, happiness stole over her. It was like being able to stand under a tree that would provide shelter from a storm. Even though he spoke crossly when she kneeled up on the seat as they set off, she wasn't frightened, because he wagged his ears at her in a comical way and said, 'Hee-haw,' as if he was a donkey, and, although they were moving slowly, showed the whites of his eyes.

Bowling through the countryside and skirting alongside a high wall overhung by trees, they arrived at stone pillars with eagles on top, and supporting a pair of rusting gates.

'Donnie is looking forward to meeting you. He and I have some matters to discuss regarding his sister Marion. Of course you don't have to be involved, but you will find plenty of things to keep you amused in the meantime. Perhaps you might go for a walk to the stables and tell me if you see a pony you like. I was thinking of changing Blackie for something more spirited,' Teddy announced. 'If things work out between Marion and myself, you might be seeing much more of Donnie in the future,' he added. Helping her father, watching his big hands clutch at the iron handle of the gate to swing it open, Jacqueline had a sudden need for time to stand still. *Mammy Marion*, she said in her mind. She made herself imagine a rosy skinned apple because her favourite fruit and the two names had a similar sound. She thought about her wet panties that morning, and about how she wanted to be grown up and say the right thing.

'If we sell Blackie, I'll never be able to ride her with Imelda in the hunt again, and she told me we would next year,' Jacqueline answered instead. She seemed to see the squat pony's wicked eyes at that moment winking at her; it was as if the devil could also be an angel in disguise.

'This has nothing to do with Imelda. You must try and live in the present, dear,' Teddy declared, and at the same time swung the gate open.

Chapter Thirty-seven

Jacqueline began to think about running away more and more. It was all Auntie Mina's fault. Every time she tried to please her, something went wrong. Recently she'd attempted to eat lumpy porridge to show what a good girl she was, because Auntie Mina had said it was important to lead by example and the twins needed to be given encouragement to eat different foods. She'd had to put a lot of sugar on it to help it go down. That resulted in one of her teeth aching so badly she'd shrieked aloud. Teddy had put a drop of whiskey on it to take the pain away. Auntie Mina said Jacqueline should have had more sense, instead of causing her father to acquaint her with alcohol. Now, for some reason, she was wetting the bed. Worse than that, she was causing Auntie Mina to have discussions with Auntie Agatha about how to cure another problem, because for some time Jacqueline hadn't been able to go to the toilet, to do a number two.

The discussion about her predicament began in Auntie Agatha's bedroom. On this occasion Jacqueline was already in there. Auntie Mina had knocked on the door unexpectedly, and marched in to join them. It was only the second time Jacqueline had travelled to her grand-aunt's room alone; she had discovered the way before.

This time, she had set out from the family quarters with more assurance. Going through the hotel, it seemed, was like doing one of those mazes in a puzzle book, when you had to find a route to reach a pot of treasure, and she padded along confidently. There were sets of steps and tricky bends to negotiate. A narrow back-stairs led to Kitty's kitchen; as she passed, she imagined herself as a spy moving stealthily, a level above the lives of ordinary folk, as though they and she lived completely different existences.

Still the magnet of Auntie Agatha's room drew Jacqueline along. To maintain her sense of purpose, she conjured up the possibility of a sweet waiting, but what she really wanted was to gaze again on the old lady's world. On the dressing table there was a silver hairbrush, complete with its dancing lady embellished on the back, and beside that a wide, peach-coloured shell. Auntie Agatha had invited her to put her ear to it on her last visit, and she had heard the sea. Even more enticing, an opened fan, in shades of red, rested against the dressing-table mirror. If only she could shake it she was sure a myriad of stars in a ruby coloured mist would drift out. As well as that, Auntie Agatha would request Jacqueline to sit in the rocking chair by the window so that they could have a talk. Jacqueline burrowed on through the hotel as her thoughts flew, and she imagined how Auntie Agatha would pause and wait for her to speak as they chatted, and how those faded puppy eyes that regarded her so solemnly would beam with delight.

Jacqueline was sitting on Auntie Agatha's bed when Auntie Mina stepped in the door. They were having a game of snap on the hilly eiderdown. Pulling herself up on her pillow, Auntie Agatha had caused the precariously placed playing cards to fall on the floor. It was time for Auntie Agatha's insulin injection, Auntie Mina declared. From that moment on, it seemed, the cosy room was transformed into a ward, because a hospital smell entered the air. A giant syringe was laid out on a tray. A sealed small bottle of clear liquid had been laid beside the needle. Jacqueline was beginning to think of herself as very grown up, because she was in the middle of an intricate procedure, when, without warning, Auntie Mina brought up Jacqueline's own condition.

Struggling to sit upright for her injection, Auntie Agatha frowned in her direction, and the room seemed to grow suddenly hot. 'If only an injection could solve Jacqueline's condition, we would have nothing to worry about,' she said, shaking her head. Her continued stare made Jacqueline squirm.

Auntie Mina winked. 'Now now, Agatha, there's no need to be gloomy,' she said, and spider's-web eyelashes flickered. 'All Jacqueline needs is a little help. She's been through a lot recently, and we must do the best we can. I've been doing my research, and a steaming bath can work wonders. Failing that, some soap slipped into the orifice will do the trick.'

'I'd prefer being made to sit on the potty and tied to the leg of the bed,' Jacqueline declared. Somehow she sensed what an orifice meant, and what was going to happen to her. When Auntie Agatha wasn't looking, she would hide the red fan in the sleeve of her cardigan and steal away. Tonight she would creep to her bedroom window when Susanna was asleep, and clamber out. Betty and Lou would come with her. Waving the magic fan would create a pathway to never-never land, where Imelda waited.

'I have nothing but praise for Jackie. I can't tell you how good she's been recently. We've become the best of friends together, Agatha,' Mina suddenly burst out. She had been putting the injection away in a case, and Jacqueline was sure she saw tears in her eyes, as if she'd miss her niece, because Jacqueline was going to run away.

She concentrated her gaze on the fan to steady her thoughts.

Chapter Thirty-eight

As well as the maze of the hotel, words were another puzzle Jacqueline liked to solve for herself. The words in her school-book, like 'sat' and 'mat' and 'Pat', were quickly digested. They hung in rows in her mind, like bunting flapping in a breeze, but the name-signs on the shops in the town were a different matter. Some of the words were written in Irish, and she had gazed, be-mused, at the strange-looking symbols, which were really letters of that alphabet. The 'T' in Tighearnaigh which looked like a teapot, was easy to identify, because she knew the sound, but the letters that came afterwards were like flyaway shapes stuck together, even if they were leggy or had a satisfyingly round shape. Sometimes she drew the main street of Tooradulla in her copybook, attempting to write the names of each shop overhead and saying them aloud as she dug in her pencil. To fit everything in, and because there were two lines of houses at the top and bottom end of the street also, to create a pretend square, her attempts changed the broad thorough-fare into a quadrangle. She allowed small roads, like funnels, to let traffic in and out, and the look of it made her feel safe, as though all that mattered existed within this daisy-chain of houses, making each tall and small drawn-in box the boundary of everything she knew.

Everyone was going to Lough Derg for a swim, Teddy had decided. It was a bright morning, shortly after Mina's talk with Agatha about her solution to Jacqueline's toilet problems. She was engrossed in one of her drawings with one twin on either side, and started with joy when Teddy made his announcement. This time she wouldn't be afraid.

'There won't be an opportunity again before the winter sets in,' Teddy said. He rubbed his hands together at the same time, and glanced out the window as though the good weather might go away. They were in the breakfast-room, and his figure was positioned in such a way that it blocked the sun, so that it poured in around him, the same colour as egg-nog, or the lemon cake Auntie Mina loved to make. The twins' unfinished lunch still remained on the table: Jacqueline had been encouraged to play with because Auntie Mina was feeding the baby, William. Now, instead of drawing in Betty or Lou into the picture of the town, as Jacqueline had been thinking about doing, she grabbed back the crayons Susanna and Tim had borrowed, and hustled them to the door. After that, loud voices and delighted cries filled the room, and soon, when it seemed they would never be ready, they were all squashed into the car. Even Floppy had wriggled his way onto the floor. In the back of the car, Jacqueline was forced to push this way and that with her elbows to create space. Outside, a hanging exhaust pipe let off gunfire shots from the rear of the vehicle, and in no time at all they were roaring out of the town. She didn't want to leave home — she would prefer to go back and finish her drawing, Jacqueline decided at the last minute — but it was too late, because Morrissey and Sons, the last shop on Main Street, had revealed its name. They had joined in with a thin trickle of traffic from the pretend square, to be siphoned out.

'It's too uncomfortable in here,' Jacqueline complained a few seconds later, but nobody was listening. Betty and Lou had come, and were sitting on her shoulder. When she got back, she had put them into her drawing. She could picture them already in their red car, lounging back on the seats and relaxing. Wriggling upwards, she made space on the edge of the seat to peer out in front of her.

'God protect us on this journey and bring us safely home,' Teddy intoned. A cigarette he threw out the window created a trail of sparks. He jammed his foot on the brakes because something had streaked across the road, making the car halt suddenly, and everyone jerked forward.

'Bless us, Teddy, that cat was well spotted. If it wasn't for your quick reaction, we could all be dead,' Auntie Mina exclaimed. 'Though less speed would be better in the future.' Her voice became louder to the girl in the back, because Teddy had revved up the engine, making the car leap, and Jacqueline imagined her aunt's clenched fingers. They might be going back yet, but although the baby wailed in Mina's arms, and the twins began to whimper, they sailed forward.

'Everybody be quiet, please. This is the thanks I get, Mina, for organising a treat. Imelda would have understood. I can't crawl to a place. It's another indication that things must change.' Teddy's voice rang out again, over the children's heads. At the same time he turned his head, as if to see the road back and return home, and Floppy barked with excitement.

'Any minute now I'll be gone, and that's another alteration that won't be undone. The last thing I want is to stand in your way, Teddy,' Jacqueline heard her aunt murmur, and then a cramp dug into her own left leg, and she groaned and had to shift out of earshot.

There was a horseshoe shape of sand on the lake shore at the picnic spot he called Jackson's Bay, where Teddy finally drew the car up. Everyone piled out, and Mina spread a rug down beside the sandy shore. Jacqueline was appointed to find a big stone to put in one corner to keep the tartan square in place. She would bring the rock back home with her, she decided, weighing her selection in her hand. It had the shape of a house, and she would paint on windows and doors, and put it on her drawing, where the hotel had been sketched in. It was a good thought to concentrate on, because the lake before her looked too wide and deep.

A few minutes after the rug was laid, Tom was in the water. Holding the baby in her arms, with an exclamation of delight Auntie Mina lifted her skirt and stepped into the shallows too. Jacqueline shrank back. Maybe she could hide in the woods and nobody would miss her, but Auntie Mina caught her eye.

'Come on, darlings, it's no shame to be naked. Take your clothes off and leave them on the rug, and we'll all paddle together,' Mina called to the twins. In a blur of movement, the pair had rushed past Jacqueline and leapt about in the shallows, splashing each other with squeals of delight. She would have to venture after them. The lake was like a sea, and Teddy's and Tom's heads bobbed far out. Floppy had set out to race round the water's edge, and Betty and Lou were perched on a rock, gazing towards the lake's shimmering horizon, when Jacqueline heard Teddy call.

'Leave the baby on the rug for a moment, Mina. Bring Jacqueline in to meet me.' The words bounced on the water towards them. Before she could take a deep breath, or say her father was out too far, she was lifted up.

The lake had some particles of weed and dirt floating in it when, dangling above the water, Jacqueline looked down. Auntie Mina's feet had a green tinge. Her legs, viewed from above the surface, seemed more like jelly, as if they didn't belong to her, or might lift and begin to float, instead of walking a steady pace. Soon, with Aunt Mina's hands grasped round her waist, she was swimming, and once, when a little wave swept over her face, she became upright again, and had to cling tighter, as if Auntie Mina was a life-buoy. It caused them both to laugh, until Jacqueline got a fright because she swallowed a mouthful. 'I want to go back now,' she gasped, but they pushed on.

'Don't worry, we're a pair of mermaids on a swim together.' Auntie Mina threw back her head to chortle, and Jacqueline seemed to see her aunt's mouth fill up with lake water. It meant she was going to let her go and they would both plunge under the slapping waves. But they were saved because they were beside Teddy. She could feel the warmth of his body as she was handed over.

'It's too deep for me. I want to go back with Auntie Mina.' Jacqueline strained her head to look back at the retreating figure. There was no point, because Teddy's arms weren't letting go, and she held on tighter. The next second, he seemed to have forgotten she was a child, and that his first job was to take care of her, because although Jacqueline hooked an arm around his neck, he uttered the words, "sink or swim" and, "being thrown in at the deep end is the only way to go". Even worse, his face beamed, as if he'd given his daughter a sweet or an ice-cream cone.

'I'm not able to swim on my own yet,' Jacqueline gasped. Out of the corner of her eye, she saw she must be wrong, because Tom was close by. He was lying on his back, his arms resting on the water as if on cushions. He even managed a wave in her direction. Things were suddenly better too when Teddy again allowed her to cling on tight to him. She was his foal and he was the Daddy horse, she thought happily, because now he heaved her onto his shoulders and they were swimming in the ink-blue waves.

'Hold on tight,' we're going out further,' Teddy spluttered.

'Bring her back. You're going too deep,' Mina's voice reached them in snatches. It was high and thin, and Jacqueline imagined her swimming out to reach them. Her aunt was too late, though, because Teddy had decided to start his daughter's swimming lesson. She was let go.

'Help, Mammy. I'm drowning!' Jacqueline screamed, until she went under.

Chapter Thirty-nine

'Just because I'm going away doesn't mean you have to get married. Have you spoken to Dorrie? She's our sister as well, and I'm sure she's in a position to take William into St Patrick's, if only for a year or two, until he's more manageable. Jacqueline could go and stay with him for a while, to stop him making strange. After all, Dorrie is second-in-command in the orphanage,' Auntie Mina said to Teddy. She placed another log on the fire in the den, dampening the flames.

'Everything will be decided in the next few minutes. Donnie and Fred are on their way here to give me Marion's answer. If she doesn't say yes to my proposal, I could consider bringing Will to St Patrick's.' Jacqueline heard Teddy sigh and saw him lift a glass of whiskey and swirl the golden liquid round. She had lifted her gaze, abandoning her game of snakes and ladders, which she been teaching Susanna how to play before the conversation began. The fire roared up. Teddy moved his chair back from the heat and turned to face them.

'I won. The game is over,' Susanna called out just then, and Jacqueline saw her slide a counter up a snake instead of the other way round.

'Auntie Mina, Susanna is cheating, she won't play the game properly,' Jacqueline said, standing up. At the same time, her little sister lifted the board to knock the counters off. It was no harm in many ways, because the name 'Marion' had leaped out at Jacqueline as Teddy spoke. If Marion said yes, it would mean Will wouldn't have to stay in an orphanage.

She could save her family, it was plain to see. Jacqueline swallowed hard, as though something was stuck in her throat. All she needed to do was to say she wanted to meet Mammy Marion. One thing was for sure: the implications of whatever she said wouldn't be taken in by Susanna, because Fred, Teddy's solicitor pal, was bustling into the room. A smell of cologne wafted towards Jacqueline because he had bent down to lift her sister up. Susanna's dress sailed outwards, and a powerful-looking white hand slapped the exposed flash.

'This is the minx I'm going to marry. Say what you will, Teddy, we're going to run away together,' the solicitor said, and held Susanna out from him in a swift movement, so that she squealed with delight.

'Fred wants to marry you, Susanna. Now you're going to have to make up your mind if you want to go with him, or stay with us and turn down the chance of having a fortune. I'd take the money if I were you,' Teddy chuckled. Jacqueline found herself stuck for words when Susanna's face crumpled in tears, as if Teddy really did want her to do what he had recommended.

The first thing Jacqueline did when she arrived at Auntie Dorrie's orphanage was to leap out of the car and run around in a giddy manner. The orphanage was in Dublin. It had been a long journey getting there, and her legs were stiff. As she ran, she took in a tennis court: a girl was cycling round inside the perimeter as effortlessly as a bird in a cage. More children were calling to one another beside a play-slide. They turned to watch her, becoming silent, as if to make her go home, as though they knew that this wasn't where Will was meant to stay, and she should sense it too. Jacqueline muttered a greeting. She would have liked to play on the slide, to see what it was like, but the children seemed to be guarding it for themselves. The building at the top of the yard was a school, she noted, galloping past, because a group of children began to trickle out, ignoring her, probably thinking she was another orphan about to come and stay. If she did come here to mind Will for a while, everybody would tell her what to do, and soon she would become a regular orphan like them, eating with them and sleeping with a big group of people. She glanced back at the car. Everybody had stood out, and Auntie Dorrie was crossing the yard towards them. She had a sudden recollection of the heat of all their bodies pressed together on the way to Dublin, and how Teddy had burst into the song, *It's a long way to Tipperary,* making everyone in the car join in, and calling them a sleepy lot, but giving up after a while, saying that the dead would show more enthusiasm. She thought about a hole in the back of the driver's seat facing her: she had worried at it with a finger until it had grown large, and then she and Tim had played a game by stuffing it with bits of straw and pebbles from the car floor until it had bulged out like a bird's nest.

'Can we play on the way home again, Jacqueline?' Tim had said with shining eyes, and she had shrugged as if she didn't care. Then he had crawled up on her knee and snuggled in and fallen asleep. Distracted from her thoughts, Jacqueline looked down. A ball had dribbled as far as her feet. It had come from a cluster of children beside the slide, and one ran to collect it.

'Hello. My name is Jacqueline. My Auntie Dorrie lives here. That's her beside my Daddy,' she said, pointing back. My brother Will might be coming here on holidays,' she continued, to introduce the possibility of a different kind of stay, and had the sensation of falling through space, as if everything in her own life, too, was out of control.

'My Mammy and Daddy are dead. That's why I'm here,' the boy who'd come to pick up the ball said. He screwed up his eyes, as if to see Jacqueline better. 'Only people who don't have parents come here.'

'I have to go to Auntie Dorrie now. Goodbye,' she said. Teddy's voice had caught her attention. She saw that he was calling and making a mad dash, because Tim had started to trot towards the opened orphanage gate.

'I can't take my eyes off you for a minute. Talk about the Good Shepherd; he'd never cope with my lot.' Teddy shook his head, heaving the little boy onto his shoulders. A smile of happiness lit up Tim's face, like a lamb in clover.

'I'll mind Tim for you. We'll all be going home soon, won't we, Daddy?' she'd called out as she rushed over, but Teddy didn't answer.

'Dorrie will have told the sisters we're coming, so you can expect a royal welcome. They are all so fond of you, Teddy, it will make me jealous,' Auntie Mina had said to her brother, laughing as if somebody had got a great big feather and tickled her, on the way up in the car, and Teddy had tapped lightly on the steering wheel, in keeping with her mood.

'You know how busy nuns can be. They have enough to do praying and saving souls in the world without bothering with us,' he'd exclaimed, but Auntie Mina was right, because as soon as the family walked in Auntie Dorrie's convent door, they were surrounded. Excited voices filled the air. Jacqueline felt herself breathed upon and kissed sweetly, felt soft cheeks touch hers, and her hands and arms caressed so much that she glowed all over, and then Auntie Dorrie brought them to a feast.

'Sister Ethel has been working hard all morning.' Auntie Dorrie had her hand on a round door-knob, and a small wiry nun made a clucking sound. Escorted by their bevy of delighted Sisters, they entered a long room. Grey light shone in through narrow windows onto a polished floor. It would be tempting to slide up and down, but that would have to be later, because cushions were found for the little ones to prop them up on their hard chairs, and these were pushed into a queen-size table. Jacqueline called it that to herself because she had already decided that the convent was like a palace full of beaming Queens of Hearts, and now they had an array of neatly piled plates to make a choice to eat from. If she had been presented with an egg sandwich to eat, in the hotel breakfast room, she would have felt queasy, but here they had a different shape and size. The egg was smooth and creamy, only lightly coloured yellow, and each morsel they ate had been cut into such a tiny square it measured the same amount as a single bite. Will was the prince of them all, because while the rest of the family ate, he was passed between the Sisters. He's so adorable you'd want to steal him and never give him back, they said as if he was going to stay in the convent forever. In the end, he rested snugly in Sister Ethel's arms.

'We'll be fighting over who is going to be out in charge of this little darling when he arrives. I've fallen in love with him already.' Ethel hugged the baby to her. Teddy seemed to get suddenly unwell, because he grew pale and coughed.

'Teddy, you must be coming down with something. Mina tells me you're working too hard. You should look after yourself more,' Dorrie said, and Sister Ethel's comment was forgotten about. It was just as well, because the requirement that ice cream must be fetched for the children was remembered, and Auntie Dorrie mentioned that perhaps Ethel would like to do the honours and cut up and offer out the fruitcake, standing resplendent on the table, which was her *pièce de résistance*, so that baby William had to be handed back.

'This is delicious. I'm not surprised the children love it here. I've a good mind to stay myself and let the rest of you go home,' Teddy quipped, and Jacqueline swivelled to stare at him.

'No, Daddy, you mustn't. We'll all miss you too much.' She felt ice cream dribbling down her chin.

'You're father is joking, Jackie, of course,' Auntie Mina laughed, but the observant girl saw her frown. 'I think you'd like to turn me into a mother and stay with you forever. Perhaps it's Dorrie's turn to help out, since she thinks I haven't been looking after Teddy properly.' She pursed her lips, and Jacqueline watched helplessly as the baby was once more taken. But Teddy stood up.

'There's trouble brewing. I know from many years of experience how just a few words spoken in haste between Mina and Dorrie can quickly develop into a full-scale row. Maybe Jacqueline could hold William for a while, and we'll begin our tour of the orphanage that Dorrie promised.' He seemed to be shouting. Although Aunt Dorrie said, "Nonsense, that's a tall tale," she handed the baby over. Jacqueline struggled under the burden. Will's trusting blue eyes stared into hers.

'He needs a proper Mammy. You said we were going to meet one soon, Daddy,' she said weakly, as they moved off. The same feeling of weightlessness she had had in the orphanage playground came over her again, but her father shot her a keen look of approval.

Chapter Forty

Nobody had said no to her before, when she had entered the walk-in larder of the hotel to sample the biscuits or slabs of jellies and other treats stored in there, but now the larder door was locked. Once, shortly after her Mammy had gone on her visit to heaven, Jacqueline had eaten so much she had had a terrible belly-ache. She didn't complain, because somebody would be bound to say it was all her fault, but now she couldn't enter the place at all. Only yesterday, Auntie Mina had driven the message home about the locked-away provisions. 'I'm taking over control of the stores. From now on, I'm keeping a ledger to account for everything that's brought into the hotel. There's money haemorrhaging out of this place, and if we don't stop it, the entire family will be out on the street,' she'd announced to Teddy. He was shaking his head when they were at the breakfast table, and complaining about always being broke.

'You can have my savings from my piggy-bank,' Jacqueline piped up, and Auntie Mina laughed merrily.

'That's very thoughtful of you, Jackie, but really it's not necessary. Instead, perhaps a certain little mouse could stop herself from making inroads into the stores when Teddy and I aren't around. It will be easier, though, when I keep them under lock and key altogether.'

'I never go in there. I don't like anything in the larder,' Jacqueline lied. She felt her face go red. It wasn't fair of Auntie Mina to bring up her faults in front of Teddy. Kitty or Phyllis probably told her aunt about the unfortunate time she'd eaten too much. They knew, because afterwards she had to stay in bed with a pain in her tummy.

'You'll have to curb that appetite, dear, or you'll turn into a balloon some day, and burst. Then where would we be?' Teddy laughed. 'Really though, Mina, you're going too far. I'm sure the small amount Jacqueline takes is hardly worth talking about. The child has to have some pleasures.' Jacqueline felt a grin tug at her mouth when he raised an eyebrow at her aunt. Even better, she caught his wink as he stood up to depart.

'We'll leave the stores open. I can hardly go against what the master decrees, can I?' Auntie Mina raised her hands to heaven but Jacqueline had sensed she meant to have her way.

Jacqueline jigged at the larder latch. Bright sun poured into the back passageway from the yard, enticing her out. Auntie Mina must have already taken charge, because earlier there was a shining new key on the bunch she'd laid on a dining-room table when Jacqueline had gone to speak to Bartholomew the waiter. 'I'm beginning to have the sensations of a jailer, or perhaps I'm the one who's starting to feel the weight of too much responsibility,' Mina had sighed to the elderly man. Even so, she smiled when she lifted the jangling array of keys to hand them over. If she came back after lunch, Bartholomew might have left it open by mistake. The need to be outside became overwhelming for the small girl, and she glanced back only once before she left.

Recently Jacqueline had been exploring the farthest-away reaches of the hotel-yard. It was bounded at the lower end by a narrow stream, with a high grassy bank on the farther side. When she negotiated the water and scrambled up the high lookout, she could sometimes see the train carriages to Dublin Kitty would take to leave, gleaming when they appeared in a gap after leaving the station, as if they were make-believe carriages from a secret place. She would watch until the movement ceased, her eyes darting forward, and continued to observe until the distant sound, too, died away. Some day soon, she would be leaving home. Auntie Mina and Teddy talked about it a lot. They spoke about what needed to be packed and what could be left behind. Some of her clothes were already put aside, to be packed in a trunk and sent ahead of them, like that train, heading for some unknown destination.

She had reached the end of the mart enclosure without meeting anyone, and climbed up onto the river boundary opposite to look out for the train, but just as soon as she reached her lookout point, she had to leave. A light mist had begun to fall. Drops clung to Jacqueline's skin and clogged her eyebrows, and she shook herself off like Floppy. She took a mighty step over the long wet grasses of the bank, before scrambling down and jumping the stream to the hotel side. Rain released smells from left-over dried pats of cowdung as she zigzagged through the cattle pens. In no time she forgot about her discomfort, because when she got indoors, and was about to race up the back-stairs, she saw that the stores door was open. She hesitated before slipping in. An array of delights met her gaze. Being inside the larder was like having a sweet-shop all to herself, and she stood stock-still. A large bowl of fruit-cocktail, soaked in juice, drew her towards it. Whipped cream formed a swirling peak in a container, and there were offerings of green and red jellies. She already knew the contents of each biscuit tin from before, but best of all a newly molded strawberry blancmange sat upturned on a plate.

There was a noise behind Jacqueline. It was the sound of the door closing, but it didn't distract her. She barely heard the key clicking before returning her attention to the blancmange. It quivered invitingly. Maybe if she sucked at it rather than bit, a small piece taken might not be noticed. She had bent forward to experiment, but it was impossible to disengage her lips, it was so delicious, and the blancmange began to break up. She pulled at a set of plates to hide the damaged article behind them, and they clattered to the floor. For the first time, she noticed that a hatch door by her side into the dining room was open. This had a rotating shelf that, when swiveled around, enabled foodstuffs to be picked off in the other room. Glancing into it, darkness met her gaze. Now and then a faint noise came from the dining room beyond. Before Auntie Mina came, nobody had stopped her coming in here. She concentrated on the thought. It had been a time when she had got her own way a lot. She might be on the floor and crying and banging her heels, and although Kitty might pick her up and tell her to shut up, it was always enough to weaken someone's will to let her see she was gaining control. Auntie Mina never gave in. Recently, she had washed Jacqueline's mouth out with soap. It wasn't fair. She'd said she had warned her once, not to tell any more lies. Jacqueline had fibbed about not playing with the matches left to light the fire in the den, and Auntie Mina had found tell-tale used ones under her niece's pillow.

To take her mind off the memory of the taste of soap, Jacqueline swirled her hand round in the bowl of fruit-cocktail to reveal the cherries. She chewed and swallowed each succulent one. Next she chose the grapes from the fruit mix, and then a piece of pear. That wasn't to her taste, and she spat it out. She mixed some green jelly and cream together, and drew it into her mouth through gaps in her teeth, giving her gums a slimy feel. Even so, she relished that bittersweet flavour when it hit her tongue. She was in her own Aladdin's cave of food, she decided, as more and more temptations met her gaze. Perhaps she would be forgotten about and left in the larder forever. Once Imelda had brought her in here to help Bartholomew out, by spooning some grapefruit into glass dishes. She had explained how much to allocate to each one, and Jacqueline hadn't spilled any juice at all. Imelda had hummed a tune about a blackbird, and said they made a great team and she must get her to help more often.

Maybe she was watching her now from the darkness of the larder-hatch. Jacqueline didn't turn round, in case her mother would go away. She called out her name. It rested in the air briefly. There was a loud rattling of the larder door at the same time, and Jacqueline heard Auntie Mina's voice asking was there anyone in there, and to open up. She had prised the hatch-door open, to allow herself to manoeuvre a way into the dining room before, and she did it again now. It was only when she was speeding away between tables that she remembered Imelda's comment, when she was spooning out the grapefruit, about being part of a team. She looked to see if she was being followed. Instead of her aunt, an arrangement of Mina's lilies on the reception counter caught her eye. The pointed tip of each was directed her way, as if her aunt had her niece's care in mind. The flower trumpets were like sword-blades, ready to take up her cause.

Chapter Forty-one

Teddy wasn't there because he'd gone on his honeymoon with Marion, and the entire Avalon Hotel was in a higgledy-piggledy state. The Clancy family was getting ready to leave for their new home. Everything that belonged to the family was packed in trunks and cardboard boxes. Each container was labelled in Mina's precise hand. There was no need to bring furniture, Jacqueline heard her aunt explain to Nurse Dell, because Marion Burke's house had all that was needed. Even so, there were some pieces that simply couldn't be left behind. It would be necessary to bring the children's beds and the ornate sideboard that had travelled with Teddy from Templederry Castle. It was an heirloom, Mina said, and she had been assured by Marion that she understood this. It would have pride of place in the spacious front sitting room of Ballyhass House. 'Of course, we've spoken about this before. Forgive me, I'm distracted at the moment,' Auntie Mina went on to exclaim.

Auntie Mina and Nurse Dell were standing in the reception hall of the Avalon Hotel when the hidden girl overheard the conversation. She was seated on a return on the stairs above their heads, waiting for a chance to slip past them and get outside for perhaps the last time on one of her journeys on her own, and she leaned down to hear more. She knew that Teddy would be here, and that they were leaving the hotel the following morning. It would be like going on a long journey, Auntie Mina had explained to the children the previous evening, but they would have something to look forward to, because they would love the first glimpse of their new home.

Her aunt was handling the practical matters of the move. Jacqueline knew this, because she saw her snap her fingers a lot, and have the answer to any question about what needed to be done, without hesitating. Today the furniture and other items would be sent ahead, and when the morning came they would pile into the car with Teddy and set off for where they would live from then on. They would meet their new Mammy and her children for the first time. 'It would all be very overwhelming,' Auntie Mina had also told them the day before. She had pronounced the word slowly, as if it would make them understand. It would be a great help for them, and being overwhelmed shouldn't matter, she went on to explain, because she would be going with them to help them settle in. Despite her reassuring words, the twins must have viewed her comment differently, because they crept close to their aunt, nestling near like chickens into a mother hen, as she talked.

Jacqueline stirred on the step where she was seated. Her attention was distracted from the chatting women for a moment, because Betty and Lou had appeared. They had slid down the banister of the stairs as far as their friend, with cries of delight, and now stood beside her, breathless. 'We're going to spend a day by the river. Lou will do some fishing, and I'm going to build a fire and cook some sausages. You can come too, Jacqueline,' Betty announced. She took the girl's hand to get her to stand, but Jacqueline shook her head doubtfully. From this standpoint, it looked as if Auntie Mina was going to block her exit from the hotel forever. Her conversation with Nurse Dell began to get louder, but just as quickly the pair disappeared into the dining room, and Jacqueline leaped forward.

'We'll drive our car, and you can run after us to keep up. The river is not too far away,' Betty said. Although she had sneaked out, Jacqueline hesitated at the hotel-front. Somehow it didn't seem right to leave her home on this last day in the hotel. Imelda was probably still in there, and feeling lonely. Even so, the idea of a day by the river sounded lovely. Beyond her, she could see that her friends were getting ready for the journey. Lou had folded a tartan rug neatly on the back seat, and Betty was already at the steering wheel. Floppy had arrived too, and was a barking beside the red car, ready to go. There was no time to think further, because Betty waved a hand out the window, and they were off.

This wouldn't be what it would be like tomorrow, Jacqueline thought suddenly, as she lifted her feet lightly and padded along. People who knew her called out her name and smiled. One or two called, 'Goodbye Jacqueline, in case we don't meet again. We hope that you will be happy in your new life.' She glanced up at buildings as she passed, and their image stayed in her mind for a few moments, like the faces of old friends. The red car turned into the pillared entrance of the river field. When she looked into it, the water was very still. Trees were reflected on the surface in an upside-down way, and the blue sky shone up.

'Help us, please. We want to find some sticks for a fire,' Betty called out, and Jacqueline saw her twirl about gaily, as though she had come to the spot to dance and run about, rather than behave seriously.

'We'll have sweets and ice cream instead of cooking. I don't want to bother about a fire,' Jacqueline announced, and soon they were all sitting down, staring into the river. Fishes came up to them to tell them about their lives under the waves, and Jacqueline asked them about the future.

'When you are like us and travel the world from the beginning of a river until you reach the sea, you know everything,' one old, wise fish said self-importantly. As he opened his mouth to speak, fierce teeth showed, and Jacqueline sank back.

'I can only tell you about all the dangers I have fought against and beaten,' he began to boast, but a current swept him under and he disappeared.

'I don't want to leave my home,' Jacqueline said suddenly to Betty. A tear she had sensed at the back of her eyes fell out, and then there were more.

'Nonsense. You'll have a wonderful time. You'll have new brothers and sisters, and you'll never forget all that you've had here. You'll still be Jacqueline Clancy, just in a different place.'

'I won't have Imelda, though, because I'll be leaving her behind,' Jacqueline wailed. But even as she spoke, she knew it wasn't true. Somehow, like those trees in the river that weren't real, but that were truly there for all to see, Imelda was beside her too. She stood up and stuck her two arms out and twirled round. Mud on the bank from the river oozed into her shoes, and she had to stop, but the movement had made her cease crying. A bird hopped at her feet. It was black with a yellow beak, and when it found a worm it picked it up and ran away. Tomorrow she would be eating food she didn't recognise at a strange table, she remembered, and when she walked to the wall of the river field where she'd come in, and leaned on it to look back at her town, she was immediately hungry, as if each door she knew there had a familiar friendly person, calling her to come inside and share their treats.

Jacqueline ran back and dipped her hands into the water to play, and as the picture of the trees reflected there wavered, the image of the houses of the town waiting for a visit began to vanish too.

Even Auntie Mina didn't complain about her wet shoes when she got back to the hotel. 'Jackie, we thought you'd got lost again. Don't run away like that when everyone is so busy. You know we have to go to your new house as a united family, putting the best foot forward. We can't have any fighting or disagreement,' Auntie Mina pronounced. Try as she could, because the words wiped them away, Jacqueline couldn't remember the still calm of those trees in the river, which had been hers a short while before. She wasn't able to recall either the jumbled skyline of buildings of the main street, of the town that was her home.

'I can't leave. Imelda might not be able to find her way about the hotel if we go,' she said.

Chapter Forty-two

It was time to depart. Teddy and Marion were back from their honeymoon and he had come to pick up Mina and the children from the hotel to bring them to their new home. They had all piled into the car. Will looked over Auntie Mina's shoulder on the front seat and waved a podgy hand at Jacqueline, and she took it and held it for a moment. He smiled at her, showing two front teeth, and bounced. He began to wriggle to get back to the children in the rear seat, and Auntie Mina declared he had so much energy even a farm wouldn't be enough space for her little boy. Then Jacqueline saw her clutch him to her bosom and hug him tight.

'Rose-Marie I love you, I'm always dreaming of you,' Teddy sang. The windows were down, creating a hurricane of wind in the back, and he waved and called out, 'Hi-ho Silver and away,' when a donkey and cart drew into the ditch to let them pass. Jacqueline would creep into his arms right now, if she could, and feel their strength, holding her tight, like Will with Auntie Mina, but the thought made her shy. Teddy had been away for a week with their new Mammy, and she didn't know what that meant. Perhaps if he had to share himself out with Marion and her children as well as his own, he might not be able to get round to everyone. She closed her eyes for a moment and the presence of everybody stuck tight in the car together grew more intense, as if they were held together by some invisible glue. Teddy seemed to recognise what she was thinking, because she saw him glance in the rearview mirror, and he called out, 'Cheer up, Jacqueline, you'll be out of the car soon and everything will be all right.' Straight afterwards, they drove over a bump in the road and everybody got tossed about, and they laughed shakily.

'This is it, Mina. We'll use the tradesman's entrance,' Teddy announced, and he steered the car outwards to directly approach a recessed gravelled entrance. There will be a gap in the stone wall soon, and you can see the old castle behind the farmhouse where you're going to live,' Teddy had ordered just before that. As they swung onto a rough laneway, Jacqueline could see the outline of a house set solidly in the fields, some distance ahead.

'We're going to be living in a mansion, like a boarding school without the teachers,' she said, and Mina laughed.

'Well noted, Jackie. When Marion's children and you all are counted up, it will be a little bit like something from Dickens.' She made a face, but Teddy shook his head.

'There's no comparison between this lovely place and anything Dickens wrote. I'm surprised at you, Mina,' he barked.

'I was only thinking it will be hard for Marion to cope with her suddenly enlarged family. You know I would have stayed on with you longer, if you had decided to do this more gradually,' she added, but Teddy still shook his head.

The car began to grind on loose stones, going up the back lane. Trees, so still they were like zigzag cutouts, met Jacqueline's gaze, and on one side a field dotted with hills spread to the horizon. A boy on a bike shot out from a farmyard gate. He pedalled madly to keep abreast with the car, sticking close to the window and peering in. His face was wreathed in smiles. Brown eyes, like those of a creature of the wilds, gazed for long moments.

'It's Anthony, the welcoming committee,' Teddy announced, and Auntie Mina waved out. That was the moment Jacqueline felt a warm trickle between her legs. It was as though part of her insides was leaking out; the town-girl with words from a different world, and faces she would never see again, all locked within her, was lost.

'I don't like it here. I want to go back home,' she whispered, but now the trickle had got more pronounced, and the other children were exclaiming and climbing up on the seat to avoid her.

'Turn off the engine at once. Jacqueline needs to be looked after,' Auntie Mina called out. She'd turned around to see what was the matter, but still the car made steady progress.

'She'll be fine, until Marion sees what she can do. This is a time for letting go of the past for all of us, Mina. I hope you don't mind,' Teddy said. Jacqueline knew he wasn't right because just as he spoke, Imelda arrived. Mina had taken a handkerchief from her jacket pocket to hand to her niece, and a picture of Imelda had fallen out with it. It dropped to the floor but Jacqueline had seen it.

The leaking stopped. A hot sun poured into the car and the smell of pee got worse. It didn't matter, because Imelda was travelling with her into this bewildering life, like somebody who could be called on always, however far she'd roam.

'I'll look after myself, when we get to our new house.' She drew herself up. In the front seat Teddy laughed. 'That's my girl,' he said and shot forward.

Part 2

Chapter One

It was half past seven in the evening before Jacqueline Clancy was in a position to get herself ready to go out. She was very tempted to stay at home and read a book, or watch a film on television. She knew that sooner or later, though, the silence that was presently a welcome blessing, now that the children were at their father's, would begin to surge around her in a different, stifling way, and she would regret not having left the house.

Jacqueline was forty-two, and she felt every minute of it, she thought, gazing at herself critically in the bedroom mirror. Out the window, the sea spread a welcoming face: an invitation to gaze, to get lost in its pearly sheen. She knew, though, that if she looked too long, thoughts and recriminations would come rushing round her, like whispering demons. It's not fair to your children to be heading off to try and meet someone. If you do introduce another man into their lives, they won't like it. Or you know what your friends say, that this is the time to enjoy your freedom, to come and go as you please and not have to think in terms of somebody else's desires and wishes. She tore her gaze away from the placid sea. She listened. No sound of waves came through to the room. She knew that the same sea could suddenly change, from being calm and inviting to a raging mass of seething waves, and she smiled. That was pretty much how she should look on this time. Nothing might happen over the next few hours, but she could adventure for a little while, like a small boat putting out, noting new places to land, and hidden scenes being revealed to her gaze, played on by sun or wind in an alluring way. Or another traveller might hail and greet her, a questing person like herself, eager for company and somebody to love. There was no time to waste because soon, like the turning of the tide, her normal life would reassert itself. There would be work and family demands.

The smell of the sea hit Jacqueline's nostrils when she opened the window briefly, then checked the fastenings, before going out. She saw a long wave break on the shore. If the wind picked up any more, it would be followed by others. She lifted up the phone. 'Hello, Anna. I'll collect you at nine o'clock. I was thinking that instead of going to Harvey's in Killrogan, we might try the Castlewarden Hotel in Dunduff. There's a midsummer festival on, and it might draw a good crowd. Jacqueline imagined her chubby friend shrugging on the other end of the phone, and she was sure she heard a yawn.

'That sounds great. You're the driver, so your choice is mine. I'll see you at nine, so.' The conversation went on for a few minutes more like that, and Jacqueline heard the other end go dead. Recently Anna's heart had been broken by a man who had initially wined and dined her. 'He was the one for her. He was kind and gentle and considerate, and not bad on the eye too,' she'd enthused to Jacqueline. At the same time, Jacqueline had been dating Peter, hungry for love, but not prepared to commit himself. Now both relationships had ended. She wouldn't let herself in for that again. She would protect her heart. Even more importantly, she couldn't bring a man into her life in a full-time way and hurt the feelings of her youngest daughter, Isobel. Jacqueline's gaze was attracted by a picture of her mother Imelda on the mantelpiece. The eyes that looked back at her were critical. She noticed a small frown.

'Don't look at me like that, mother. I'm doing nothing wrong,' she said. As if in answer, this time the phone rang. It was her daughter Isobel.

'Can you come and pick me up, Mum? I don't feel well. Daddy says I can come out to you tonight if I want to.' Jacqueline registered the sixteen-year-old's pleading tones. *She's unhappy. It's not on to be thinking about meeting another man at this time. Isobel needs all my attention*, she thought.

'I was going out tonight, but I can change my plans. It won't matter for once. I'm coming to collect you now.' There was a loud noise from the flat upstairs, as though a door had been banged in someone's face, when she hung up.

Chapter Two

Jacqueline sometimes wondered how so much sand got into the house. It seemed to settle into crevices as though that was where it actually belonged, and constantly covered windows and ledges like a fine layer of dust. The sea sheds sand like a dog moults, she thought, and sighed. Although she loved this house, which she had bought with the help of a small mortgage after her marriage breakup, she sometimes thought of it as a weight around her neck, something that needed constant attention and reassurance, as though it was a needy child. That didn't actually matter, because an expansive feeling of being perfectly at home in her new place always reached inside her when she stepped into her hallway. It was as if they were invisible friends, she and this recent abode, ready to protect each other forever.

'Mammy, I can't find any clean underwear. Can I have some of yours?' Isobel called from her room on the landing above. Pat Kerrigan, her upstairs lodger, passed Jacqueline in the hallway at the same time. She wanted to shout, *Of course, but next time make sure you have something ready the night before.* Instead she kept her voice even.

'Go ahead, you know where I keep them.' Jacqueline smiled at the man moving by. Pat was a single tenant in a neat flat she had had created under the eaves of the house. This should have been a golden opportunity for her to assert herself against her daughter, to say that they were going to have to help each other by co-operating more in household matters, such as putting a wash on, for instance.

'Did you close the Velux window on the top landing before you left, Pat? It let the rain in yesterday,' she said, addressing her tenant directly. There was something close to hysteria creeping into her voice; she shook herself, as though even the elements were conspiring to wrest control of her life from her.

'I think it was Isobel who opened it. She's taken to calling in to me to say hello recently, and she said there was a stuffy feeling in the place. I'd keep an eye on her if I were you, Mrs Delahunty. She's growing up fast.' Pat shook his head. He began to whistle as he opened the front door, and the sound stayed in the hall after he left, free as birdsong in the air.

'She's forbidden to be in the top of the house. Let me know in the future,' Jacqueline called out, but it was too late: Pat wasn't coming back.

'Were there any reports on what it was like in the Castlewarden on the night we missed?' Jacqueline asked her friend Anna later that day. It was lunchtime, and they'd met in a local café for something to eat. Rain had sprinkled a thousand diamond drops on Anna's black coat. They flew onto the seated Jacqueline, as her friend shook it out.

'A pity we didn't go. My friend Thomas — well let's call him a friend, even though he behaved like a bastard — was there. Sheila told me. You know her. She's as thin as a beanstalk. She said he was even chatting her up. The cheek of him.' Anna sat down heavily. 'But wait until I tell you. Wasn't there a message on the phone from him this morning when I got back from the shops. He wants to make up, and he'd like to meet and have a chin-wag.'

'Where's all this leading to? Don't tell me. I think I know,' Jacqueline said. Her face had a fresh glowing feeling because she'd walked by the sea to get to the café from her work in the office of St Colmcille's school some distance away, and she was hungry. She noted the gaze of a man, seated at a table behind Anna, linger on her. Anna laughed.

'You've guessed it. We'll go there next Saturday night and play it cool. I'll say I'm with you. It will be obvious from him straight away if he wants to make up. Immediately after Anna had spoken, Jacqueline felt a presence hovering.

'I wonder could I use your milk jug, please? I seem to have run out.' The man who had given her the long glance was bending over her.

'Of course. Be my guest. It often happens in this place.' She found herself pulling back as he came too close. There was a heady smell of aftershave. Before them a group of schoolgirls Isobel's age were chirping at the café counter. They had spilled their money together in one girl's hand and were counting it and laughing. There seemed to be no way forward, or back, they suggested. She was no longer the safe married woman she had been, and yet her life was too conscribed to allow adventure.

'He likes you. Why didn't you ask him to join us?' Anna said when the man had left. 'If you don't want him, I'll have a try!'

'Don't be silly. It is a pity, though, that lunchtime is so short. Otherwise we could stay and chat forever,' Jacqueline said. She kept a trained eye on the schoolgirls. She remembered the tenant Pat's remark from the day before. She would have to be more vigilant. Isobel was only sixteen. It was an age fraught with danger. *Mother, what should I do? I want to meet somebody for myself but I can't let my daughter down.* The thoughts welled up inside. She had a picture in her mind of Imelda, from the days so long ago when Jacqueline was small and her mother was alive.

'I'll never leave you. You can depend on me to look after you.' The sharpness of an image, resurrected, seemed to assert itself. But it wasn't what had happened, because Imelda had died. Perhaps that was Jacqueline's fault too.

Chapter Three

She would find out more about her seaside town of Cloonva-ra, Jacqueline had promised herself, when she first went to live there, and now she was in the newspaper archives section of the National Library in Kildare Street. It had been impossible to know where to start, so she chose the *Cloonvara Gazette* of September 1950: the month and year she was born. It was a large room, but stuffy, and a sensation of invisible dust in the air made her want to sneeze. Silent figures, bent over screens illuminating columns of newsprint, leapt into view. Rotating the newspaper pages in front of her also, Jacqueline was a prisoner of the past. She gazed, mesmerised. Black-and-white figures looked out from photographs. She was being sucked into a world the page revealed, and yet wasn't part of it; she was gauging photographed people as though she might suddenly see a familiar face — one of the many walkers by the sea who passed by her window every day, for instance — and she smiled. The instinctive response relaxed her. It had been a difficult morning. A couple who had only recently moved into the basement flat, which came, fully converted, with the house, had given notice they were about to quit. Jacqueline hadn't expected it of the quiet middle-aged pair, but it seemed they both liked to dabble in landscape painting in their spare time, and needed the light of a north-facing room to pursue their art. She wanted to be a humane landlady, not to penalise tenants for a situation she completely understood; even so, it was hard to let them go without a complaint or a fight.

'I'm sure I won't have any trouble finding a replacement for you in a short time,' she'd said in the end, and they'd nodded at her gratefully. A woman beside her in the archives room murmured to Jacqueline, and she looked across.

'I'm leaving my notepad here, but I'll be back in a second. Do you mind looking after it?' the stranger asked, and Jacqueline raised a hand in agreement. It was the second favour she had been asked to do that day. When she turned back to her screen, though, she almost cried out with delight. She had been scrolling down without paying much attention, and her eyes widened. A seaside scene of picnickers and children splashing at the edges of rolling waves leaped up at her. An air of ease pervaded the picture, as though this day of sunshine, of abandonment to play and carefree pleasures, would last forever. Even more importantly, as a background to a summer's day by the seaside, the camera had taken in her own terrace of houses. The first thing she decided was that they hadn't changed, as though the time that had intervened between the snap being taken and now meant nothing. This wasn't the case, though, because there was a B&B sign in the front garden, and deckchairs on a lawn; tarmacadamed in the present day. A girl in an apron stood at the basement door, as though she had stepped out of the kitchen from her duties to take the air and bask in the sunshine for a few brief seconds. From the start, though, Jacqueline's gaze had been drawn to a man who stood by the front gate. She guessed he was a commercial traveller — as they would have been known in those days — because he was alone and was dressed in a suit and tie, rather than the open-necked shirt and sandals of a seaside visitor. There had been a sense of familiarity about his face the instant she saw it that eluded her now, and she had to dismiss it. She couldn't possibly have known the man from that far back, she grinned at the daydream. Still, it was lovely to see her own house.

The woman returning to her seat beside her made Jacqueline check the time. Isobel would be home from school soon; the present began to surface. Before standing up to leave, she had a peek at a few more pages and then, going out the library doors, had to pause. One of her shoelaces was untied, she saw, but halting to fix it, something else caused her to stay put. The face of the commercial traveller had only been familiar because it bore an uncanny resemblance to the man who had borrowed the milk jug from the day before, at lunchtime. Perhaps they would get to know one another better. Jacqueline felt a shiver of anticipation. She was meant to see the picture. It was a definite sign.

Chapter Four

S he had alighted from her bus, which left the city at two o'clock, and Jacqueline was about to walk down a windy street that would quickly lead to Cloonvara's open vista of beach and sea when she felt some drops of rain. Glancing at the sky above the buildings opposite, it was a smoky grey colour. A heavy shower was about to erupt, and she veered into a charity shop beyond the bus-stop to avoid getting wet. There was a faint smell of stale clothes Jacqueline didn't like, but outside the rain had started in earnest, and she began to move around the cluttered interior. She was at the back of the shop, rummaging in a basket of £1 bargains, when she heard her name being called out. Turning, for a moment she was puzzled.

'Hello Jacqueline. I'm Theresa, Anna's friend. The first time we met was at Isobel's parent-teacher meeting,' the woman approaching said brightly. Even before she had begun to speak, Jacqueline had recognised her. A shopper passed between them, forcing her to step back. As if some sort of dance was taking place, the newcomer put her hands in the air to avoid being touched, and swayed sideways. Jacqueline had an urge to use the excuse of the intervening stranger just then, to turn and walk away.

'Of course, Theresa,' she said instead. 'How could I forget? Even if I did, Anna often mentions your name. I suppose you know about Anna's fortieth birthday coming up. Her daughter Sinead is organising a surprise party. I'm sure she'll get in touch with you.' Jacqueline nodded her head. Out of the corner of her eye, a man had taken a coat from a rack nearby and put it on. He flicked the collar up in a debonair way as Theresa leaned in to her.

'I think I should come into charity shops more often. Maybe you get a free man with every coat you buy,' she said with a wink. Jacqueline wasn't listening, because a scene from the recent past had forcibly taken her mind over. She was sitting alongside Theresa on a row of chairs outside Isobel's classroom, waiting her turn to go inside. She was worried about her daughter Clara taking ecstasy tablets, Theresa had just confided. Jacqueline had also remembered a conversation with Isobel. It had taken place earlier that day. Isobel had asked her whether she could go to a party at Clara's at the weekend, and she had said no. Any minute now, Theresa would make the request again, on her daughter's behalf.

'That suits you. It's a perfect fit, and it looks like a good make too.' She turned to the man beside her, and he stared at her blankly.

'Oh, I just came in to pass the time. I don't usually buy second-hand clothes. It's not my style. It looked so comfortable, though, I thought I might try it on,' the man stammered.

'Hello. I'm Theresa, a friend of Jacqueline's here.' Theresa nudged her to move sideways.

'Nice to meet you. I'm Ronan. I suppose you two married ladies come in here from time to time. You look as if you're familiar with the place.'

'Oh, I'm not married. I divorced a few years ago. Jacqueline here is separated.'

'This is my lucky day, so. I'm being spoiled for choice.' Jacqueline was sure the man was about to say more, when another shopper intervened.

'Thank God that shower is over and the sun has come out. I thought it was down for the day,' the recent arrival said. An umbrella began to dribble water on the floor at Jacqueline's feet. Here was her excuse to go, before Theresa got a chance to mention Clara's party.

'Perhaps you might recommend a good gentlemen's outfitters in the town. It might be no harm for me to look into getting a decent coat.' The hazel eyes of the man who had first addressed her were turned in her direction. They twinkled. She saw shapely lips curve upwards.

'Sorry, I have to go. Theresa has been living in the town for a long time, I believe. She'll be able to help you.' She began to back away. By the time she'd got to the door, she knew she'd made a mistake. It was the second time this week she'd been presented with a golden opportunity to speak to an attractive man, and each time she'd turned the chance down. As though it was meant to be, at that moment Isobel entered the shop. She was linking arms with Clara. The other girl must have known her mother would be in here, and had come to meet her.

'It's your lunchtime. We'll go home together, Isobel,' Jacqueline said, reaching for her daughter's bag, and the girl stiffened.

'I saw you from outside, Mum. You were chatting up a man, and now you won't let me do what I want. If you can lead your own life, I have the right to as well,' Isobel stormed.

'My apologies. I seem to have caused some distress. I'm going now. Perhaps we'll meet again. You have a delicate matter to discuss here,' Ronan said, and he slipped past.

'I have no desire to meet you again. We're only strangers in a shop,' Jacqueline replied. Somehow, though, she had waited to speak, until the shop door had been shut behind the retreating man.

'I can see we're not wanted here. If you didn't want our daughters to be friends, you should say it to me,' Theresa shot back at her.

She was about to chase after the departed man, Jacqueline was sure.

'Clara and I are doing our homework together. You said to me before that it would be a good idea to have a friend to go over things with. Is that all right, Mum?' Isobel asked sweetly. *I can't do being a mother on my own*, Jacqueline thought.

'Go now. But we'll have a talk about all this later on this evening,' she said weakly. If she couldn't manage her own daughter in crucial matters like this, when she didn't even have the complication of a new relationship to add in, she certainly wouldn't be able to look out for her with a man around. It was impossible not to look surprised, because Ronan had come back into the shop.

'How would the prettiest woman I've met in a long time like to go for a cup of coffee?' he asked.

Help, Imelda. What should I do? she thought.

Chapter Five

Making a cake or some sweet delicacy always settled Jacqueline's mind. There were certainly plenty of offers to sample what she cooked, even if Amy, her eldest daughter, now twenty years old, was more often than not away, sleeping overnight with a friend, and her son Isaac, just a year younger, spent his every spare moment out on the sea. It would take just one raid by Isobel, carrying the treat on a tray, like bearing a trophy, into a group of friends who had gathered in her bedroom, for all that she had baked to be gone. Jacqueline shook her head, gathering her ingredients together. On occasion, she would drop something into Isobel's bedroom herself, for the group of girls; Jacqueline fetched eggs from the fridge. It might be a drink or some other treat, and an image of young swans would arise in her mind. The girls were mute in her presence, but they were graceful, and flushed with the bloom of youth, and their future gleamed with hidden promise in their eyes. She had been like that once, but she wouldn't think of the man she had married, who had said he no longer loved her. Jacqueline counted out four eggs. That grief had barely gone away. She began to measure flour carefully for a Black Forest gateau.

Vaughan, Jacqueline's husband, was from her home town of Tooradulla. He hadn't been the boy next door, though, because after

175

Imelda died, when Teddy and Marion married and they'd moved onto Marion's farm, she had rarely visited that pleasant setting of her early childhood. It was of no consequence that Vaughan was from there, really, because he was an only child of older parents, and when she had met him, both his mother and father were dead. It was strange, though, that shortly after they met, he reminded her, in a peculiar way, of her Auntie Mina.

Jacqueline put butter and sugar in a mixing bowl. She broke in the eggs. This was a recipe she knew off by heart, so that sometimes she introduced variations: less sugar, or more chocolate. If she had been wrong with her calculations, she would whip some extra cream and add more sugar to that. Her mouth began to water and she started to mix.

Jacqueline had met Vaughan when they were both doing voluntary work for Vincent de Paul. They had volunteered to work for a youth club, and from the start, the cheekier kids were pairing them up.

'You can't fool us, Miss. We know why you're not going home yet,' one of them would pipe up, when the drama session she had conducted was over. She'd be chatting with them, sitting down in the club kitchen, before leaving. 'You're waiting for Sir,' the taunt would continue. 'We'll tell Mister Delahunty that you love him,' another voice might chime in. Later on, when Vaughan at last arrived in, flushed after a strenuous session on the football field, she would feel like passing on the joke, until his sharing of some amusing incident on the pitch with her, or an insightful comment into one of the boys in his charge, checked her facetious remarks.

Jacqueline turned the oven on to the required temperature, and gradually warmth from the cooker began to seep into the kitchen. She splashed some boiling water into a mug, into which she had spooned the required amount of cocoa powder, and a rich smell invaded her nostrils. When the children were younger, it had been impossible for them to resist putting a finger into the cocoa mix to have an experimental lick, and she remembered their screwed-up faces of disgust when the bitter flavour registered. Taken off guard now, still enveloped in those moments from the past with Vaughan especially, she had to stop herself from plunging her own finger in.

I love you, Vaughan. The words hesitated on her tongue. It had been easy to say before, but now the wellspring of the source of that feeling had dried up and faded away. It would only need a little encouragement from him for it to return, though, she knew. What really kept it in check was the presence of Nuala, his new girlfriend: the woman he'd left her for, and who was by now continuously by his side, like a pretty ornament he would stroke and pet, worse than any adoring slave. He would act like this even in the sight of the woman he had left.

Jacqueline slowed the electric cake-mixer, and her quick deft movements as she worked, absorbed her attention. It was funny how, from the start, Vaughan had reminded her of Auntie Mina. Her mind darted back once more, as the mixture began to cream. Auntie Mina had been the one to step into the breach to take care of her brother Teddy and his family when Imelda had died. Now Jacqueline wished she herself could learn some lessons from that painful past. She would like to know, for instance, if she had fallen in love with Vaughan because he was a spar to cling on to as she moved into her adult existence, just as Auntie Mina had allowed herself to be for Teddy, or was he somebody she loved for his own sake? He even had the same penetrating blue-eyed gaze as her aunt, and those high cheekbones and sandy complexion. Jacqueline shook her head. She should concentrate on what she was doing. Ingredients were added, one at a time, and finally the mixture was placed in the oven. For a moment, when she glanced up, it appeared as if Vaughan really had arrived back in her life, but it was her son Isaac framed in the doorway. Three good things had come from her marriage, and here was one of them, the silent thought arrived. His face had grown ruddy and his frame was filled out from his outdoor life; she gazed at him lovingly. He looked excited, unable to contain himself, and punched the air with a closed fist.

'Dad has just rung up, Ma,' her son said breathlessly, hopping about. He wants me to get to know Nuala better, and he's booked the three of us onto a yacht-sailing training course in Cobh, in Cork. He says that after that, he'll probably buy his own boat and we can go sailing together. He'll even get me driving lessons so that I can use his car to drive to the yacht, if ever I want to sail it. It would mean living with him, though.' Jacqueline realised Isaac's voice was trailing off, as though his dream had taken over, or maybe he realised it was better to stop talking now.

'That would be lovely for you, dear. I'm sure you'd enjoy it very much,' she said as evenly as she could. *It was the way of life*, the thought stormed. Sometime in the near future, Isobel would come in with her own story of an escape-route from her mother. There were steps to this existence of hers, the same as there were to making the cake she had put in the oven. 'Just so long as you remember that I am your mother, and not that ornament Nuala. She hasn't kicked me out of your father's life completely yet. I could have him back tomorrow, if I wanted to.' She heard saccharine tones in her voice, and grimaced.

'I love you, Vaughan.' This time the words resounded in her mind like a hunting-call.

Chapter Six

A sensation of love returning began to fill up Jacqueline's heart for the next few weeks. It was as if the tide of it had gone very far out, but was on the cusp of coming back; maybe it was still lapping out of reach, but not gone away. Nuala usually made herself absent when she brought Isobel and Isaac over on Saturday mornings, and the last time, Vaughan had said Nuala was gone with her girlfriends for a long weekend to London. Behind him, she had spied unwashed dishes in the sink and smelt burnt milk. More than that, she had sensed light-heartedness in his manner. Here was the Vaughan she had known before their terrible sundering: loquacious and with a merry glint in his eye, as if life itself was one long madcap adventure. She found her hand reaching up to push back some hair that had fallen over his forehead into place, in her usual way of trying to bring him back down onto earth, and had to move her fingers to her own face and rub her eyes instead.

'I'm tired,' she said to him. 'The washing machine broke down yesterday, and it was all hours before the mechanic who came to fix it, left.'

'So a broken washing machine is the excuse you're using now, Jacqueline. Maybe that wasn't all he was fixing.' Vaughan grinned, and she blushed. The conversation was intimate, risqué even.

Vaughan went on to say that whoever he was, having to work late wouldn't have been a problem, with other compensations at hand. All in all, she had left the house with a gleam in her own eye after the chat, as if Vaughan and she had shared some secret liaison together, to be repeated again in the future.

'You look happy, Mam. It's nice to see you and Dad talking properly again,' Isobel had remarked when she said goodbye at the gate, and her mother's smile widened.

Jacqueline slumped down on a chair. She was suddenly tired and let the heat from the oven wash over her. There was too much to do, though. It was impossible to relax: Isobel had a badminton match that afternoon and wouldn't be home 'til teatime, but she had left a trail of untidiness behind her, after her morning exodus. Jacqueline had already almost fallen over an abandoned racket press. Dishes she had piled into the kitchen sink clamoured for attention, but she turned her back on them.

A whistle blew in Cloonvara train-station, arriving faintly through the closed windows like a call to action. It was at times like this that Jacqueline felt the vacuum in her life most — that absence of a companion Vaughan might yet come back to fill — and she shifted in her chair. It was a pity she had sat at her ease, though, because a shiver ran through her. Nuala's face had come into her mind, and that first time she had the stark evidence of her deceit, when she and Vaughan had paraded themselves, as if they were a married couple on a night out.

It was Vaughan's solicitors' firm's Christmas dinner- dance. Right from the start, Jacqueline had said she wasn't going to go. That decision had been reached reluctantly, but it clashed with the first night of an eagerly anticipated visit home by her sister Susanna, who lived in Australia. Jacqueline had offered to pick her up at the airport so that they could have as much time as possible together. They were arriving early for their function, and as she passed by she saw some of Vaughan's colleagues, in their cars, nose into the car-park of a fairy-lights-festooned hotel.

'Surprise him and arrive late. It doesn't matter that you've missed the meal, and you know how you love to dance,' Susanna said to her a few hours later. The airport pickup had gone like clockwork, and Jacqueline shook her head as her sister winked. 'You've been telling me in your letters you feel you've been drifting apart recently. Now's the time to change all that.' Susanna yawned, but her demanding blue eyes held Jacqueline's in a steely gaze. Even now, Jacqueline had to spring up and rush around the kitchen sink to attack the dirty dishes there, to help absorb the barbarous nature of the sight that met her gaze when she walked into the music-filled party-room. At that late stage, the tables had been moved back, and dancing couples were dotted about the floor. A wrenching pain in her gut had rendered her almost lifeless, and she had reached blindly for a chair. The face of a woman she barely knew mercifully blocked her vision from the sight she had just been confronted with. A hand was put under her elbow, there were firm words in her ears, and she was led out of the function-room door and into a nearby ladies'. She was made to sit down, and soon a cup of tea was brought in. She had seen Vaughan snuggle into a new fellow solicitor, Nuala, on the dancefloor. They were kissing. She had a flash of them being naked together, as if this had happened before. The woman's hand had reached into his hair; had delved into its curly depths, like a siren of the deeps, to pull him down. The memory of it rocked Jacqueline now, and she stood and gripped the kitchen sink and swayed.

'Show him the red card. Anybody who makes you cry like that isn't worth it,' a male voice said behind Jacqueline, and she spun round. It was Pat, her lodger. A charming lopsided grin came and went. 'Sorry for bothering you,' he said with a shrug. 'The door was open and because I'm going to be away for a few weeks I thought I'd pay my rent early and get it out of the way. It removes the temptation of spending it.' His smile turned to a frown. Normally well-fitting jeans were slipping from his waist and Jacqueline watched, fascinated, as he hitched them up.

'I'm sorry. I was cutting onions for dinner, and you know the usual effect.' Jacqueline sniffed. A white handkerchief was handed to her.

'Blow into this. It will take the worst of it away,' she was ordered. The handkerchief smelt of male cologne. Her breathing had become funny, almost non-existent, and then her heart began to beat too fast. Pat had stepped closer.

'You're very beautiful. I suppose you know. Lucky man who was married to you. I wouldn't have given you up.' Dark eyelashes lowered and raised over chocolate-brown eyes. 'Perhaps a hug might help you forget the onions,' he said. Lips were lowered towards hers. Much later, when they were in bed, she heard Isobel call out downstairs.

'Mum, I'm home early. I'm starving. Is there anything to eat.' Jacqueline leapt onto the floor. She grabbed her clothes.

'Not a word of this to Isobel,' she whispered back to the bed, fiercely.

'You'll have to give me a kiss to make me promise that,' Pat said.

'This is a terrible example from a mother,' Jacqueline said, and then felt her face widen in a complicit smile. It was alarming too, when she looked back before fleeing the room, to notice that her seducer's skin, which had been so hard to resist, had the same honey-coloured tones she remembered of Imelda's.

She would have to forget this had ever happened.

Chapter Seven

Susanna was home in Ireland for another trip, and now they were sitting together in Jacqueline's seaside home, looking out to at the coastal scene. Susanna had given her sister very little notice of her coming. As if to reinforce the point, the older sister waved the letter she had received from Susanna in front of her sister's nose, she hadn't had time to tidy away, moving other papers to one side on the coffee table before them. A sunbeam played through dustmotes, which were dancing merrily, and Susanna picked up her glass. White teeth gleamed in a tanned complexion when she smiled. 'If I'd known you'd bought a place as nice as this, I'd have come back from Australia and moved in with you straight away. You have the house looking a treat,' she said, raising her drink in a toast. On her visit, Susanna had brought her boyfriend Dave with her. He had gone for a walk, and Jacqueline imagined him striding along the seafront as if he'd made a mistake in coming, and wanted to walk to the continent he'd left behind.

'You'd never be able to come back here. You must be in Camberwell for twenty years by now. You probably have plenty of friends made, as well as the library staff you work with,' Jacqueline responded. This wasn't meant as a rejection. It was her way of softening the blow when, in a few seconds' time, her sister realised the futility of her wishes about Cloonvara, but Susanna frowned.

'If you don't want me to live here, you should say so. You know how I always prefer straight talking. A person would want to be a mind-reader to know what you're thinking about,' she snapped. Susanna leaned back in her chair and a hush fell on the pair. It was filled with the sound of voices as they passed the sitting-room door to go upstairs to Pat's flat. Jacqueline recognised her lover's voice but a woman's laughter interspersed their chat, light as a tinkling stream. Simultaneously she seemed to feel Pat's warm hand touching hers, as he'd pressed it on the stairs that morning.

'Don't feel under pressure. I'll wait for you forever,' he had murmured to her. She had shaken her head, trying to stop a smile. Probably the woman with him now was a sister, or an old and trusted friend. Even so, she felt her neck getting hot. She leaped up and opened the door. Slim legs in elegant red high heels were disappearing from the first landing. A retreating heel kicked the air. Last weekend, when the children were away, Pat had proposed a date. He had told her at the same time about a girlfriend he had just broken up with. Perhaps that was her now.

'On second thoughts, it might not be so nice living here. I know you don't mind sharing your house with strangers, but it wouldn't suit me,' Susanna went on. She gave a mock shiver. 'Imagine turning round some day and one of them is standing at your shoulder with a knife in his hand.' Susanna must have found the image amusing, because she laughed immediately afterwards. 'I'm sorry, Jacqueline, don't mind me. It's the wine. I shouldn't drink in the middle of the day. You're right to keep tenants if it helps to make ends meet,' she continued, but Jacqueline knew she'd spoken the truth. She hadn't told her sister about Pat yet. Maybe he couldn't be trusted either: the remembered blow when she had seen Vaughan on the dancefloor flashed before her. It was impossible to stay in the house with whatever might be happening going on upstairs, and she stood up.

'You're right in some ways. I should be more careful.' She raised her glass once more, and nodded.

Turning to the sea, Jacqueline saw a single ship impaled on the horizon. Despite its stationary appearance, if she had looked again in ten minutes' time, it would have moved on. She had to view Pat in that light. He had said to her when he first arrived that he didn't know how long he was staying. He had taken his current job in the local Castlewarden Hotel until he was offered something better.

'Look at the time. Dave said he'd ring from a coinbox on his way back from the walk to bring us out for lunch, and here we are chatting.' Susanna struggled up. She fluffed out her hair, taking a mirror from her bag to examine it, as if Jacqueline wasn't there at all.

The sisters were leaving when, a short while later, Isobel came into the house. She stamped some rain off her feet and removed her coat and shook it. 'Hello, Auntie Susanna,' she said, and then her eyes flashed. 'If you're going out, Mum, would you mind buying me some underwear in Pennys. I can't keep wearing yours all the time. Anyway, I can't stand all that lace. If my friends saw it, they'd think I was on the game.' She grinned at her aunt as if they were conspiring together.

'Whatever you say dear,' Jacqueline struggled to sound normal. By the sound of her words, Isobel must have sensed there was something between herself and Pat. Now she would have to pretend otherwise. The affair couldn't go on for another reason. It was too soon to let Isobel feel she was unwanted, that she didn't come first in her mother's affections.

'Let's get going,' Susanna said. On her way in through the porch, though, she picked the local Advertiser from the letterbox and brought it back.

Castlewarden to close with loss of fifty jobs, a headline screamed at Jacqueline.

Chapter Eight

'Promise me you'll go for some counselling,' Susannah said at Dublin Airport. She had turned back on her way through the departure gates, and Jacqueline had nodded. It was only three weeks after she first sat in that window seat looking out to sea, on her much-anticipated visit to Jacqueline's new home, and now, all too soon, she was leaving.

'Yes, of course. You're perfectly right. I'll search around for somebody who's recommended as soon as I go home. I promise.' Jacqueline pressed her sister's hand. There had been a longing to help in Susanna's voice when she had made the request, Jacqueline realised, but she knew she herself hadn't been honest in her reply. *I can get through this on my own*, had been her first thought, and I don't want somebody else telling me how to run my life.

It was ironic, all that had happened, because at this very moment Jacqueline was in a counsellor's waiting room, about to unburden herself to one of those enigmatic creatures Susanna had talked about. The counsellor's name was Magda Carroll. When Jacqueline had entered the house, from the beginning she had felt her soothing presence. There was a sense of peace and restfulness: some candles in the porch and a calming scent in the air. Shortly after her arrival, Jacqueline was brought to a wood-panelled converted garage with oversize cushions and beanbags scattered about, and a low glass table where tea-lights flickered. Magda left for a few minutes to file away a form about Jacqueline's general health, which she had just completed, and her new client closed her eyes and relaxed. Unexpectedly, because she had not had a minute to draw breath recently, never mind to talk about the person she had been married to, the first face that floated into her mind was Vaughan's.

'I love you, Vaughan,' Jacqueline said aloud, and her arms twitched. Her eyes opened abruptly. Even seeing perfectly, gazing ahead of her boldly at a picture of a forest scene on the wall opposite, the image of Vaughan wouldn't go away. She blinked, and still nothing changed. Perhaps she should leave now, before the real truth of her heart's condition came out. She began to panic, but Magda had returned. Jacqueline had a ridiculous thought: *she's a dentist, about to extract something precious from inside of me.* She clutched her arms, in case they might betray her in a different way, because now she felt like lifting them over her head in a languid manner, as though the surge of feeling that had rushed through her a few seconds before needed to be marked by a dance, or a gesture of celebration.

Magda had chosen a hard-backed chair, and as she sat, Jacqueline was forced to look upwards. As soon as she got home, she would speak to herself sternly, Jacqueline promised herself. The counsellor beamed. It was a professional smile, Jacqueline knew, meant to put her at ease, and it was working: despite herself, she began to sag. 'Now, Jacqueline, we can settle down and have a chat. Take your time. There's no need to talk at length. It doesn't matter if a silence develops. Tell me all about yourself.'

'I'm not giving up my husband. He can stay away from me as long as he likes with whoever he likes; I'll always love him,' Jacqueline announced.

Chapter Nine

'*Out beyant Finglas he was found,*' Jacqueline let herself sink into Isobel's school performance of *Juno and the Paycock*, which was unfolding before her. A background hum of rustling sweet-papers, whispering voices and cheerful cat-calls and whistles from the rear of the hall, filled the air. Jacqueline craned her head to see between backs. The age of the young players seemed less important as the human story unfolded and Jacqueline let the drama draw her in, acting like a balm to help her forget her troubles.

'*Give us a song, Jockser, one of your shut-eye ones,*' Mrs Madigan's lines rang out, and Jacqueline heard Isaac mutter the rest of the speech, beside her. Isobel was playing the part of Mrs Madigan; it was understandable that Isaac would know the words too, because bits of paper with her lines from the play had been stuck onto doors and presses for the past few weeks.

'She's good, isn't she? We might have an Abbey Player on our hands yet.' Jacqueline found herself beaming, but Isaac had forgotten about her. He was reading a note in the half-gloom, which had been passed up to him from a few seats behind, and she saw him glance back quickly and wave. Even Isaac had romance in his life — or at least the possibility of it — and for some unaccountable reason she found tears welling up in her eyes.

It was much later, when the performance was over and the invited audience of parents, as well as students from the school, had gathered in a classroom next door for tea, that Jacqueline spotted Nuala. The woman's self-possessed air made her stand out, and Jacqueline stepped back into the partial concealment offered by a set of lockers, to observe her better. There was no mistaking the mass of red hair. Almost at the same time she saw that Isaac had also spotted his father's girlfriend. He looked towards his mother and grinned and shook his head. It was the first time Jacqueline had seen the woman alone in any setting, and by instinct she took a step forward. This was a golden opportunity to confront the schemer who had stolen her husband away.

'Excuse me, please. Can I get by?' a young voice said at her elbow, and Jacqueline had to retreat. At the same time, somebody called out behind her, and she found that she had upset another guest's cup of tea.

'My apologies. I shouldn't be so clumsy,' Jacqueline exclaimed.

You're missing your chance to talk to that bitch Nuala, another voice said inside her head, but everything was suddenly getting too big for her. It was meant that she should withdraw strategically, Jacqueline decided. She was right, she found out a few minutes later: turning to see where the hateful woman was, she had disappeared.

There was a teacher bearing down on Jacqueline when she next surfaced. At least that was how she described it to herself. Recently, she had begun to realise, after the counselling — ever since Vaughan had told her he didn't love her, in fact — she had been living like a marooned sailor adrift in a fog, trying to get her bearings. It was like wide-awake dreaming. That was how she had described it to Magda. She and Vaughan were on the same sea, in different boats, and this fog was preventing them from getting back in the same one, together. Minute by minute, she said, she could feel them drifting apart. If she was patient, though, she knew her day would come again, and they would be reunited. When she had said that to the counsellor, she had felt her own face break into a wide smile and the relief of feeling in love had blown through her like a perfumed breeze.

'Lovely to see that you could come along, Mrs Delahunty. Isobel wasn't sure if you could make it. She said that you've been having severe headaches recently, and that you often need to go to bed early.' Jacqueline gazed blankly at the teacher opposite her. Rather cold-looking eyes gazed into hers.

'Perhaps you should let Vaughan take the children more often. Forgive my saying this, but I myself have been in the same situation as you. At one point my wife ended up in hospital and I had to take them over for a month. It was hard going but I think we all got something from it.' The teacher smiled. 'Sorry, perhaps you've forgotten my name: it's Simon Fitzmaurice.' He stuck out his hand. To her horror, Jacqueline felt tears pouring down her face.

'Forgive me for all this. I have to go. I must find Isaac and Isobel,' she sobbed. At the same time she spotted Nuala again. She had come into the hall, and this time Vaughan was with her. Isobel and Isaac had made their way over to her and they stood in a circle together, like the perfect family, Jacqueline had a sudden irrational thought. 'Maybe you're right. I shouldn't always put myself first . . .' she began.

A sudden hush descended in the air before Jacqueline could explain further. There was a sharp clapping of hands to call for silence, and she found herself slinking back. Now was the time to leave, to allow her children to bond with their father and this new woman. She caught sight of her face in a mirror in the toilets used as a cloakroom when she went to retrieve her coat. Her cheeks were flushed and her normally tidy hair had a tossed, windswept look. 'Imelda on a beach,' she said aloud. She had had a hazy recollection of a summer holiday long ago. She was between her mother and her father and they were swinging her in the air. Jacqueline trembled. Somehow she would have to get through this. She had experienced love disappearing before, and had been able to survive.

'Mum, what are you doing here? I've been looking for you everywhere. I'm going to be presented with a prize for best actress. You should be with me.' Isobel was by her side. She was pulling her forward. Inside the hall a way had been paved for them both to walk to the top table. 'You're the best Mum in the world. I couldn't accept this without you,' Isobel whispered.

'It's wonderful. But if only we all and Vaughan could be one happy family again,' Jacqueline sighed.

Chapter Ten

Ever since she had seen Nuala at the school play, Jacqueline had found herself becoming more and more marooned in her seaside home. Even Isobel had remarked to her mother that she should plan to go out, and now her cousin Bernie was arriving in ten minutes to pick her up for a dance date and she wasn't even half ready. Jacqueline swished through the clothes in her wardrobe again. The trouble with Bernie was that she always had an ulterior motive for going out. She had her eye on someone who went to a particular venue, in this case Harvey's, and as soon as she arrived, she would place herself in a good position to be viewed by him. This would invariably include Jacqueline playing her part, by dancing with her cousin so that Bernie could show herself to her best advantage on the dancefloor. And then, when her ploy had worked and the man she was chasing after had succumbed to Bernie's charms, Jacqueline would be left to fend for herself.

I'm not going with her this time. She can find somebody else to help her land a man, Jacqueline thought morbidly, as she continued to flick. Bernie had come into the house already though. In a moment, her laugher rang out from downstairs. It penetrated the bedroom's silence and Jacqueline knew she was wrong. Dressing quickly and arriving to stand in the sitting-room doorway, she saw that her cousin had turned on the television and had begun to chuckle at a comedy. This was just the woman she needed. Bernie was light-hearted and lived for the moment. Life was never dull when you were with her. As well as that, she was a connection to Jacqueline's past, keeping her stable by linking her to that long-ago world before she had got married. She had another thought: Magda would approve of her doing this. That one and only time she had been to her, she'd reminded her that she had to look at her childhood to see if any unhappiness she had experienced then was creating upset in her life now.

'Ready, Bernie? I went for that little black number in the end.' Jacqueline mustered up happy-sounding tones.

Moonlight speckled the sea grey and, emerging from the sleeping house, the two women paused, charmed. At the same time, Jacqueline saw Pat arrive in his car. He was on the steps in seconds, before she could hurry on. He'd been away on another trip, he explained: this time to Cork, to see about getting work there. *'Darling, you look wonderful tonight,'* he crooned in an exaggerated way, and before Jacqueline could pull back, a finger brushed her arm. He's safer to ignore, she decided, but skipping down the steps, the sensation of his touch remained.

'Aren't you going to introduce me to your friend? I don't think we've met.' Bernie was tugging her arm at the same time. Fun-filled eyes flashed and flirted. 'Maybe we shouldn't go out. Your house could be far more interesting.' She directed a restraining gaze at Jacqueline, attempting to turn her round.

'This is Pat. He's staying with me on a temporary basis. I'll see you during the week, Pat. There's no time to delay now,' Jacqueline was forced to call back, until she could haul the curious woman away.

'I've been to a counselling session with a person called Magda Fitzmaurice, and I still love Vaughan. I can't get him out of my mind. He's the father of my children too,' Jacqueline said to her cousin a short while later. They had stopped at traffic lights going out of Cloonvara, and the dark mass of a mountain loomed ahead.

'If counselling is having the effect of pushing you back to a time that is past, and to a love you have no hope of rekindling, you should give it up,' Bernie said briskly. She had shot forward because the traffic lights had changed to green, and they emerged onto a country road. A stream of cars with dazzling headlights bore down on them. 'Of course you could be like me and go out for fun and not take any man you meet seriously: that way you wouldn't have to forget about Vaughan at all. He'd be like a phantom love in your life, never going away.'

'I want to forget about him. It's not doing me any good,' Jacqueline said. She meant the words too, for long moments. It helped that she had had a sudden remembrance of Pat's touch, but now she folded her arms, as if to make that go away. A large moon beamed over the clear horizon of the mountain, spilling light on the point like icing sugar. From now on, she herself would be cool and remote, just like that inaccessible peak, she decided. Neither a man she had been married to or one that was about to go off to Cork were much use to her. A cat was trapped in the beam of the car for a second and a sense of her own helplessness swept over her. The puss vanished from sight.

'I meant to say to you that the man we said hello to on your doorstep reminded me of Teddy. He had the same shape face. I'd advise you to keep away from him. It's not a good idea to be going for somebody because they have a familiar appearance. You need to get to know them first. I could suss him out for you, if you like.' Bernie laughed. There was a stretch of darkness and they slowed down to make their way.

'I have no interest in him. Teddy would be much happier if my marriage was mended,' Jacqueline said. But Bernie had been right. The next time she looked at Pat, she would recall his similarity to Teddy even more. She was attracted to him for the wrong reasons. She would tell him that too.

Chapter Eleven

Somebody else came into the ladies' toilets in Harvey's nightclub when she and Bernie were in a cubicle together, and Jacqueline put her finger to her lips. Bernie coughed and spluttered. She wet her fingers to stub out the glowing tip of a marijuana joint and put it in her purse. Her face had gone red with the effort of coughing, but she cast pleading eyes at her friend. *She's worried*, Jacqueline thought shaking her head. Somebody she knows might come in here at any moment. It wasn't just that. There might be a policeman in the nightclub who would somehow guess she had been smoking cannabis and lie in wait for her.

She would have to get rid of all evidence, Jacqueline guessed her cousin was thinking, because Bernie whispered, a few seconds later, 'Oh my God, I bet you'd know from my eyes I was smoking dope.' She brushed shreds of tobacco from her clothes onto the cubicle floor and tried to wipe them out of sight with a wad of toilet paper. The toilets made too loud a noise as the residue was flushed down. *There isn't anything wrong with a piece of fun*, Jacqueline made herself think, but when a voice beyond the cubicle asked if there was anybody there, she fled from the ladies' in relief, with her cousin in tow.

An hour before, Jacqueline had reluctantly left her home to go to the popular nightspot. On her arrival, as they swung into the driveway, the place had been lit up like a fairy-tale palace set into the Dublin mountains, and she had insisted to herself that the night must be enjoyed. Even if she was still in love with her husband, it was great to have an opportunity to unwind. She and Bernie had sat in the car for a while and talked. Overhead, that full moon continued to pour light from an ink-stained sky, and gradually the entrance area to Harvey's filled up as passengers emerged from cars, like moths attracted by bright beams of light.

Jacqueline's first thoughts were on Bernie's safety now as they dashed from the toilets. She herself didn't like the idea of taking dope — not because it was forbidden, she often explained to Bernie, but because it removed some of the self-control from your own life — and she sighed loudly, hoping her cousin would hear.

'I'm feeling like somebody who's about to meet her Prince Charming. Sorry, not true. As a matter of fact, he'll be the lucky one.' Bernie grinned widely, as though nothing was amiss. She floated onto the dancefloor.

'And now. A special request for a birthday boy. It's Ronan O'Dwyer, and he's forty today, or is it twenty-one again?' the DJ called out, just as Jacqueline stepped onto the dancefloor. A familiar-looking figure met her gaze. She had been right about not wanting to come to Harvey's, because the same Ronan she'd conversed with when she'd met Theresa in the charity shop was standing behind them. He noted her glance and smiled and waved. There was a loud cheer from his friends. A floor-to-ceiling mirror acting as a wall of the dancefloor allowed Jacqueline to observe Ronan approaching. Its reflection might have trapped them all, because Bernie was doing arabesques in the mirror, temporarily removed from the world around her, and she saw that her own face had a dreamy expression too, like a princess in the tower of that fairy-tale palace bathed in moonlight she had imagined Harvey's to be when they'd sat outside. In real life, her palace had a solid quality to it, though, and those lights represented busy goings-on. It was the home of her children, of course: the three people who mattered most to her in the world.

'I hope you won't refuse me a birthday dance. I'll be the happiest man in the world if you say yes.' Ronan took her hand, and Jacqueline seemed to see him bow before her. It was a pity that at that moment a small packet of something wrapped in tinfoil fell on the floor at Bernie's feet.

'Mind my Moroccan Blue,' her cousin said, and her voice rang out in a break in the music.

'Sergeant, I've had a call from the station. They want you to ring in as soon as you can. Somebody has agreed to take your early-morning shift.' One of Ronan's gang had arrived beside her at the same time.

'Oops. I think we're in trouble, Jacqueline,' Bernie said. She swooped low to pick up her package.

'You mean *you're* in difficulties, Bernie,' Jacqueline, said too loudly. She felt the castle that was home tug and lift away, as if it was just something pegged down, that could drift up to the moon and disappear. She shivered as though hit by a blast of cold air, but struggled on. 'I'm still your cousin but sometimes it's necessary to leave the past behind,' she said stumblingly. At the same time, a tear fell from her eye. It seemed to come from nowhere, but it might act as a distraction for the policeman while Bernie hopefully vanished.

'Shall we dance, so?' she said brightly, and turned to the man beside her. Instead of offering her his arm this time, though, his gaze was focused on the top pocket of her tailored jacket. Looking down, she saw a packet of Rizla cigarette papers Bernie had put there for safe-keeping, sticking up. *He thinks I'm an addict*, she thought.

Chapter Twelve

'I'm glad that Dad is going to Cork to look at a yacht today. It's good to have Saturday with you alone, Mum,' Isobel said to her mother brightly. It was breakfast-time in the seaside house, and mother and daughter were in the kitchen together. 'We might be able to go to Dundall Shopping Centre,' Isobel added in the next breath. 'I believe Marks and Spencer's have opened a new store, and there might be some early bargains. I met Clara yesterday and she said a whole gang of them were going along.'

Why don't you go with them, so? Jacqueline was about to say, but had to stop herself. The less her daughter had to say about that hussy, the better. She reached an arm around Isobel's waist and kissed her cheek. 'You're right. And we'll make it a good day. I haven't been in Dundall for ages. I believe there are some new charity shops in the village we could take in as well.' Jacqueline's eyes twinkled.

'If we're that badly off, we shouldn't go shopping at all. The days when I wore second-hand clothes are over.' Isobel pulled away. 'You go to those places and I'll find my friends. Then we'll do some real shopping. Some of the boys from school will be there with Clara, and we might stay on and go for a stroll in the local park. The fresh air will do us good.' *She means for herself and some rascal from her class to slip away to and be alone.* Jacqueline pasted on a smile. She raised a plate of scrambled egg on toast to her daughter's nose.

'Look at that. You wouldn't get better in the Gresham,' she said. 'No more talk about your friends. I'll go to Marks and Spencer's with you and we'll come straight home,' she said firmly.

A pleasant odour of cooking filled the air in the kitchen. A silence developed; Isobel glowered. Blue skies showed through the high narrow kitchen window, though the sun would not reach the back of the house until much later. Filtered light rested on some open presses and a sink cluttered with unwashed dishes. Jacqueline heard a fly buzz loudly about, until it landed probably somewhere suspect. She swung a bottle of tomato ketchup onto the table and tackled her creamy-looking egg and crisp toast with gusto. 'I'm inclined to believe a plate of good food is a perfect substitute for having a man in your life. Give me a well-cooked meal any day. What do you think, Isobel?' Jacqueline licked her lips.

'Don't be daft, Mum. You left a letter you were writing to Dad open on the sitting-room table yesterday, and I'd read the first two lines before I realised what it was. I'm glad none of my friends were in the room and got a glimpse of it. You were practically begging to take him back. He'll never give up Nuala. She's got her claws in him now. You should have stuck to your guns in the first place and not left the house, even if he did bring her back that weekend we were away. He was completely out of order.' Isobel shrugged at last. She upended the ketchup bottle, allowing a large blob to fall on to her eggs, and pushed the food round with her fork.

'We'll have to put the past behind us and learn to be happy with changed circumstances. Anyway, you should never read a private letter,' Jacqueline said, frowning. There was no time to complain, though: a knock on the door was followed by Pat Kerrigan's voice, and the pair in the kitchen started. At the same time, Jacqueline found herself fluffing out her hair. She used the back of her hand to try to cool a suddenly burning cheek. She had shaken her head at Isobel, but her daughter stood up and was strolling away from the table.

'Is something the matter? Can I help you, Pat?' Jacqueline leaned out the door. 'Oh, I see, you want some sugar. Give me the bowl and I'll get it for you,' she said, almost closing the door in his face.

'Tell Pat to step inside. Don't be so rude.' Jacqueline jabbed a finger in the air. Her daughter was bound to notice her agitated state; she continued to try and eat.

'Don't be silly, Mum. It's plain for all to see, he fancies you. You can't tell Dad one minute you want to make a go of things and string along another man at the same time. Anyway, Pat Kerrigan has a girlfriend. I've heard a girl's voice going up the stairs quite a few times with him recently,' Isobel said in a quick undertone. Before Jacqueline could stop her, she had bolted out of the kitchen, holding the filled sugar bowl in her hand.

'Don't let your breakfast get cold,' Jacqueline called as the door banged shut.

* * * * * * *

'Did you know Pat has a son called James? He showed me a picture of him yesterday. He was going to meet him for lunch, in Killrogan. He said I reminded him of James because we have the same happy disposition. He'd come down with a bag of sugar to replace what he'd borrowed. Dad was picking me up at the time, but you were out,' Isobel said to her mother the following day. She had turned back to say goodbye on the house steps before going to school, and they had both spied Pat Kerrigan pull up outside. He had wound the window down but looked straight on, as though ignoring them. 'He probably thinks James and I could be friends, but I much prefer older men. They've lived life and know how to have conversations. Boys of my age are stupid,' Isobel prattled on. She hugged her mother briefly and wobbled down the steps in a pair of high heels, which she would take off and put in her bag when she arrived at the school door.

'Pat, can you give me a lift?' she called to the seated figure. Her clear tones travelled back to the house and a sea wind lifted her hair like a mermaid's. The same breeze blew around Jacqueline's ankles and she hunched her shoulders. Recently, when she wasn't working she had got into the habit of not getting dressed until noon. She knew there was still mascara on her eyes because she hadn't bothered to wash her face properly the night before, and the skin of her face felt tight. Down on the seafront, a father and his children were playing with a kite. Soaring in the air, it tugged, as if eager to escape. That was Isobel, thirsting for life and determined to experience it to the full.

'Come home straight away after school,' she called. The cool wind picked up her words and tossed them aside.

'I forgot my purse, Mum. I need it for a new book today.' In a moment Isobel was back. She had left Pat's car and, despite her high heels, had bounded up the steps. 'Love you, Mum. Don't look so glum,' she said, poised on the top step, before leaving.

'Enjoy school, and don't worry about me. I have to give this house a thorough cleaning. I've been neglecting it recently. Now go along or you'll be late.' Jacqueline blew her a kiss. The gesture raised her spirits, until she saw that the kite had broken away from the man's grasp and was sailing away.

Chapter Thirteen

Time to hunker down and appreciate the cosiness of being at home alone, Jacqueline thought happily. It was Sunday morning and everybody was still away. Although it was June, as often happened in her coastal location the weather had turned squally. Stepping into the shallow conservatory at the back of her home as she took a walkabout, a steady downpour gave the impression that the house had broken its moorings. Elsewhere, though, in the bedrooms and the elegant, carefully restored front room, the only sense of a storm outside was the discreet sound of falling rain, muffled because of double-glazed windows, and a deserted seafront with the churned-up sea tossing spume into the air, reaching defiantly towards a lurid sky. She shouldn't have done so because she needed to be thrifty, but Jacqueline had turned on the heating when she went for a shower, and warmth filled the air, as though that blocked-off sunshine had come indoors. She brought a cup of coffee and an out-of-date *Irish Times* into the sitting room, placed them on an occasional table and arranged a foot-stool so that she could relax completely. *Cloonvara, the second most popular place in Ireland to live*, an headline inside the paper declared, and she sighed happily.

The heat must have caused her to doze, because when a loud banging on the door made her leap to her feet, for a few seconds she was disorientated. She was aware enough, though, to see a police-man's car on the gravel outside and, struggling out to the hallway, noted a burly figure through the glass panels of the porch. Some-thing told her to cool the place down, that she would need to keep her head in order to deal with whatever was going to be said, and she flicked the boiler-switch beside the coat-rack. Ronan O'Dwyer was outside the door, she was sure of it, but when she opened it, a policeman she had never seen before met her gaze.

'Jacqueline Delahunty, am I right? Is it OK if I step inside?' the policeman asked, and dropped the coat which he had been holding over his head to keep out the rain, down onto his shoulders.

'Of course.' Jacqueline had an instinct to laugh. It often happened to her when she was nervous — as when she was confronted by a policeman — but she coughed instead.

'Is there something wrong? Has something happened?' she spluttered, but the policeman was smiling.

'Sorry for barging in on you like this. My name is Philip Reilly, by the way, and I've come on an errand from Ronan O'Dwyer. He asked, if I was passing by, to call in and ask for your telephone number. He wants to get in touch with your friend Bernie,' the new arrival said mysteriously. He stamped his feet on the hall-mat and rubbed his hands together.

'Come inside. You're drowned wet. I'll get you a towel,' Jacque-line exclaimed. Bernie was in trouble. She'd have to stall this man and give herself time to think. Bernie had her own problems. Once, a long time ago, her husband had been arrested for selling drugs. Bernie had been pregnant when she got married, and although her parents had begged her not to tie the knot, she had said she loved her boyfriend and that everything would be all right. Twenty years later, he had given up that trade, but some of his bad habits had been picked up by her. Even so, she had to protect Bernie. Her cousin had brought up her family almost single-handedly and now they were all doing well. She would give the policeman her number, and with a beating heart changed the last digit. The lie would give her time to talk to Bernie.

'This is a lovely house. I've seen the work going on to restore it, as I've driven up and down. Despite what people say, sometimes a policeman can be very unobservant, but I take an interest in old houses myself, and always notice when they are being worked on.' Garda Reilly was glancing about. He used a knuckle of one finger to tap the wall in the hall.

'Come into the sitting room and look around,' Jacqueline gushed. She drew a shaky breath and stepped ahead. Perhaps she could say something to put him off the scent of Bernie altogether. That favourite picture of Imelda stared at her from the mantelpiece. It had been the first thing she had put in place when she had moved into the house: a smiling face gazed back. A slant of sunshine patterned the floor at her feet. The sun had come out while they were talking. At least Imelda was on her side: the brightening of the room and a blue patch in the sky beyond was helping her relax.

'I'm about to go out, as a matter of fact. I'll bring Bernie's phone-number down to the police station and give it to Ronan myself. We can have a chat together. I think it might iron out some bad impressions he has of my family,' she called out. She had had to return to the hallway because Garda Reilly was disappearing up the stairs.

'Sorry. I couldn't resist having a look to see if the coving on your ceiling went all the way up the stairs. My apologies for snooping.' She saw him emerge onto the landing. There was an apologetic grin on his face, and Jacqueline found herself smiling back. 'As a matter of fact, I have a confession to make.' The intruder came downstairs slowly and, for the first time, Jacqueline noted his cheerful good looks and how the quiff of hair on the crown of his head created an urge in her to pat it down. 'I grew up in Cloonvara,' the policeman shrugged. 'And I remember my father pointing this house out and saying that it used to be one of the most prestigious places on the seafront. There was a mystery attached to it nobody had been able to solve; got to do with money. It seemed the people who owned it had amassed a considerable sum from their business. They both died within a short space of one another, but no bank account was found in their name, and wherever they had hidden their money, it was never recovered.' Garda Reilly shook his head. 'Ronan told me his grandfather had stayed here from time to time too, as a dealer in high-class ladies' underwear. I have to report back to him if I manage to get a peep into the place.'

If she had any sense, she would ask this man to leave now, Jacqueline tried not to stare at the policeman. He could have made up the story about concealed money, as an excuse to go upstairs and see what he could steal. This was the problem about being a woman living on your own. Even the police felt free to take advantage of it. Irresistibly, though, a vision arose of finding that cash. It would solve a lot of problems. She could take Isobel shopping in a proper way, not just for bargains and second-hand clothes. Then there was the yacht Vaughan had decided to buy. She could compete in her own way, by bribing Isaac. She would pay for a course in underwater exploration, for instance, if he agreed to continue to stay with her. There was still a room to be renovated. It was a small room, which had probably belonged to a servant, below Pat's flat. It was funny how she had been born in a hotel and had ended up in what had once been a rather grand bed-and-breakfast. She had a vague recollection of a room under the attic of the hotel, where the servants used to sleep. As far as she could remember, 'Kitty' was the name of one of them. Kitty was given charge of her when Imelda was too busy, and after her mother died. 'Kitty and Phyllis.' She said the names aloud, suddenly recalling that there was a pair of them.

'I haven't heard those put together by anybody before. Perhaps it's a coincidence but they are the names of my mother and her friend.' The policeman was by her side.

He's snooping again, trying to find out more about me, Jacqueline thought. Escape, Kitty had said. She and Phyllis were going to start a new life in Dublin together. If Philip helped her find the money, right now, they too could run away together. She glanced at the picture of Imelda to steady herself, but a trick of the new light was causing her mother to wink in agreement.

Chapter Fourteen

The Victorian railway station at Cloonvara had been one of the things about the place that had appealed to Jacqueline from the start. 'Mum, you can't be thinking of buying a house in Cloonvara. It's full of toughies, and people who pick fights with you.' Isobel had looked at her askance when she had first told her about the house, but Jacqueline had other instincts concerning it; somehow, the railway station was one of the buildings to confirm her view. Gazing in from the entrance when she first arrived, she was back in Tooradulla again. It was more of a country station than just a way of bringing workers into Dublin city, and it was a mainline station too, for trains going further south. It gave the town its own special identity, just as her seafront house did, and the mountains stretching out behind. Sugar granules from a sachet rustled, before Jacqueline opened it and poured it into a cup of coffee. She was in a café close to Cloonvara station with her friend Anna: they had been discussing their home town. She picked up a spoon to stir her steaming liquid.

She could see what her daughter meant about Clonvara, though, she began to elaborate: only a night ago, Isobel said a gang had travelled to the seafront from a nearby suburb and had started a fight. She had been lucky to get away from them before a knife was drawn. Vaughan was *"going to do something about it."* Jacqueline shuddered. The friends were in a different coffee shop than usual. It was a place that Jacqueline had suggested, because she thought both of the policemen she had become associated with would know the one she normally went to and had to be avoided. They might even be heading there now. At last, Anna patted her arm.

'I don't know why you bother with a bungalow when you could be living in a big house by the sea,' she said, out of the blue. 'That's what you should say to Vaughan if you want him back.' Her face brightened. 'Tell him his daughter is in danger and that he'd never forgive himself if something happened to her. You could also let him know about the money that's hidden in your place. That should make him want to live with you pronto,' she nodded and laughed.

'This is all just fooling ourselves. I know I'm on my own from now on. Even if he did get down on his knees to beg forgiveness, I should say no to him,' Jacqueline sighed. Even so, despite herself, she had a vision of Vaughan's face drawing near and his soft and desirable lips coming close for a kiss. 'I'm beginning to hate the man, as a matter of fact,' she added weakly.

'Don't say anything, but your tenant Pat has just walked in,' Anna announced a few moments later. She had been getting up to go to the ladies', but bent down in a rather exaggerated fashion over Jacqueline. Her voice was loud enough to carry to the far corners of the place, Jacqueline decided, and now, just as she was about to ask her to wait with her, she had abruptly disappeared. The buzz of the café took over. Jacqueline swilled her foamy coffee to cool it. Normally she liked to create a heart-shape on the cup's surface, and now she had ruined her efforts. This was all Pat's fault. By rights, she should go to him and say that she had destroyed her coffee because of him. She grinned at the thought. The action made her relax, and she sat back into her seat. Anna would be back at any moment, and she would sit opposite and let her know all that was happening at the other table. Pat deserved to have a girlfriend, she decided. She herself hadn't given him any encouragement to pursue his interest in her, after that passionate encounter a few weeks ago. A memory of the alacrity with which she had jumped into the lodger's bed — and her subsequent embarrassment at her precipitous conduct — swept over her.

Fortunately, none of the children had been about. If she had continued to encourage the liaison, they would all be with Vaughan now. Isobel had more or less warned her that she wouldn't be able to cope with any more people departing from her life, just yet. The problem was that it seemed as though her daughter hadn't got over the fact that her father and mother were living in two different locations. The ideal for her would be that, somehow, Vaughan would realise his mistakes and ask her mother back.

'That pair are oblivious to the world around them. Even from here you can see they're an item,' Anna said as soon as she came back. She pulled in her seat and nodded to her side. She cut open a scone she had ordered, and buttered it thickly.

'I wish they'd leave. What are they doing now?' Jacqueline asked, despite herself. Somehow she had gone off the idea of eating, and she imagined her coffee turning cold and unappetising. That was probably how Pat viewed her. After their romantic encounter, he had made enough overtures for her to be sure he would like to see her again, but she had continually turned him down. It was no wonder he was sitting with another woman in her company and didn't care.

'Shush, he's coming this way to pay the bill. He'll have to pass us out,' Anna said. She cut the bottom half of her scone neatly into sections and popped a piece into her mouth.

'And now, the end is near,' Frank Sinatra crooned through a café speaker. Pat hadn't paused to talk. *He mustn't know I'm in the café*, Jacqueline thought, but at the last minute he turned to face her.

'Hello, Jacqueline. I'm glad you're here, because I wanted get a chance to speak to you,' he said. She noted how he spoke in measured tones, as if weighing his words, and how at the same time his eyes seemed to caress her face. 'I've been looking for somewhere else to stay. My sister,' he indicated behind him, 'would like us to share a house together, and it seems a sensible thing to do. It would mean living in the city, since she'd like to be close to her work and I've already accepted a job in the vicinity. Of course I could change my mind, if I felt there was any reason to.' He rushed out the final words, and Jacqueline saw his neck take on a pink tinge.

'My friend would prefer to be left alone at the moment. She's still very much in love with her husband,' Anna burst in, before Jacqueline could answer. The sound of a horn, signalling that the train was about to leave, arrived clearly into the café. The face of Kitty floated into her mind from long ago. She remembered her eyes shining at the thought of being able to escape. She saw the train from Tooradulla ploughing a confident line through the countryside. She had her own destiny to change right now.

'I've often thought of running away myself,' Jacqueline said, and wrung her hands together.

Chapter Fifteen

Isaac was in the Harvey's Hotel swimming pool with Jacqueline. She needed to be able to swim properly: if she learnt, they would be able to go away together. He could bring her for a week on Vaughan's yacht, where they would just have each other for company. Otherwise it wouldn't be possible to have a helpless person on board whom Isaac would have to rescue, if she fell into the water. He would be happy enough if she just managed to stay afloat on the waves without panicking; at least then he could throw a life-belt to her, Isaac had assured her before they arrived. They had been looking for a spot in the busy hotel car-park to manoeuvre the car into, and Jacqueline had mumbled an answer. Now that sensation of a rapid heartbeat she had had when they spoke, returned, and she shot an arm out in the ice-blue swimming pool and flailed about.

'Perhaps you could leave me on my own for a few minutes. I want to take a breather. It's ages since I've been in a pool,' Jacqueline gasped. Chlorine-tinged water rushed at her in a nasty wave, and she swallowed some and spluttered. *Get a grip on yourself. You're supposed to be the adult here*, she told herself, but Isaac had shunted her over to one side of the pool and was gone. Relief poured over her. Watching her son swim strongly up and down, Jacqueline was reminded of a fish, powerful and ready to seek fresh waters; to explore beyond man-made confines.

I need you to protect me. Stay close to me forever. I can see how strong you're growing, she had an urge to say. The words reverberated in her head. Another swimmer touched off her and pushed her aside, grasping at the side of the pool she'd been clinging to, to heave herself out.

* * * * * * *

Jacqueline was seized by long moments of happiness, sitting on a bench in the pool reception area some time later. She had left the swimming quarters before her son, and observing him coming through the doorway had caused her loving looks. A column of kids arrived at the same moment, chatting and pulling at one another and constantly breaking line. It took some effort on the part of their minders to keep them in place, and Jacqueline heard raised voices. She saw that Isaac had recognised one of the escorts: instead of coming to her, he made a beeline away from her. He enveloped the unfamiliar girl in a hug. Flattened down, his wet hair gave his head a sculpted look. His mother imagined how, close up, his eyelashes would look charmingly spiked, darkened by their prolonged ducking. *I will hold on to him, even if he has grown into a man almost overnight.* The thought took root, and she called his name softly. Instead of hearing her, though, his arm lingered for longer than was necessary on the girl's shoulders. He was pressing her close, and Jacqueline stood up.

'Isaac, I've set the oven to have lasagne cooked by the time we get home. I'm ready to leave,' she called. Her voice had a squeaky sound, she decided, but that would have to be ignored. This time, Isaac planted an awkward kiss on the girl's cheek and whispered something in her ear, causing Jacqueline to stare, mesmerised, rather than being sensible and looking away.

'Maybe you should get swimming lessons from a professional. It would increase your confidence, Mum. I don't mind doing it, but I don't know all the steps it needs. I remember I started off with a buoyancy aid,' Isaac suggested some time later. They were in the car on the way home. Jacqueline pressed her foot on the accelerator by mistake, making the car shoot forward. She had had a sensation of being ducked under the water by some force greater than herself.

'I should have learnt when I was young, but there were no convenient swimming pools in my day.' She gripped the wheel and braked. Perhaps she should ask the boy to get out and walk home, he was causing her such trouble, but Isaac had dropped his head forward to dry his hair. He tossed it back carelessly and settled into his seat, as if the car was his.

'I forget to tell you Mum, that Dad gave me a present of some driving lessons. He said you might lend me your car to practise, because it's better to start with an old model.' Isaac flexed his shoulders. His words arrived with the squealing of brakes behind, and Jacqueline found herself at traffic lights she hadn't even noticed were red.

'You mean he's saying my car is a bit of a has-been, like myself, and it doesn't matter if it gets bashed about.' Despite herself, Jacqueline's tone was sharp. Her gaze swivelled to take in her son. There was silence from the boy beside her. 'I'm sorry, Isaac. I shouldn't be asking you to take sides between your father and myself.' Jacqueline found that her grip had tightened on the wheel, but she reached out and touched her son's hand.

'A family break-up affects all of us. It's not a matter of taking sides,' he said eventually. Despite the shampoo he had used, Jacqueline was reminded of the chlorine in the pool: the skin of his hands had a flaked look when he stretched them out, like a body left too late before coming up for air.

That evening, the sound of Isaac's voice in the porch, and the lighter tones of a girl, made Jacqueline pause when she was heading for the sitting room for some welcome rest. Earlier, she had found the energy after her swim to make Isaac's favourite chocolate cake. Unfortunately, too, she had sampled it herself, taking a large slice, and couldn't help pausing at the hall mirror to study her figure. She was forced to suck in her breath. Outside, the voices had ended in a melodious duet of laughter, and she continued into the sitting room, to get a better look through the bay-window. Isaac and the girl he had encountered at the swimming pool were perched on the step railings.

He's just like Vaughan, around for as long as it suits him, she thought, frowning, but her gaze lingered. However much her expression contorted, love for the boy was swelling in her heart, as though it might drown her in its warmth. She took a deep, happy breath. He had taken her hand and was small again. They were running down a grassy slope, and at the bottom she would scoop him into her arms and he would call out, *The next time we can touch the sky*. There was barely time to see them bound down the steps, because the phone was ringing. Jacqueline hurried into the sitting room.

'You know the way my birthday is next month and I'll be seventeen? Would you mind if I had a party in the house, Mum?' It was Isobel. 'Dad said I could use his place but I'd prefer to have it in Cloonvara.' The eager tones slowed down. 'The only thing is, it would be better if we could have it to ourselves. Daddy wouldn't agree with that, but I thought you might,' she said, rushing on again. 'I promise I will look after everything, and if there's a mess I'll tidy up afterwards.' Jacqueline held the phone away from her ear, to cut off the words. *I'm only a convenience to Isobel too*, the thought stayed. She resolved to have another slice of that delicious chocolate cake to soothe her, but out on the front gravel Pat had arrived. He went round to the passenger side of the car and helped his sister out, leaning in to take her hand and hold it, as if they weren't related at all. Even when she tapped on the side bay-window to get his attention when he was coming up the steps, he ignored her. An auctioneer was putting a for-sale sign up on the house next door.

'Take me back, Vaughan. We have a lovely son and daughter for a few years more,' she murmured aloud. *But you are denying yourself too much happiness*, the opposite thought competed. This wouldn't be like the time Imelda left her and it wasn't possible to bring her back, she fought back, because she would make sure she retrieved Vaughan's affections, in the end. She would go on a diet. She would use her old allure. They'd be a happy family again. Everything was going to be all right.

Outside, a gust of wind took the for-sale sign from the sales-man's hands. It bent towards her as if she was the thing for sale, and everyone knew it.

Chapter Sixteen

Those beautiful new bay-windows of the front room, with their double-glazing, must have prevented Pat hearing Jacqueline tap the window, she realised, because he didn't approach the family rooms for the rest of the evening. It was true she had gone out with Annie for a glass of wine, but he would have left a note if he'd called. *He's probably the type who likes to communicate in person*, she concluded, but for the next few days she would stop what she was doing to listen for his voice. She became more aware of her house being a place of secrets, where lives were conducted that would remain foreign to her, and that even a house's past was shrouded in mystery, full of old longings, love and defeats. She didn't believe in ghosts, but sometimes, when a floorboard creaked unexpectedly or the noise of a joint settling in the old place came to her ears, she had visions of an Edwardian clientele, tripping about in their superior accommodation, and saw a silverware setting and a fine bone-china tea-set gleaming as they sat down to eat. Then, as now, the sea would have presented a curious face to all who came and went, taking in the rich array of changes day by day, in this multi-layered place.

Thoughts about the many existences that her house had accommodated, and new ones about to arrive, came into Jacqueline's mind a few days later. She was in her sitting room, and a multitude of wallpaper patterns and paint colours was spread on the floor. That morning, she had received a letter in the post from America. It was from Auntie Mina, telling her she was sending a cheque to Jacqueline, and that she hoped to make a visit home, some-day soon. The gift she was forwarding, she explained, had come from a grateful client of long ago. They were dollars bequeathed to Mina in a will; it was a bequest she felt Jacqueline could avail of in her new circumstances. Now Jacqueline spread the brochures on the floor in front of her further, to match shades, and sat back. There was a noise in the hall, and she imagined Pat outside. She would make a cup of tea before studying the display catalogues, she decided.

She nearly collided with Pat as she stepped out of the room. He had hoisted a coffee table over his head, and she took a step back. 'Sorry, Jacqueline. I'm afraid this table is more awkward than I thought. I'm trying to get it out without damaging your paint-work.' Pat's voice was strained with effort, and he swung the table dangerously close to a Rembrandt reproduction Jacqueline loved, on the wall behind him.

'It's a nice table.' She kept her voice as even as she could. She had had an instinct to shout, because of the possibility of damage to the picture, and now the full implications of what was happen-ing sunk in. Pat was leaving. His rent was paid well in advance and he was a free agent, perfectly entitled not to take advantage of the weeks he had in hand. 'I remember you bought it in the sales in Arnotts. You thought it would be a good idea because it was a piece in its own right and would fit in, in most places, if you decided to move,' she stumbled on. At the same time she felt her lips pout. It would suggest disappointment, or even disapproval, that he could be so flippant about departing from her life, swinging a table over his head like a removal man.

'I'm reorganising my room. The flat is beginning to feel cluttered. My aim now is to create more space.' The man before her spoke cheerfully — so much so that Jacqueline started to feel she was some sort of clutter in his life too, that even now she was in his way. He was lying, though: she could see it in the way he avoided her gaze.

'Let me know when you're ready to move. I certainly wouldn't want to stand in your path if you choose to take everything belonging to you away. It will help you leave easily, when you finally decide,' she said, and swept past him. Her voice was beginning to shake. *Some men have the effect of making me very angry*, she thought.

Jacqueline was forced to shove the incident with Pat about which she had been brooding to the back of her mind, an hour later. She was at the police barracks and, as she had half anticipated, had encountered Ronan. It was the only place to get a form to renew her driving licence, and she had come face to face with him, emerging into the sunshine from the front desk. They had almost collided, and he had put out a hand to protect her, making her move back. 'I'm all right,' she found herself saying, and her gaze wandered. 'My head was down, or I would have seen you. Going into a police station can be a serious business,' she quipped.

The man opposite frowned. 'I was wondering when we'd meet again Jacqueline' — Ronan shifted but didn't budge — 'since a smile from you would lighten any man's day.' His face grew serious, as if he had issued a warning rather than a compliment. 'My apologies about not getting back to you about the matter relating to your cousin,' he said at last, grinning. 'The possession of hashish can be a serious offence. I'm hoping if I delay putting it into a report — after all, Bernie was never charged with anything — it will be forgotten about. For your sake,' he added earnestly, 'I wouldn't like to see you coming under police scrutiny because of somebody else's indiscretion.' The sun was beating down on them as he spoke. Jacqueline suspected that Ronan belonged to a plain-clothes division: an open-necked T-shirt revealed a tanned neck, and her gaze rested for a moment on a partly revealed manly chest. Pink lips parted, to reveal pearly-white teeth. 'I think we can safely say, as a matter of fact, that the whole affair has been forgotten about. Your cousin should be careful, though, not to be so indiscreet in the future. She might not always be lucky.' The policeman's nose crinkled.

'I'll tell Bernie what you said. She's a lucky woman.' Despite herself, Jacqueline felt a glow suffuse her body. It would lend her face a faint flush, she knew, and then she found her right hand raised in an elegant gesture, and she fanned a partly exposed bosom. The nearness of the man before her was making her weak. A delicious lassitude was causing her to sway, as if she might fall down, and she sashayed past him. 'I'd better be getting along. The station will be closed to the public. It must be nearly five o'clock.' She turned, unable to go any further. Ronan had taken her hand.

'I can't let the opportunity go without asking you out,' he said. That was when she saw the wedding ring on his other hand, before he plunged it into his pocket.

'I have a date with my lodger, Pat Kerrigan,' she whispered.

'I know Pat. I meet him in the Castlewarden on a regular basis. We're both members of the Manchester United Football Club. I'll be getting together with him later on in the evening to discuss going to a League match in Old Trafford, I'll congratulate him on getting a date with the smartest lady in town, first thing,' Ronan said, with a shrug.

Chapter Seventeen

Isobel was too preoccupied with her existence as a fledgling adult to fully understand the seriousness for everyone of this family break-up. All Isaac wanted to do was to glory in his own strength, pitting it against whatever physical challenges the world had to offer, but Amy was different: she was more mature than you would expect a twenty-year-old to be, and she oozed sympathy for her mother. Of the three of her children, this daughter was the one who was going to bring them all together again, Jacqueline decided.

It was Saturday afternoon in Dublin, and Jacqueline had to search through aisles of clothes in Penny's department store to find where her daughter had disappeared to. Amy was going to her friend Marguerite's hen-party, and she had to get something suitable, but not too gaudy, to wear. When the subject came up, Jacqueline had to stop herself from offering advice. There had been no such a thing as hen-parties in her day, but now she had a secret longing to put on something with allure and daring, and launch herself into a glittering party scene, like a lit-up goddess.

'I found a black dress and a pink belt to tone in with whatever's going on. There's bound to be lots of people flaunting pink. It's not my favourite colour, but there's nothing wrong with compromising sometimes,' Amy announced. Her blue eyes danced with mischief.

She towered over her mother and leaned on a railing. Jacqueline was sure she caught a condescending note in her tones. 'That's it for me. I'm ready to go when you are, Mum. There's nothing here you want to get, I presume. I know you were invited to the hen-party, and Marguerite's mother will be there for a while, but it's hardly your scene. You're more the book-club or sensible-hill-walking type.' She shook her hair out into the stale department-store air, impatient, as though freeing herself from any mundane thoughts of the present, and already experiencing scenes of the party ahead, and seeing herself as a calm and collected presence: somebody who had already taken charge of proceedings. 'Unless you'd like to come as a retired hen, getting old gracefully, now that her chicks have more or less left the nest.' Amy smiled broadly.

'It's still possible for me to have another child. I might surprise you all yet.' Jacqueline tapped her daughter on the hand.

'So long as you don't mind looking after it yourself. There must be babies in the air. Nuala was saying last night she and Vaughan should start a new family, Isobel told me. You'll have to find a father somewhere else, Mum,' Amy said. Instead of delaying for her mother, she turned on her heels and made a beeline for the queue to pay at the cash-register, as though she couldn't wait to get out.

'I was thinking of having a party for Isobel for her seventeenth. I know she wants to invite her friends around, but I thought it would be nice to have something more intimate. We haven't seen your Uncle Tim in ages, and I'd invite my brother Tom too, of course. Granny Delahunty would help, and she would make sure Vaughan was there. It's nice to have something to celebrate, instead of gloom in the house all the time. It will raise our spirits,' Jacqueline said brightly. They were outside the department store after their shopping, and she had to raise her voice: a preacher, entreating passers-by to repent and confess their sins to the Lord to be saved, had set up stall beyond them, and his ringing tones made it difficult to be heard.

'It sounds like a good idea. Let me know what date you're planning it for. Dad is bringing us all out to dinner next week. He has a lot on his mind at the moment because he's very busy at work, but he's putting some time aside especially for us. It's a pity you can't come along, but Nuala will be there. I don't know how they don't get fed up with one another. They work together and now live together. It must be a bit of a strain. At least you only had to put up with his moods for half the day.' Amy lowered her voice to normal speaking tones: the shop's security man had approached the evangelist to move on, and a space became cleared round him.

'I never minded your Dad's bad humour. It's difficult being nice all day, having to smile at clients when sometimes you feel like throttling them,' Jacqueline joked. She reached a hand towards the sky and felt rain. 'We'll talk about the party again,' she said. 'If we don't run for the bus, we'll get soaked.'

'God can see into your heart and he will strike the wicked down.' The preacher had set up stall further down, as they ran past. *He can't mean me, can he?* Jacqueline thought. She had a vision of the revealing dress she planned to wear at Isobel's party, and she saw herself too, at a candlelit table. She would place Vaughan opposite and, accidentally on purpose, would toss a shoe off, to let her toes wriggle for a moment against his leg. The little red dress her husband loved had to be her choice. Diamantes sewn on the neckline — if you could call it such, it plunged in the front so much — would glitter as she regaled the table with her witticisms or learned talk. It was her body, though, not her mind, that Vaughan loved, she knew, and that would send out unmistakable signals of sultry desire. Jacqueline ran her tongue along her lips as she darted and sucked in rain. It had a salty taste coming from her upper lip, and she smiled and flushed at another thought. She and Vaughan were in bed together. The time of the month was perfect. There would be another baby.

'I'm terribly sorry,' Jacqueline said. Somehow a buggy with a toddler had been in her way and, running along, she had almost knocked the child out. It wasn't her fault, though, because the buggy had been brought to a halt right in her path.

'Go, then! You're only a part-time father anyway. You're no good to me or the child. We're better off without you,' a harassed-looking woman was shouting at her companion opposite. Jacqueline saw him dig his hands into his pockets and slouch off.

'Why did she bother getting pregnant when she knew the sort he was, right from the start? That's what I want to know,' Amy said when she had helped her mother right herself, and they stood shivering at traffic lights.' Nobody would want to bring up a baby in those circumstances. I know Nuala is talking about it, but that's different. She and Dad are an item now.' Jacqueline looked at her daughter's face to see if she realised how hurtful her words were. Amy shrugged. 'Sorry, Mum, but it's true.'

'Your father has never stopped loving me or his children. He has no interest in replacing us,' she said bravely. She knew that her words had sunk in, because Amy linked her arm.

'Maybe we could have that birthday party. I was thinking of going to London, and I was hoping Dad would buy my ticket. It would be the perfect time to ask him for money. After all, he needs to remember that his obligations lie with us, the real family. Right or wrong, Mum?' She smiled.

Chapter Eighteen

'*Slean leat a Mháistir Cinneide. Beid me arais go laithreach De Luan.*' Jacqueline called out her goodbyes to her boss as she pulled the office door of St Colmcille's School closed behind her.

'*Dia is Muire dhuit,*' a pupil who was seated on a chair outside the office greeted her.

'There you are, Leonora. Mr Kennedy will be with you in a minute,' she answered, and hurried along. She was paid to be a school secretary for a half a day, but she could be there until closing time, she told herself, as she let herself out. Sunlight bathed the school-yard. A slate-grey cloud had lowered itself onto a hill rising beyond the gates, ominously, but soon a piping of luminous light appeared around the edges. It was a promise of good times ahead. She was free. Jacqueline eased her shoulders back and felt tension flow out. Slipping into her car, she hesitated. '*Mum, I asked Dad for the money to go to London yesterday, but he hasn't lodged it in my account yet. Could you lend it to me? I promise I'll pay it back.*' Amy's telephone call from that morning came back to her. Jacqueline fingered the cheque that had arrived from Auntie Mina, pushed deep into her coat pocket. She pressed her back into the car-seat to get more comfortable. That cheque had been earmarked already to buy some expensive flock wallpaper and matching paint, but Amy had conveniently forgotten that. Jacqueline sighed. In fact, she had already engaged Claus, her Polish odd-job man, to come and do the work this Saturday. The only way out of it was to charge the paper and paint to the bank account she and Vaughan still shared, which was supposed to be used only for the children's college expenses. After all, Amy not having the money was partly Vaughan's fault.

'Yes, that's it,' Jacqueline said aloud in the car. The words gave her an agreeable sensation of being looked after, and she said them again, more slowly. The truth was that Vaughan wouldn't miss the cash. She could let the amount she would pay for her decorating items rest in the account for months. She began to glow, as if it had already happened. Yesterday, too, she had seen a beautiful Regency-style sideboard in Finnegan's store-rooms in Cloonvara. If she paid out for the paper and paint, she couldn't afford that as well, she had thought at the time, but if the other items were charged to the joint account, she could. Amy could still wait until the birthday dinner to ask for the London money. *First stop, the Glenview wallpaper shop*, she thought.

'You're almost there. Just a fraction more to the right, Claus,' Jacqueline called out to her Polish workman, perched on top of the ladder in her high-ceilinged sitting-room, the following morning. At the same time, she placed a phone, with its extension lead, with which she had been about to make a call to Bernie, on the floor at her feet. Hiring Claus had meant agreeing to pay him extra to get him to work on Saturday morning, but it had been worth it. She could manage the extra money from Auntie Mina's windfall, just to have the place looking well for the dinner party, Jacqueline had thought, and now the first sheet of wallpaper had already been hung. Dotted here and there, as part of the pattern, were golden cupids aiming arrows. *Vaughan is bound to get the message*, Jacqueline decided. She held the ladder tightly as the workman dabbed and pressed on the paper with a dry cloth. As he descended slowly a few seconds later, he slipped on a rung of the ladder and instinctively reached for her shoulder to break the fall.

'My apologies. I'm so sorry, Jackie,' he murmured. Jacqueline noted the creamy tones of his broken accent — which she hadn't observed before. The name 'Jackie' rang through to her from the past, and surprise registered. Auntie Mina had been the first to adopt that practise: Jacqueline heard her auntie's ringing laughter in her head.

'*We must all learn to live with one another, now that the past has gone. You're a clever girl. Wake up to all that is around you*', she imagined her murmuring. Trying to extricate himself from her supporting arms in the real world, though, Claus was getting more entangled. Suddenly they were both on the floor, and his body was covering hers. At the same time, the phone rang. Claus was the first to sit up, and he automatically reached for it. He pushed it at her.

'Hello there, Vaughan,' she said. The familiar voice was at the other end. 'To what do I owe the honour of this call?' There was laughter in her tones as she shook herself free from her entanglement. 'Sorry, but that was very funny, Claus.' Her whisper was louder than she had intended: she heard Vaughan sigh.

'You're in good form. That's the wife I remember: always there to cheer me up. Things are rough at my end,' Vaughan said gloomily. 'I tell you what, I'd love a chat. I'll come over and we'll go for a cup of coffee.'

'Bring your chequebook while you're at it. Every girl has her price,' Jacqueline giggled, and Vaughan laughed.

Chapter Nineteen

Jacqueline had felt a little extra pressure on her hand as Vaughan was leaving. She couldn't be mistaken.

'I love you, Vaughan,' she said to his picture on her dressing table. She had fallen asleep for a few minutes, and rubbed her eyes. Normally the framed photograph of Vaughan, looking flushed and happy after a game of rugby, was pushed into the back of her wardrobe, but a while ago she had taken it out and put it standing beside her face-cream jars. The bedroom door was open, and she glanced at her watch, because now the noise of the radio was louder, coming through the floorboards from below. Isobel was back. Normally she would hear her arriving in the hall door, but this time it must have been left open, and she had come noiselessly through. Jacqueline cherished her few moments to herself.

Claus had finished up at lunchtime and would be back tomorrow. At the moment of their collision, when he had stumbled on the ladder, she had felt some sort of obscure delight soar through her, and the kind of happiness one experiences after coming out of a dark tunnel, but Vaughan appearing not long after had overshadowed all that. He had arrived at the door with some newly cut hydrangeas in his hand. They were blooms from the bush she had planted when Isaac was born. She imagined Isobel now, noting the familiar-looking blossoms, and wondering how they had got there. She had keep her revelation about what Vaughan had said, though, until dinner-time. 'You naughty man,' she murmured at the picture, and smiled. It was surprising that Isobel hadn't called out to her. Just as well, because she needed a few more minutes before coming downstairs, to remember. She allowed all of Vaughan's words to surface at last. Now was the time to be dispassionate, when her ardour had cooled down, and before she committed herself in words to her youngest daughter. They were short of a supervisor for the office in the solicitors' premises, Vaughan had said earnestly: with her obvious skills, she would be perfect for the job. Her laughter on the phone had brought the realisation home to her forcibly. In fact, he couldn't do without her, he had admitted.

'What about my school-secretary job? I can hardly leave that on a whim. We need to think this out,' she had said, but had been distracted by his hands. She had forgotten that they were so big, like a working man's hands, not those of someone who seemed to have been born in a suit and tie; they suited him so well. Still, he had thrilled to the rough and tumble of a rugby match, and he had held her. Those hands had brought her to heaven and back only two short years before.

Her body had shouted yes to Vaughan's request when he had made his suggestion, Jacqueline recalled. They were in the kitchen and she paced for a few moments to give the impression she was deep in thought. She loved her school job. There was the parade of children's faces every day, which acted like a tonic to pep her up and keep the world a fresh place to be in. She sighed.

'I take it that means no,' Vaughan said. He must have heard the resigned sound, but she spun round.

'It will necessitate my taking some files home in the beginning to familiarise myself with the job. You'll have to visit me here some evenings to talk me through matters. I hope that's acceptable,' she said, and he nodded slowly. Something had got into one of her eyes at that moment, and she had had to blink rapidly. She had reached out for a kitchen tea-towel. When she was finally able to see again, Vaughan had gone.

Jacqueline rubbed her lips together in the mirror. She had massaged some face-cream into her skin, and let the oily sensation sink in. She had to pause because Isobel's voice distracted her. It was coming from above rather than below, and she opened the door. 'Pat has borrowed a metal detector and we're going to use it in the spare room in case that money that went missing so long ago has coins in it. He says that treasure that's found like that belongs to nobody, and finder's keepers,' her daughter announced. Isobel was on the stairs to the attic. She was pointing something in the air, that looked like a spade with a flashing light. She leaned against the banisters, to stare.

'I didn't hear you come in,' Jacqueline said.

'There was a problem with the school water supply, and we were let home. I've been in Pat's flat. He's helped me with my homework I couldn't do. I should have asked Dad, though. I saw his car outside. Is it OK, Mum, if we go into the spare room? I told Pat all about the money that wasn't found.'

Once a thing is gone, it can never be found again. That's the problem about time. It has the effect of changing everything. If only we could turn back the clock; how great it would be. 'Go ahead and try if you like,' Jacqueline shrugged. She had tried turning back the clock once before, hoping against hope that Imelda would return to her life. She was doing the same with Vaughan, but this time she would succeed.

'You have a very clever daughter here. I could barely keep up with her, doing her homework.' Pat appeared. He had paused beside Isobel and held Jacqueline's gaze. 'Have you got something in your eye?' His tone was concerned; once again she began to blink rapidly.

'Nothing so bad I don't recognise a real friend when I see one,' she said, blinking again, and smiled.

'You only have to call my name and I'll be by your side,' Pat said.

Chapter Twenty

'Get the mousetrap quick, Mum. There's one in the wardrobe. I saw it jump in and I banged the door closed. First I threw a shoe at him, but I missed. He's a goner now,' Isaac enthused.

Let me have a gawk. I want to see what he looks like. He's mine. He was in my room first. Mum, tell Isaac not to kill him,' Isobel exclaimed, jumping up. The family were in the kitchen. It had been Isaac's turn to wash up, but he had said he was late handing in a project for the physical-education course he was studying, and that he would do the washing-up after. Now plates and cutlery were piled higgledy-piggledy over one half of the table, and Jacqueline observed a trail of gravy congealed into splashes of brown on the smooth wooden surface.

'I don't blame a mouse for hanging around. There's rich pickings in this house. If we kept a tidier, neater home, there wouldn't even be talk of a mouse. You can't just kill it in cold blood, Isaac,' she said, turning to her son, but he had already pulled a mousetrap from the back of a press. He grabbed a piece of leftover meat from a dinner-plate, and set the spring. Isobel reached to try and get it.

'Mind your fingers!' Jacqueline yelled, but before Isaac could be stopped, he had dashed up the stairs. 'Maybe we should let him look after it, Isobel. Boys have their uses,' Jacqueline said. She smiled at her daughter, to try and settle her down. Isobel glared.

'That's typical of you, Mum. You just let things slide until there's no choice but to take the easiest solution offered. I'm going to stop him. He's cruel. He doesn't care what pain he inflicts on a poor dumb creature.' Isobel went red in the face. 'Tell him not to, Mum,' she demanded, clenching her fist, but Jacqueline shook her head.

'When I need your advice, Isobel, I'll ask for it,' she declared, but her daughter's words had sunk in. She still hadn't written her letter of resignation to Scoil Colmchille. If she delayed much longer, Vaughan would change his mind. Even now, he might have mentioned it to Nuala. A picture of the other woman came into her head. Instead of Vaughan opening the door the last time she was over, that floozy had. *Time to move on.* The words that had materialised in her head when she received the money from Auntie Mina had stolen into her mind as soon as she had reached the house that day, but the moment the shock of seeing a friendly face smiling at her from what should have been her own front door subsided, Jacqueline had glared. She didn't respond with any words to a murmured greeting but kept her lips sealed tight. It all would have been discussed between the two later, and she would have been the devil in disguise. Her shoulders sagged.

'He's gone, Mum. Isaac pulled everything out of the wardrobe but there was no sign of a mouse. There's probably a hole in the back, and it escaped. Isaac is down on his hands and knees looking for it.' Isobel was back in the kitchen, laughing.

'Can we have some peace in this house? You and your brother are forever squabbling. If you thought more about sparing my nerves and less about the fate of a mouse, I'd be happier,' Jacqueline exclaimed. She picked up her son's pen — which had thrown on the table — beginning to tidy up, but when she looked at her clenched fingers, it had leaked. 'This whole house is coming apart at the seams and you and Isaac just make use of it. As soon as you've grown tired of it, you slide off to your father's. Instead of sending you back, of course he indulges your every whim. Well, I demand some respect. I'm a single parent now: I need some help in this house.' Jacqueline began to groan. Her voice had rung out in the beginning, but now she knew she could cry.

'You're just feeling sorry for yourself, that's all, Mum. The sooner you forget Dad and get on with your life, the better. He's exactly the same. Every time something goes wrong, he says, "This would never have happened in the past." He forgets all about the rows you and he had. I'm surprised you stayed together for as long as you did.' Isobel flicked her hair back.

'I loved your father, and I still do,' Jacqueline said, recovering her composure. Now let's all calm down and forget our words spoken in haste.' She smiled, but her skin felt tight, and she could sense a headache beginning.

'I boxed him in a corner and killed him with the base of my locker lamp.' Isaac burst in the doorway. 'That's what you women lack, the killer instinct.' He swung a mouse by the tail, allowing a drop of blood to fall on the floor. Isobel cried out and leaped back.

'I hope he had a good life, for the brief time he was on this earth,' Jacqueline said. She was amazed at her continued calmness, as if she had done the deed herself, as though she could perform just such a daring act as her son had — like hitting Nuala on the head. A carving knife gleamed dully on the sink. She had used it to cut up some raw meat earlier, and she spied some blood on the handle. Another drop from the mouse fell on the floor. Her hand reached out.

Chapter Twenty-one

It was Tom who told Jacqueline that Mina was in a position to return to Ireland. Her job as a social worker in the parish of St Michael's in Philadelphia was changing, their aunt had explained in an unexpected phone-call. Up until now, she had spent a lot of time visiting and ministering to people in their houses, but more and more the paperwork in the office was being left to her, while the younger staff were being directed to perform tasks on the street. Working in an office did not require any particular talents or skills, and perhaps this was the time to make a clean break with her fast-changing employment, and relocate herself to where she could be of some use to her family. *If such a need should arise*, she had added to herself. 'She's asked me to use my contacts in the auctioneering world to get her somewhere to stay. Her pension will be modest, but with some careful management she'll be fine,' Tom went on.

Tom had made tea for them both when Jacqueline arrived in his auctioneer's office in Dublin city centre. She noted how his cup rattled when he put it back on the saucer. He took a few sips before pushing it across the leather-topped desk where he worked, three floors above a busy street. *He's been on a drinking binge again,* Jacqueline thought. *If he's not careful, he'll lose his job once more.* She knew this was his second position in the space of a year. Tom gave her a jolly smile.

'By the way, you're looking wonderful, Jackie,' he chuckled. 'This broken-marriage business has been a blessing in disguise, as far as I can see. You're positively blooming. A man doesn't know how lucky he is to have such a sister as you. I'm blessed, you see, to be the uncle of those three rascals. Life would be dull without them.' He shook his head as if not believing his own good fortune, stretched his hands over his head and sprang up. As he began to pace, Jacqueline noted with despair that his thinning hair had created a small bald patch on the crown of his head. Her brother was growing old; they all were; and now Auntie Mina was coming back to join the pack.

'She can stay with me. After all, she came to look after us in the hotel all those years ago, and the least we can do is return the favour,' she said. Tom beamed, and rubbed his hands.

'That won't be necessary.' He shook his head, and paused. 'Though she will be in a position to pay some rent.'

'I'm expecting a tenant called Pat Keegan to leave soon. His flat would suit Mina perfectly,' Jacqueline said brightly.

Jacqueline would have driven into the city and parked her car in the space, allocated to her brother, he had never used, but she had noticed a flat tyre when she went to get into it, and decided to take a bus. It was raining now, when she emerged onto the footpath after her visit. 'Stay and have some lunch,' Tom had urged before she left. Although Jacqueline loved his up-to-the-minute flat, overlooking the Liffey, she had shaken her head.

'There's trouble at work. I've told my boss I might have to leave my job, and he's refused. He said it would be impossible at this time of the year to get a replacement with my experience.'

'Leave it and to hell. Or ask for a rise and see what he'll say to that. He doesn't deserve you anyway. Come and work with me.

Even better, we could set up a company together. Soon anybody involved in the auctioneering business will be making a killing. There's another boom just around the corner,' Tom had announced. 'Let's drink to that,' he declared, and took a bottle of Tullamore Dew from his desk drawer, in a flourish. A pair of drinking glasses materialised in a flash. 'To a perfect brother-and-sister partnership.' A finger of whiskey gurgled into the glasses for both of them, and Tom raised his own and downed it immediately. The smell had tickled at Jacqueline's nose, and she sniffed the air. She and Tom had stood shoulder to shoulder before, when Imelda had left their lives, before Auntie Mina came. They could present a united face to the world again. The sharp odour of drink began to choke her.

'I suppose a small drop would be no harm. It might help me think.' Jacqueline grimaced and picked up the glass. Looking at her brother, she saw Imelda in the line of his jaw and those deep-set lustrous eyes. He would look after her; she would have no more troubles ever again. She sighed. 'Vaughan wants me to work for him. He has a job ready for me to step into.' She swilled the fiery potion.

'Don't waste that. It's precious stuff. Give it to me and I'll drink it if you don't want it,' Tom said, and reached out. A wedding ring from his marriage to his wife Rose, ended years ago, gleamed on his finger. He hadn't given up his belief in her either, she thought. His fingers grasped the proffered glass. 'Vaughan is an old friend of mine, and I hope he will always be. I'd like to see him again,' he mused.

'I'll think about your idea of a partnership. At least you know the business. We could do well,' Jacqueline said slowly after that, and left.

'I'll be getting off in a few stops. You can have my seat.' A young man with a suitcase beside him stood up to give Jacqueline his place, a few minutes after she had boarded the bus home. It jolted forward. Stretching up to hold onto the hand-rail, he crooked his arm over a pretty girl in front of him, and she leaned back. They were talking to each other too quietly for her to hear, and the girl laughed. Perhaps if she did work with Tom, Amy could come and join them, and later Isobel would swell the ranks. A doting uncle was a perfect substitute for a shallow father. Jacqueline noticed a bump in the girl's dress beside her, as they prepared to dismount, and wondered why she hadn't been sitting down. *Young women are very independent these days*, she thought, *but they shouldn't ignore the conventions of the past.* The man took the case off first and then straightened to allow the girl to leap awkwardly into his arms. Jacqueline felt her own tummy, instinctively. It was weeks since that last mistaken capitulation in the lodger's bed, but soon she wouuld have Vaughan in her arms again, and then the world would see. Every moment after that on the journey home she seemed to see pregnant women, wheeling buggies, or walking serenely, and sitting at bus-stops.

If Jacqueline hadn't been so observant in these matters, she would not have noticed Nuala coming down the pathway from the gynaecologist's rooms of a big house near her bus-stop at the journey's end. She was smiling radiantly and turned to look back. Vaughan emerged to join her.

Chapter Twenty-two

A wind seemed to blow Auntie Mina in the door of Jacqueline's elegant house three weeks later. Not long after that you would think she had lived in the house forever, because she had found the spare room Jacqueline had got ready for her, and soon was sitting at the kitchen table, looking round. 'This is a change-about for us, dear,' Auntie Mina said. 'You'll hardly remember when I arrived in Tooradulla, but it was to look after you all for Teddy. Now the shoe is on the other foot. However, it won't be for long.'

Coffee fumes wafted in the air. There was a smell of baking from the brownies Jacqueline had made for the occasion; her aunt picked one up and nibbled at it. 'Well done, Jackie, these are delicious,' Mina said. Some crumbs had started to fall, and Jacqueline could see that the brownie was about to break in half. But the younger woman could feel herself glow. She could be little again, and was deliberately courting her aunt's favour. The timing of this visit had been poor — Isobel's party was coming up soon — but she began to relax.

'I had a good teacher in yourself.' Jacqueline found herself smiling. It was just as well, because the woman opposite her had begun to hum, and a faraway look came into her eyes, as if this leaving of America had been a mistake and she should go back.

She reached over and touched her aunt's hand. 'You're probably missing your old friends, and places you knew so well, in Philadelphia.' Jacqueline shook her head. Her aunt was pretty, still. That curling red hair had grown grey and was cut short but it framed a wide-awake face in a becoming way. *Auntie Mina has left behind somebody she loves. There's been a falling apart, or maybe he died*, Jacqueline thought suddenly. The woman opposite was blushing.

'I appreciate it even more being here,' she said, 'because now I know what it must have been like to find yourself being bereft of the thing that mattered to you most in your life: a mother's love. I could never have hoped to replace that.' She lifted the coffee pot to pour some, and tapped the table with her spare hand, as if still thinking.

'I never minded you being in the hotel. Perhaps I wasn't as welcoming as I could have been,' Jacqueline stammered. A blind flapped on the kitchen window, which Jacqueline had opened to let in some air. The sunset shade of the walls, picked by her to bring some cheer into the cold back room, created an air of distant places, as if whispering adventures.

'Isobel, come in and say hello to Auntie Mina,' Jacqueline called out, a few minutes later. Her youngest daughter was standing in the kitchen door shyly when Jacqueline looked, but then sauntered in.

'It's lovely to see you, grand-aunt,' Isobel said. 'Welcome back to Ireland. It's a pity everyone isn't here to meet you. Amy is in London for a week and Isaac spent the night at Dad's.'

'Darling Isobel. What a surprise. You're home from school early. But look at you. Aren't you pretty!' Auntie Mina stood up from her chair and held her arms out, but Jacqueline saw her sway. She noticed fatigue deeply etched on her face. 'I've longed for this moment, to meet you.' Auntie Mina's tired eyes sparkled. 'You're a fully grown young lady. How the years have flown.'

'I'm almost seventeen,' Isobel grinned. Although the way Mum treats me, you'd think I was seven.' Isobel bowed in her mother's direction.

'Your mother knows what's best. But we all think we know everything when we're your age.' Auntie Mina, still at ease, strolled to the kitchen sink and cleaned a plate before placing a brownie on it and handing it to her grand-niece. *She'll be asking us all to wear hairnets next*, Jacqueline thought, and grimaced, but her aunt hadn't noticed her reaction, and Isobel was munching happily.

'You succeeded in doing what you wanted to, all the same, Auntie Mina. Not like me. I feel like a chained dog. Mum's afraid I'll run away and never come back.' Isobel sat beside the visitor and leaned into her.

'I agree that sometimes it's no harm to escape, as I did,' Auntie Mina said. 'But now I've come home.'

Auntie Mina has an opinion about Vaughan and me. She thinks I'm running away from all that happened. Jacqueline had another quick revelation. *She probably believes I ran away from everything, even Imelda's death.* 'That may be so, but I'm sure you manage to find a bolt-hole every now and then, Isobel,' Auntie Mina continued, and hugged the girl beside her.

A voice calling to Isobel made them all pause to listen. 'Mum, it's Pat. We're going for a walk along by the sea. I'll introduce him to Auntie Mina.' The girl stood up. Galloping out the door, she was back with the newcomer in a few minutes. 'Pat, I'd like you to meet my great-aunt Mina,' Isobel announced. 'She's staying in the spare room at the moment, until you go. I'm sure you don't want to keep her in the damp room Mammy has given her.'

'Your mother has made her feelings in this matter plain enough,' Pat said coldly. Perhaps your Auntie Mina was put into the worst room on purpose.'

'This is nonsense. Nobody has to move. I know I'm a nuisance but I'll only be with Jackie for a few weeks,' Auntie Mina said. She gripped the edge of her chair, as if she was about to rise.

'Don't be ridiculous, you can stay as long as you like,' Jacqueline heard herself say. At the same time, she saw Pat was looking at the brownies on the plate. 'Perhaps you'd like some coffee, Pat. Do sit down,' she said. She found herself melting, just like one of the delicious treats, herself. Isobel had placed a seat beside her, so close that when Pat sat down, their thighs touched.

'Give in, Mum. You know that you like him. There are some treats better than chocolate,' her daughter said, with a grin.

Chapter Twenty-three

'The phone is ringing. I'm in the hall if you want me to answer it.' Auntie Mina's voice arrived faintly in Jacqueline's ear. She paused on the upstairs landing.

'Don't worry, whoever it is will call again,' she shouted back down, quickly. She was sure it was Vaughan, and since she had told her aunt she was expecting to hear from him, Mina had probably guessed it too. She couldn't talk to him anyway, because she was outside Pat's door. She needed a clear head to conduct a conversation with her husband about his proposal, she told herself. Already, she was under pressure for time. Vaughan wouldn't understand if she had to make the conversation brief. Pat was out, she knew, but somehow he might return. It seemed like an underhand thing to do to go into his room, but the water tank needed to be investigated, and his flat was the only place from which to access it.

Jacqueline glanced about hurriedly as she crossed the carpeted floor. She had chosen the flooring's red shade deliberately, she realised, because she wanted a sense of luxury in a space so high up, as if to say that riches can be found in the most unexpected places. Being tucked away from the gaze of the rest of the house gave the room under the eaves the unmatched appeal of being a welcome surprise, removed from domestic worries and strife. She had run up the stairs in a hurry but now she kicked her shoes off. Being here would give her the strength to look Pat in the eye the next time they met. She would be cool and calculated and say that it wasn't fair to have somebody with such an independent nature as Auntie Mina living in a poky hole, while one of the best rooms in the house was not wanted by its tenant. The time had come for a definite date for his leaving to be decided on.

Jacqueline glanced at the double bed she had been in all those weeks before. For some reason, one of her fists had been clenched, and she opened it out. She patted the bed experimentally. A corner of the duvet hadn't been properly arranged, and she fitted it back into place. Below her, she knew, water was no longer coming into the middle-landing toilet. Perhaps if she looked at the stopcock here, she might fathom the reason why. Her heart skipped a beat. There was a man and a woman's voice outside the door, and she leaped up and flattened herself against the wall beside it. Pat had come back. As soon as he walked in, he would see her. Even so, she had every right to be here. She had an instinct to return to the bed, as though she had made a big mistake by leaving it, all those weeks ago. Pat wouldn't understand her urge to nestle in. He just saw her as somebody convenient, a landlady who was there for him whenever he wanted her, and that he could leave whenever the fancy took him, just as he was about to show with this new conquest. Her heartbeat was beginning to slow down, and then the voices stopped.

'There's a key in the door,' she heard Pat say, and Jacqueline put her hand on the handle. When she opened it from inside, Pat and Auntie Mina were there.

'Here you are, Jacqueline. I thought I'd show your aunt my room. She hasn't seen it. I think it would be perfect for her. That is, unless you would like me to keep it on. I have grown very fond of it.' Pat smiled ruefully.

'What a wonderful view of the sea.' Auntie Mina clapped her hands. She had walked over to a small window, like a port-hole in the roof, and was gazing out. 'You're a lucky man to be living up so high. I don't know why you want to give it up, Pat.' She wheeled round.

'It does have some precious memories, and one in particular I'm loath to abandon,' Pat said. The house-phone on the locker was ringing, and he lifted the receiver.

'It's Vaughan. For you.' His voice had grown quiet, and Jacqueline blushed.

'Vaughan must like you a lot to keep on ringing. He should have remembered that when you were married.' Auntie Mina shook her head and grinned.

'It can get complicated. I have an ex-wife who seems to have forgotten she betrayed me too. She lives in London now but wants to come home, and has asked that we start all over again.' He shook the phone in the air.

'Don't do it, Pat. There can be no going back,' Jacqueline found herself saying, but Vaughan's voice was coming through, for all to hear.

' . . . your answer to my proposal?' The faraway tones had a boyish ring.

Chapter Twenty-four

Oh, why couldn't it just all be as simple as this? Jacqueline thought, and a shiver ran through her. Her teeth chattered and her body convulsed, but she was in the strong arms of a man. She stared at her rescuer gratefully and Philip Reilly, whom she remembered had once visited her house and admired it, responded to hers with an equally keen look. She was sure she saw purposeful lips move down towards her almost-blue ones. *It's the kiss of life again*, she told herself; she let herself drift off for a few moments. *'If you want to know if he loves you so, it's in his kiss,'* the words of a hit song rang through her head. This second time would definitely tell her, but the rescue effort wasn't going to happen.

'We'll have to get you inside. That looks like a painful cut on your leg. Relax and I'll carry you,' Philip said, and they both glanced down at a line of blood trickling from underneath a make-shift bandage he had made from his shirt. He pulled his police-man's coat around her more fully. 'Hold on tight,' he said, and she draped her arms round his neck. A large wet stain appeared on his vest when she snuggled in close. He swayed as he carried her over stones, as if she really was on that rowing boat she had planned to take out from the harbour below, to become more at ease with the sea before her trip with Isaac.

The warm air of the Anchor Bar above the pier in Dunduff wafted over them as the policeman carried Jacqueline inside. Although she righted herself to sit down, her rescuer pressed in close. 'It's so your temperature doesn't drop,' he said, frowning, when she pulled away. 'You've had a shock. A whiskey would help,' Philip continued, and raised a hand towards the counter. 'Then we'll have to get you some dry clothes.' Looking down at herself, forcing her shaking to subside, Jacqueline noted that her wet dress was clinging to her body. It had outlined the shape of her breasts and thighs. She tried to straighten up, but when she pulled her dress out with white fingers, it slapped back into place, even more becomingly. 'Do you have a husband or boyfriend I could ring?' the policeman asked. 'Not unless you'd like to be a stand-in one,' she joked weakly; Philip Reilly caught those poor frozen hands of hers between his huge ones and rubbed them.

'I could think of a lot worse things to be.' His voice was low and intimate.

'Oh my God,' why did I take such a risk?' Jacqueline suddenly shuddered. Philip had stood up and she saw him speaking to a woman behind the counter, and he seemed to sway before her. It was because the sensation of her stepping into a boat with a life-jacket in her hand — which she had planned to put on as soon as she sat down — had returned. She hadn't expected a speedboat to come swinging towards her. It had caused her to lean and grab an oar to push herself out of the way, making the boat rock and precipitating that fall overboard. By the time the youngster in the speedboat had seen the disaster he was causing, she was drowning. Only the quick action of the policeman, who happened to be on the pier above and had thrown her a life-belt, had saved her.

Beginning to compose herself in her seat, watching the bar-woman come towards her, carrying a coat that must be for her, Jacqueline let her thoughts drift. Perhaps the accident was saying something. The first thing she would do when she was recovered was to send the policeman a thank-you card. There was no point in believing you can direct the course of your own life by willpower alone. Chance had almost caused her to drown, and the unexpected could happen at any moment.

The woman with the coat had reached her. Her name was Leslie, she said, and proffered the bulky coat to Jacqueline. 'Put this on. You must have got a terrible fright. You can return it to me later. If anyone asks, say it belongs to the bar-owner.'

'Thank you.' Jacqueline's teeth chattered. Her words dried up: tucking the coat around her the policeman was reminding her of Teddy. The grin on his face was the same lop-sided one her father wore, if she'd said something to amuse him, as though the world was a brighter place for her presence. She could pretend to faint now, and snuggle into her rescuer's arms, and the conquest would be complete. She saw herself floating down a church aisle too, a radiant bride. It was a pity that, unlike her father, Philip's legs were long and gangly, and his face was broad.

Leslie was watching, and nodded at them both. 'You two look a perfect match together. This might be the start of something new,' she said. It was Teddy coming back again, pointing the way ahead, Jacqueline decided.

Chapter Twenty-five

As she watched, the kitchen ceiling bulged and the flow of water pouring through a newly made hole, got stronger. 'You'll get a bucket that's filled with toilet rolls in the press at the bottom of the back stairs. Empty it out and bring it to me fast, Isobel.' Jacqueline squeezed her daughter's arm roughly, so that Isobel jerked away.

'Don't fuss. I'm going. It's only a leak,' she said, but even so, Jacqueline heard her clatter down the uncarpeted stairs, at some speed. *This is happening to test me. One week I nearly drown myself and the next the house looks as if it could fill with water,* Jacqueline thought. 'Hurry up, Isobel, it's getting worse,' she called. *It's just as well I rang Vaughan and told him I'd take his job. It doesn't mean anything more than working with him, and a better salary will be needed now,* her thoughts continued.

* * * * * * * *

'There was something wrong with the toilet on the middle landing, but I never expected it to come to this,' Jacqueline exclaimed to Claus, half an hour later. Isobel had left for school. Thanks to Auntie Mina's efforts, a cheerful neatness prevailed in the kitchen — apart from the water-stain that was spreading on the ceiling. A hole, as though a finger had been poked through, had formed, and a thin dribble of sour-smelling liquid continued to flow through. Claus quickly removed the kitchen table and chairs away from the leak, and stacked them in a corner.

'I think the water has been gathering overhead for a while. If the family had somewhere to stay for a couple of days, I could get the repairs done more efficiently.

'My husband will put me up. He likes Auntie Mina and he owes this to me, at least,' Jacqueline said.

'Mum, I forgot to tell you. Nuala bought me a new wetsuit. You can borrow it when you go out on the yacht.' Isaac yawned and stretched as he sauntered into the kitchen. He stared at the dripping ceiling. 'What's this? We're about to float away. It's the sinking of the *Titanic*.' He grinned.

'That's just like something Vaughan would say, turning everything into a joke,' Jacqueline snapped back, and she sighed. Contrary to her previous thought, here was a reason why she shouldn't take his father's job. She had forgotten how impractical and facile Vaughan could be. She could still change her mind.

'Come on, Mum. Whatever you say about Dad, you're going to need his help now, to repair all this,' Isaac said, shrugging. 'What's for breakfast?' he continued, and skirted around the buckets and some saucepans on the floor, as if they didn't exist.

He's right. I can't survive on my own, Jacqueline thought. Tomorrow was her birthday. She would tell him then.

Chapter Twenty-six

'*Happy birthday, dear Jackie, happy birthday to you.*' Auntie Mina's singing tones penetrated Jacqueline's sleep. 'I have a suggestion. Why don't we have a proper celebration for you and Isobel on her birthday? We can combine them both together,' her aunt continued.

Jacqueline had been trying to open her eyes to remove herself from a pleasant world of warmth and no cares, and she struggled upwards. 'Thanks, Auntie Mina, you're great to think of me.' She rubbed her eyes. A breakfast tray with toast and a boiled egg caught her eye. It was placed on a bedside chair, and soon an extra pillow was tucked behind her back. Outside, a wind was roaring past the house; Jacqueline blinked, and pulled the duvet closer round her.

'Somebody has to make you feel important. Now I don't want to see a scrap of the food left. Diet is an easy thing to neglect, and I'm a firm believer in an egg a day.' Auntie Mina placed the tray on Jacqueline's flattened knees. 'Vaughan would approve of this,' she added, and Jacqueline looked at her in surprise.

'You know what I mean. He never got round to serving you breakfast in bed himself, I gathered from your complaining letters. Maybe he thought it was a job for someone else.' Auntie Mina smiled, to take the sting from her words. 'Let's forget it. Today is your birthday, and you need to enjoy it,' she added, but her words lingered when she left the room.

Jacqueline began to butter her toast. The comment would niggle at her, she knew, like the inevitable hard crumbs that would invade her sheets after this repast.

'Vaughan always knew I understood that his time was precious. Everybody complains, but they don't really mean it in the end,' she would say to Auntie Mina when she got downstairs, but then she had to concentrate on her egg. It was barely set — the way Auntie Mina liked it. She had a vivid recollection of a similar one almost being forced down her throat when she was a child. *I don't think I'll be able to take this woman in my house for a day longer.* Her shoulders sagged as she stared at the congealed mess.

'Auntie Mina said I should come in and say happy birthday before I go to school,' Isobel said, bursting in the bedroom door. She leaned over to give her mother an awkward hug. 'I hope she stays forever. Tell her to, Mum. She cooks the best boiled egg ever.' Isobel beamed before she slid back upright.

'Auntie Mina won't want to outstay her welcome. She's already mentioned that being here is only a temporary arrangement until she gets somewhere else,' Jacqueline said. She had visions of her aunt struggling to stay warm and staring at the four walls in some lonely bedsitter. 'Our lives could change in the near future again, anyway. I can see new developments ahead. I'll let you know about them as soon as they become more clear,' she added mysteriously, and her eyes became slits. She could feel her toes curl up deliciously, like those of a prowling cat.

There was a card on the table when Jacqueline went downstairs some time later, and she grabbed at it eagerly. She really was glad she had said yes to Vaughan's offer of a job: she had recognised his handwriting straight away, and placed the envelope carefully in her bag. She would delay the lovely sensation of opening it, until the right moment came. She would bring it to work at the school, and when the principal took his morning break to have coffee with the teachers, she would slip into his roomy chair and slit it open. Vaughan had even chosen a card for her birthday that came with a yellow envelope, her favourite colour. She peeped in at it in her bag before she left, and saw it snuggled into place between her purse and a letter that had arrived yesterday about an overdue Visa bill. Better still, the yellow glowed, acting like a cheerful sun.

There was a picture of a heart on the outside when Jacqueline slit open the envelope and turned the card over an hour later. *Maybe he thinks this is Valentine's Day,* she thought. For some reason, instead of feeling that rush of delighted anticipation she had expected before reading the words inside, she was overcome by a sense of unease. When they had been married, Vaughan had never sent her a card as explicit as this. 'I'm a man for understatement,' he would laugh when she'd stare in bemusement at a piece of plain graphics on a card, or a simple illustration, to express his care. The heart was embossed and seemed to leap out at her, as if it had become engorged with blood that might begin to drip onto the desk before her. Her fingers tingled, as if ready to mop it up. A cheque slipped out from between the folds of the card. She stared at it in dismay: it was for five hundred pounds.

'Many Happy Returns for the day, from Vaughan and Nuala,' the card said inside. There was a drawing then of what should have been a star but was more like a stork carrying a bulging cloth in its beak. Vaughan had always been useless as an artist, but even so, Jacqueline shuddered at the sight.

Chapter Twenty-seven

'I'd say there's a nest of wasps there,' Auntie Mina craned her head back so far to look, she had to hold onto the hand-railings at the front of Jacqueline's house. Her niece gazed up with her. The eves were too high to see anything properly, but Auntie Mina nodded. 'I saw them coming and going that time I visited Pat's flat, and now one or two have appeared in my room. There is no time like the present to investigate,' she murmured. 'I know you're busy getting ready for the birthday party, dear.' Auntie Mina glanced at Jacqueline, who had hurried out to the steps when she was asked, and was lifting her apron to clean her hands, which were covered in flour. 'But perhaps we could have a look at the attic. It might save somebody getting stung.' Auntie Mina stopped looking to rub her eyes, as if something had fallen into them, and Jacqueline blinked. High overhead, she had seen a bird crossing the sky, almost indistinguishable from the blue. Freedom. The word had echoed in her head momentarily, like a clarion cry. *It's telling me to break away. To be glad that my children are growing up and my responsibilities are getting less, and that I'm not tied to a man. There's so much in the world out there to discover,* she thought. When she closed her eyes, the image of blue stayed there, like a sea calling to be crossed. The infinite possibilities the world had to offer stayed with her for some time.

'We'll try the attic. I know you like to take these matters in hand yourself, but it's no problem for me to tag along, in case you need a second opinion,' Auntie Mina said when they went inside. She took Jacqueline by the elbow and steered her away from the kitchen.

'Up here is worse than being in an underground cave,' Jacqueline said loudly a short while later to Auntie Mina, who was holding onto the base of a ladder below her. 'I don't know why I agreed to do this,' she continued, turned away from the upward-gazing face of her aunt, and looked around the dim space. Beneath her she thought she heard footsteps on the ladder. It was probably Auntie Mina, but the footsteps paused and retreated, suggesting a change of mind.

Gradually the sensation of being in a black hole began to disappear for Jacqueline, and she focused her gaze on the far corner. Chinks of light were appearing through slate, helping her see better, and she found that she was getting more used to the weak light. There were boxes stored up here, the contents of which she had already forgotten about, and rolls of insulation that Claus had yet to lay. She would speak about them to him next week.

A voice called out to Jacqueline, and she veered round, away from her squinting at the point where the attic roof met the house wall; where she and Auntie Mina had looked up at from outside. She stared at the trapdoor. For a few seconds a torch-beam dazzled her eyes. It was Pat. For some reason, Auntie Mina hadn't called out that he was coming. Jacqueline put a hand up against the glare. *He wants to ambush me, to get me on my own,* she thought and had a memory of a figure lurking in the kitchen as she had passed.

'It's you. I'm having a dinner party for Isobel and myself, but I thought I'd better take a few minutes off to search for a wasps' nest. It's here somewhere.' Her voice had a squeaky quality, and she coughed. Pat's free hand was behind his back, and now he brought it forward.

'I'm sorry I missed your birthday yesterday. I've been trying to think what to get you, and your aunt mentioned this.' His fingers opened.

She's interfering in my life; she'll have to go, Jacqueline thought, but her pulse began to race. 'It's a ring of your mother's Mina had as a keepsake, and I got the two of your names inscribed inside,' Pat said. They both heard the wasp coming in their direction at the same time, and ducked.

'The ring has fallen,' Pat exclaimed. 'We'll have to find it.'

This is all Imelda's fault. She should rest in peace, Jacqueline thought stupidly, and found herself groping around on the floor. It should never have happened, but she was on her knees looking for a ring. Even if she wanted to rise, she couldn't, because the angry wasp had been joined by a companion, and was continuing to circle. *Marriage is forever.* The words pounded in her head. Imelda had lived those vows until her death, and she would too. Finding that fallen ring would declare her intention. Auntie Mina's voice called from below, asking whether everything was all right.

'Better than I expected,' Pat murmured in Jacqueline's ear. That was when one of the wasps overhead chose to find freedom by means of the trapdoor. It dived. 'Move back towards me!' Pat yelled.

Chapter Twenty-eight

How did the party of yours go?' Anna asked Jacqueline, a week later. The two friends were out walking and the heady smell of pine trees filled the air.

'It was a success, thinking about it now.' Jacqueline nodded. 'Vaughan got an evening call from a client whose court case had been brought forward at the last minute, and had to work late on the file, but everybody else had a good time. It was lovely to see all of the family sitting down at the same table, and I met Glenn, Amy's new boyfriend, for the first time,' Jacqueline gushed, but had to force a smile. 'Vaughan has arranged for us to go out to dinner together, to discuss my new job. That's the most important news of all.' She placed her hands in her pockets, as if the wind had grown chill. The two friends slowed their stride to look around. The panorama of Glendalough spread out before them. 'This is the place where you can hear an echo. Do you want to see?' Jacqueline asked, and without waiting for an answer from her friend, began to clamber down a path towards a shining lake. Branches rustled overhead and there was a sudden confused movement as a hidden bird broke from cover.

'Wait for me. I'm coming,' Anna called. She created sharp sounds of bracken crackling as she stumbled.

'Don't bother. I'll be back in a second!' Jacqueline yelled. She wanted to be alone here. Teddy had first told her about this place. He and Marion had come here on their honeymoon, he said, and she had been so taken by an echo that travelled across the lake, just opposite from the famous site of St Kevin's Bed, that he could hardly get her to leave, he had chuckled. Remembering his words, Jacqueline became still. Her father had been weak; he had forgotten Imelda far too easily. Well, she wasn't like that. '*Back in a second,*' her reply echoed already from the opposite shore, to prove it.

An hour later, the sun was sinking when the two women hurried towards the only hotel in the valley; alone, and skirted by a stone-laced swift-flowing stream. Behind them, a fog was beginning to envelop the steep hillsides they had left, settling onto trees and meandering upland paths. It blanketed Glendalough's twin lakes like a barrier, to shut them out. Jacqueline shivered. This valley would be an eerie place to find yourself lost in. She turned to her friend gratefully. 'Who needs a man with a friend like you to go for a walk with? We must do it again.' She linked her arm.

'And what about all the lovely men you fancy at discos when we go out? You have something different to say then,' Anna replied, laughing.

'Hello, girls. What are you doing here?'

Jacqueline wheeled round at the sound of a familiar voice. She had just splashed some cold water on her face in the ladies' at the hotel: she had been burning hot from the exertion of the walk. She exclaimed loudly, 'Bernie! I don't believe it. This is the last place I expected to run into you.' She groped for a towel and dried her face and blinked. 'You look happy. What's going on? By the way, this is my friend Anna. I don't think you've met.'

'We did once. At Harvey's.' Bernie waved a hand. 'You won't believe what I have to tell you.' She grinned. She wore an air of satisfaction, like somebody who had just eaten a good meal. *Any minute now, she'll tell me she's scored a perfect piece of dope and ask me to go into a cubicle to let her smoke some,* Jacqueline thought. But Bernie was pirouetting on the tiled floor.

'Myself and my darling husband Luke have consummated our marriage again. I'd forgotten how good he was in bed, and who can resist that forever?' she said in a stage whisper to Jacqueline. Anna laughed.

'Lucky woman. Now it's your turn to get Vaughan back, Jacqueline. The gauntlet has been thrown down.' She grinned.

'We'll leave the love-birds alone,' Jacqueline said when they sauntered into the hotel bar a few minutes later, but Luke was waving them over. He stood up and gave Jacqueline a hug.

'Bernie told me she met you. I haven't seen you in ages.'

'How do you do, Luke? This is a coincidence. Meet my friend Anna,' she said.

'Where have you been all my life?' Luke said, and pressed Anna so close to him, Jacqueline thought she would have to prise her away.

'Luke knows quality when he sees it. I'll have to agree with him. You are stunning, Anna,' Bernie said, but Jacqueline saw a frown appear between her eyes. *At least he does it to her face. Vaughan sneaked behind my back for his cheap liaison,* she thought.

'I'm afraid my good looks are fading. A man would have no interest in an old person of forty like me.' Anna threw her head back and revealed a creamy neck.

'There's no hope for us, so. It's no wonder I want my husband back.' Jacqueline grinned.

There was a handwritten envelope in the letterbox of the hall-door when she arrived back in her seaside home that evening. Twilight clouds infused with pink banked in frothy layers on the horizon. She had had an urge to stay out of doors. But duty beckoned. Tomorrow was her last day of freedom before taking up her new job in the solicitors' office, and she had to cook some meals for the freezer for the times ahead. She would begin with a few days of orientation, when she need only go to work for an hour or two. That would be coupled with this evening's business discussion over dinner, when she could ask all the questions she wanted.

Jacqueline turned the envelope over in her hands. There was no clue from the front about who it might be from, and she didn't recognise the handwriting. Whoever it was, was familiar with where she lived, and had probably wanted to meet her when they dropped the letter in. She thought about calling Auntie Mina down, but remembered that her aunt would be away that evening. Cold air from the sea invaded the hall and she pulled her coat around her.

Dear Jacqueline,

I hope you are keeping well since we last met. I'm writing to you in this informal manner, as a friend. My intention is to keep what I know in confidence, so that we can discuss it together and see what you think about it all. Perhaps we can come up with a plan together.

Jacqueline's eyes began to open wide as the contents of the letter started to reveal itself.

Your son Isaac has been seen with very unsavoury company recently, by some colleagues of mine . . . .

The words ran on and she skipped the signature below: *Ronan O'Dwyer.* She would have to get in touch immediately. She would go to bed with the man if she needed to, to find out more. Jacqueline groaned. She put the letter on the hall-table and grabbed at her hair, in despair. She recalled the wedding ring on his finger, which he had shoved into a pocket. It would be wrong of her to betray his innocent wife, but it was the only way she could keep Isaac away from trouble. If Vaughan found out what was happening, he would take the boy over completely. She was exaggerating, she knew, but the timing of this was all wrong.

'Is something the matter? You look fit to kill someone,' Pat said. *This man has habit of creeping up on me,* Jacqueline thought. The letter was open on the table and she sidled over to hide it.

'I wonder why all the best men are married. Even you have an ex-wife you can't say no to,' Jacqueline said.

'I found that ring, by the way. I searched for it afterwards.' Pat wore a preoccupied look, as if he hadn't heard her. 'You could slip it on and we'd run away together, into the sunset, as if the past has never happened,' he said.

'I'm going to live with Vaughan again. He and I have a son to take care of now,' Jacqueline said.

Chapter Twenty-nine

She'd run out of cocoa; at least there wasn't enough to make the chocolate brownies Auntie Mina had expressed a special fondness for, the first time Jacqueline had made them. Jacqueline began to take some tins and packets out of her provisions presses, just to make sure. It created a bare look on the shelves. Her brown-sugar glass container was quite low too, but she wouldn't get depressed. Recently, she had only been able to buy sufficient for basic grocery needs. She had been going to the local shops as well, in order to spend less. That was false economy, she knew, but her poor cashflow meant she could only buy small amounts at a time. She had had to put off working with Vaughan, to concentrate on the Isaac problem, and this morning Pat had left. It might take her a few weeks to find a replacement lodger. She had refused to take rent from Auntie Mina, and her savings were quickly running out. Jacqueline began to rummage at the back of the press for a chocolate bar, left over from Christmas. The cocoa she had would be enough to make a decent batch of brownies. Her fingers clutched it. *Something will present itself to help my money problems,* she thought.

'Only sissies stay at home in bed when they have a cold. I don't want to miss my course, Mum,' Isaac had said that morning when Jacqueline had held his arm to keep him from going out.

A racking cough shook his frame, belying his words that he only had a cold.

'If you don't stay at home for a while, you'll end up hospital,' Jacqueline declared. She had been amazed at her resolute tones. Recently, her son had been unapproachable, a silent figure in her presence, as though an invisible wall existed between them. This time, when she approached to give him a hug to show that she cared, that she was there for him if he had anything on his mind, he shrank away from her.

An appetising odour of newly baked chocolate treats spiced the air, and Jacqueline laid them neatly on a wire tray. She had made them small to allow the mixture to go further. Isaac was generally indifferent to any chocolate temptations his mother conjured up, but even if they weren't touched, there would still be enough left if she brought some to the sick-room. She made some lemon tea with honey, to add to their appeal.

The curtains were closed when Jacqueline went into Isaac's room, and when she pulled them across to let daylight in, he asked her to stop, in a strangled voice, and she returned them to their closed state again. Even so, she left a sufficient slit of light to allow her to see him. He lay huddled up in bed. After a few seconds, though, he shot up into a sitting position, stiff and startled-looking.

'You never told me you were coming into my room, Mum. Why are you here? I want to be alone,' he moaned.

'Nonsense. Look what I've brought you. These are just made,' Jacqueline said briskly, but something was stopping her from approaching the boy. She could never tell his father about how she and her son had become strangers, about the way he was staring at her now, for instance, as though she was more a threat to his peace of mind than somebody who loved him to bits; because Vaughan would blame her. *You spent too much time in that school of yours when he was a baby. You cared for your work more than him,* he would say, or accuse her of neglect — that she never had the place shining like a new pin, so that the boy wouldn't be able to wait to get home.

'What's the matter? You look done in. I think I'll call a doctor.' Jacqueline reached out a hand, as though to touch her son, and let it drop away. She placed the tray on her knees. 'This will make you perk up. You need sugar for energy.' She nodded brightly, but her son shifted so that the cup slopped over and liquid fell on his duvet, and she had to snatch it back. Despite herself, tears were welling behind Jacqueline's eyes. She couldn't bawl now. As if to reinforce the thought, Auntie Mina was calling out downstairs, wondering if anybody was at home. At the same time, she spied a packet of cigarette papers on her son's locker. Isaac was so conscious of the risk to his health of smoking, years ago he had even forced her to give them up; she stared, mesmerised. Auntie Mina was coming up the stairs; she grabbed at the papers and hid them up her sleeve. Isaac gave her a sickly grin. *He thinks I'm on his side now,* she thought.

'Hello, Auntie Mina. I wonder could you bring up the phone to me to plug in here? Mum forgot it. I told her earlier on I wanted to ring Dad. He forgot to give me this week's pocket money and he said he'd drop it over. Mum won't mind. You like any excuse to meet him, don't you, Mammy?' He grinned at her in a charming lop-sided way. It would be a perfect opportunity for her to tell Vaughan all about the cigarette papers she had found, but he would whisk Isaac off straight away. Jacqueline's thoughts jumped ahead.

'Of course,' Auntie Mina said. 'By the way, I met somebody called Ronan O'Dwyer who said he was a friend of yours, when I was out walking.' She turned to Jacqueline. 'He's a policeman, I believe. He said they were on the lookout for a member of a well-known criminal gang who had been sighted in Cloonvara.' She shrugged. 'I don't know why, but he even gave me a photocopied picture to show you,' and she placed the face of an unshaved dark-haired man on the bed.

'Take him away. I don't want to see that ugly mug.' Isaac dived under the bedclothes.

'We need a man in the house to protect us. You're right, Jackie, about Vaughan being back in the fold. I think I can help you do it,' Auntie Mina said.

Chapter Thirty

'You're going to spruce yourself up. I'll pay for a hairdresser to give you a cut that would make any man's head turn. We'll buy a stunning new outfit that shows you off, and you're going to start that new office job,' Auntie Mina declared. 'After a week of posing and simpering round, Vaughan won't able to resist you. That first flush of passion he experienced for Nuala must be wearing off by now.' Her eyes glinted. At least that was how Jacqueline described the look she saw in them, to herself. *You would think Auntie Mina was the one who had been married to him*, the idea persisted.

It was a wet day in Cloonvara and condensation was beginning to creep up the window of the back conservatory, where Jacqueline had been sitting reading, until a cup of coffee was placed on the wicker table beside her and she was forced to look up. Even this cut-off retreat wasn't sufficient to provide means of escape from her aunt, Jacqueline thought disloyally, and she beamed her thanks, to make up for it. Every day Auntie Mina came up with a scheme to help her get Vaughan back. But this was the most daring one. As soon as she announced it, Jacqueline knew it would work. Vaughan was a secret woman-watcher. She used to admonish him for it when they were married, without really believing anything could happen, but then there had been Nuala. Now it could be her turn to be the femme fatale. She would be irresistible.

Rain pattered on the glass roof of the small annex. In contrast to the spacious view the front of the house enjoyed, here the presence of paving and a high back wall created a bleaker aspect. Adding in the streaming rain, it seemed that she had been cut off from the world, so as to be forgotten about. Only Auntie Mina's vision of a brighter her, moving voluptuously through a drab office, lighting up the scene like a neon sign, invaded the glass room. She shifted in her seat to become more comfortable, and the harsh conservatory light presented Auntie Mina in sharp focus. Somehow Jacqueline had thought of her as never aging, but now she noted the fine lines on her face, how her years of hard work in America had stooped her shoulders and the way her eyelids had grown thin and transparent when she closed them, like delicate bat-wings. Auntie Mina sipped her own coffee. She was waiting for her reply, she thought, but instead she daydreamed.

Jacqueline was back in the hotel when she was very young. It was an incident she must have shoved to the further reaches of her mind, because it hadn't surfaced for years, but now she remembered. Teddy had an ease about horses, as if he and they spoke a secret language together that cut her off from him when he was in their company. She had said she would love to ride a horse, and he had believed her. It must have been before Blackie arrived, because he put her up on what he called a 'tame' roan mare. He would ride alongside her on his own horse, and she would be safe as houses. Besides, he would only go at walking pace, he had assured Imelda, when she came into the hotel yard to investigate.

Her mother's protests were in vain and they had clattered out of the hotel confines together. High-up windows, good for looking into, were at Jacqueline's eye-level, but she had to concentrate hard not to fall off, and they slipped past. She was a boat perched on the waves with a lake-bed far below, or a trapeze artist without a net, she decided; the ground was impossibly out of reach. She pressed her ankles into the hard saddle to try and get a grip, and clutched at the reins, pulling back the horse's head. She could feel her heart fluttering like a bird in her chest when the horse charged forward. They had reached a country road, treading a grassy margin, when a rag on a bush caught the roan's eye and it bolted. By the time Teddy reached her and plucked her into his arms, his daughter could only bawl with fright.

'She's a brave girl and a natural horsewoman. Anybody else would have fallen off,' he boasted to Imelda, allowing Jacqueline to stay in his arms for longer than usual when they got back. Teddy had been cruel, though, to put a sprat such as herself on an adult-size mare. Jacqueline had an uneasy feeling that his sister Mina might be showing the same streak of cruelty now. Supposing that, when she went into the office, everybody laughed at her and, instead of admiring her full figure, they called her fat, behind her back. In a few weeks too, the fashionable streaks Auntie Mina had put in her hair would be dotted with strands of grey. She was getting old as well, she thought moodily. The pert twenty-somethings in the office would be the ones Vaughan would have eyes for.

'Can I join you? I'm tired. We had a hard day at school, from the minute I went in this morning.' Isobel arrived with a steaming cup of hot chocolate and perched herself on a conservatory chair. She tucked her feet underneath her. 'You two are very quiet. What's going on? Can I join in the conversation?' she asked. 'It's bound to be better than the talk about football. I got stuck with Charlie Meagher on our way home from school. In the end I walked on and left him.' She shrugged. 'There are more important things in life than sport — to me, anyway.' She blew on the hot chocolate and sipped.

'We were discussing a new look for your mother. She has to get out there and show the world what she can do. She can be confident, bright and smart at the same time. There's nothing my niece can't do if she puts her mind to it,' Auntie Mina said. She stood up from her chair and plumped the cushion behind her so that, when she returned to her position, she was balanced like a bird.

'I'm not saying anything yet. Your grand-aunt has a plan for me to win back your Dad,' Jacqueline said, blushing, but Isobel had lost interest. She had opened up a fashion magazine on the wicker table and was leafing through it.

'What's so good about having a man? Aren't you happy the way you are? I don't know why all females harp on about boyfriends. It's not the be-all of everything. I'm going to be free and independent.' Isobel stretched up, like a flower unfurling. 'Anyway, Dad has other things on his mind. I heard him having a row with Nuala last weekend. Well, maybe it wasn't a row, but their voices were raised. She said there was no point in being in their relationship unless they had a child.'

Jacqueline was back on that horse again and she was falling, falling.

'And what did he say?' Her voice had a paper-thin quality.

'She's bluffing. She'll let Vaughan make a decision on that,' Auntie Mina said. Suddenly, Jacqueline saw right through her. She had guessed that something like this was about to be said. Maybe something like it had happened to Auntie Mina herself once. Jacqueline pushed away the distracting thought. Her aunt had deliberately advised her to go back to work because she knew that, when she began to order Jacqueline about, just as when she had been a child, she always resisted.

'Dad said one family was more than enough to manage,' Isobel began to make swimming movements with her hands, as if she was underwater, reaching for the surface. She looked sideways at her mother.

'Don't worry, Isobel, we'll look after ourselves, even if he does have another family,' Jacqueline gasped. She couldn't take that job now, of course. The rain got heavier outside. Soon it would find a crack to come in. There was no doubt either: she needed a salary.

'I have worked for a brief period before, in Vaughan's office,' she said bravely.

Chapter Thirty-one

Despite herself, Jacqueline couldn't get rid of that secret glow inside, which Auntie Mina's provocative words about drawing all eyes to her beauty in Vaughan's office, had provoked. Although she had changed her mind about the red dress being a good idea, and had instead gone for a more sedate black number, she had been unable to resist the suggestion of a good hair-do. Now she was leafing through a magazine in Top-Knot, the local hairdresser's, waiting for her turn to come round.

She hadn't given a thought that the place was unisex, and was startled when a man's voice addressed her by name. Claus stretched out his long legs beside her. He saw Jacqueline glance at his thinning locks, and he grimaced and shoved a hand through curls which were more abundant at the sides, making them stand out. The bench was short; just as Claus greeted Jacqueline, another prospective client sat down close to him, making him push along. Their sides touched briefly until she wedged herself into the wall. 'Hello, Claus. I didn't know we shared the same hairdresser. Paolo,' she nodded towards the stylist, 'gives a very good cut.'

Beyond them, a slim dark-haired man was peering into a mirror over a customer's head. 'There's nothing like a good hair-do to cheer a person up,' she went on, as though talking to a best friend.

In a way, though, Claus was her friend — somebody she had been able to call on over the past few difficult months, however small or large the job.

'I've been invited to a wedding in Portlaoise this weekend, and I thought I'd better take care of my looks.' Claus's husky voice, and his charming accent, made Jacqueline grin, despite herself. This was what she liked about hairdressing salons: somehow, the holidays she read about in their magazines seemed to create an air of escape, as though it was possible to slip into a make-believe world like theirs, if only for a little while. She batted her eyelids at the man beside her.

'Lucky for some. I'm afraid it's shopping and cleaning the house for me. I'm taking up a new job next week,' she lisped. She was being girlish and yet a mature woman at the same time; she tossed back her hair as if it was already sleek and blow-dried.

'I have an idea. You need a break, and we could go along to the wedding together. It will be good fun, and you'll have something to look back on, during the hard weeks ahead.' Claus returned her looks with an enigmatic smile. *He's afraid I'll say no. That's why his tone is light,* Jacqueline thought, and she dwelt on the expression 'hard weeks ahead'. There was still time to say no to the offer. If she went to the wedding, though, she would be exhausted, and badly prepared to start any job.

'Next please, Jacqueline,' Paolo called, and she stood up.

'Come to the house later. I was thinking of doing up the back room for Mina. She doesn't want to inconvenience me by taking up one of the rentable flats,' Jacqueline said, turning to Claus, but his gaze had drifted to a blonde coming in the door, and when his eyes returned to hers, they had lost their lustre. Of course she was too old for him, she knew that, but she could pretend.

'Certainly, whatever you wish,' he nodded. But this time his smile was false.

It was some while after her conversation with Claus, and Jacqueline was at home, staring into the fridge. She would have to shop for groceries, and she did a quick calculation. Combining that with the cost of the hair-do, and an unexpected sum she had had to hand out to Isobel for extra violin classes, so that she would pass her next grade exam, she wouldn't be able to pay Claus. She took a deep breath to avoid panic and moved a litre of milk aside to see better. The remains of yesterday's pot roast was revealed, and she spied some tomatoes and a jaded head of lettuce. She could make a nourishing pie with a salad on the side. Then she wouldn't have to buy anything big, and Isobel would be delighted with the savoury treat.

A can of beer attracted Jacqueline's attention when she opened the fridge, second time round, on this occasion to take out margarine for her pastry. The can had been stored in behind the milk cartons, to hide it, and for some moments she thought it might be Isaac's. It was an expensive can of German beer, though: she knew he wouldn't buy that. Isaac would go for quantity rather than quality: he would be able to buy three cheap beers for the price of this one. Maybe Auntie Mina had bought it for some reason, but her drink, if she bothered at all, was whiskey. Now and then, she would have a bourbon with ice — she had developed a taste for in the States, sitting at the bay-window at dusk and staring out at the view — but Jacqueline had never seen her drink anything else.

Auntie Mina cleared up the mystery a short while later. 'I hope you don't mind. An old friend of mine, Fred Noonan, has been living in New York for the past three years, and he's arrived in Ireland for a visit. We've kept up correspondence and he's coming out to see me this evening.'

Jacqueline shook her head. 'Of course not. It's typical, though, isn't it? I'm having Claus over as well, to look at doing something to your old room, which you said you wanted to return to. I thought I might be able to fit in a shower and toilet in the walk-in cupboard at the back.' Jacqueline felt herself tense. It wasn't fair. Even Auntie Mina was using her. She herself was having to take up a job tomorrow she didn't really want, when nobody else seemed to care where the price of anything that was provided for them came from. She spied a note from Isaac on the top of the microwave a few seconds later. Beside her, Auntie Mina tapped an impatient foot.

The back wheel of my bike has become too buckled to use it. Could you lend me the money to get a new one and I'll return it to you as soon as I get it from Dad, Isaac had written. Vaughan was impossible to get money from for small matters like that, and yet for her it could break the bank. Isaac knew that as well, yet he persisted in asking.

'Be my guest. I'd be delighted to meet your friend, Auntie Mina,' Jacqueline said, turning to her aunt at last.

The other woman frowned. 'Don't worry. I'll be able to look after him myself. Perhaps he could sleep in the spare room tonight; though if Claus is working on it, we can put a mattress down on my floor. It wouldn't be the first time we've slept in a room together.' Auntie Mina grinned.

'I think I remember you talking about Fred Noonan before. You mentioned him in a letter to me and said he was one of the first divorcees you met when you went to America,' Jacqueline said slowly, and Auntie Mina turned as if to hide a smile. *She had an affair with him,* Jacqueline thought.

She could easily have a fling herself with Claus, Jacqueline decided that evening. Sunset was tipping some gold through a high-up window into the small back room as they worked. She had started to pull down strips of wallpaper from the upper part of a wall onto the ground, and uneven pieces curled up. The work would be in lieu of payment. She poised herself, ready to step down, and backwards into his arms, when he walked past the table she stood on. This was the pot of gold Philip Reilly had talked about. It was the best kind of treasure, something money couldn't buy: the gift of friendship.

'By the way, that offer of coming to the wedding with me still stands. I even got some money out of the ATM before I came, in case I didn't have time in the morning.' Claus seemed to have read her thoughts. His red cheeks when he smiled reminded her of Father Christmas, and he waved a bundle of money in the air. *There must be a hundred pounds there, at least,* she thought. She looked at her watch. Auntie Mina's friend would have arrived at this stage. She would have to give them some space to be with one another; she couldn't go down to the bottom part of the house now.

The genial giant beneath her had her trapped, and she shivered with delight. A piece of paper she had thrown on the ground rustled and moved slightly, and she stared, mesmerised. It was a mouse underneath, but when it scurried away, something glinted on the floor. There was a ring. Maybe it belonged to Auntie Mina and she had worn it to pretend she had been married when she went away on those weekends with her friend Fred Noonan. Whatever the truth was, the spell was broken. She herself was a real married woman. It hadn't been her fault that her marriage had broken up, and now she must repair it.

'Is this a proposal?' she asked lightly. 'Are you trying to buy my favours?' she added.

Claus shrugged. 'If that works, why not?' He grinned. 'Nobody could put a price on you.' It was what Jacqueline wanted to hear — something Vaughan had forgotten about. He must have said it to Nuala, though, and that was the reason why she stayed with him.

'Money is at the centre of everything, isn't it, Claus?' she said. 'I wish I didn't have to go to work on Monday, but I do.'

'By the way, did I ever show you a picture of my girlfriend?' Claus said. Unexpectedly then, he took a picture from his wallet, and Jacqueline stared down. Even Claus was ready to two-time.

'Let's get on with the work. Unless the mouse has shredded them, there are banknotes behind the wall somewhere,' she said.

Imelda and Jacqueline, Pat had had inscribed on the ring he had wanted to slip onto her finger, Jacqueline remembered. She would give him a call in the morning and ask his advice about her problems. Unless he had fallen under the charms of his former wife again. Everybody else in her world seemed to have a second love, except her, she sighed.

Chapter Thirty-two

'Allowing time to dry-line and plaster the walls, I should be finished in a week,' Claus said. 'Including materials, it will be around five hundred pounds.'

The words came back to haunt Jacqueline. She was sitting in Stephen's Green, immersed in watching the passing parade, beguiled by the steady flow of cosmopolitan life, coolly assured office girls and laughing young men, all perfectly set off by the park's scenic backdrop of a glinting duck-pond and amber-tinted autumnal trees. She shook a hand in the air, as though to swat those thoughts away. She moved over on the park bench to accommodate another sitter. A pigeon pecked round at her feet and she cast the remainder of the crumbs on her lap, gathered as she finished her home-made sandwich. The pigeon was joined by another busy member of that species. Their neck-feathers gleamed in rich hues of turquoise and grey. She would have to draw on her small savings again. This year, she had hoped to give herself a holiday, but now that was out of the question. It was a warm day for October, and Jacqueline bathed in the heat. She closed her eyes, and a need to sleep assailed her.

'Excuse me, please. You have dropped this.' Her fellow sitter was speaking; she opened her eyes again. One of her gloves was being proffered in her direction; she must have dislodged it when she was throwing the crumbs. She nodded her thanks. She didn't get much time to spend outdoors. She had agreed to work for an hour in the afternoon in Vaughan's office. She stood up to go. 'Take care now. Have a lovely afternoon,' her park companion continued. He was a Dubliner, she decided from his accent, and his clothes were neat but shabby. For him, St Stephen's Green was his retreat from the world, like a miniature but much loved city back-garden, a token gesture of all the world of nature had to offer.

'A pleasant day to you too. It looks as if the weather will stay fine.' Jacqueline smiled. The man doffed his cap. He turned into a side path and was gone. She too could disappear like that, Jacqueline thought. The worst thing about being in Vaughan's office was that it was having the insidious effect of drawing her back into organising his life. Her instinct to be methodical and set up an infallible administrative system was already taking over. She could feel the possibility of her becoming indispensable. She kicked at a pebble at her feet as if she was a small child: the old Jacqueline, ready to rebel at any moment. She should be proud of herself and all she had the ability to achieve, but she felt weighed down, as if a chain had been attached to her ankle, and she was stumbling forward. Leaving through the park gates, a bunting-bedecked van with its complement of smiling girls had been parked to dispense free samples of a new yogurt. She paused to take one. 'Thank you, that looks delicious,' Jacqueline said.

'Here's a voucher if you want to buy some more. You can get them at half price,' the cheerful yogurt promoter said, waving a slip of paper in the air. *She has kind eyes for me,* Jacqueline decided, *even if I'm a complete stranger.* Then, suddenly, Jacqueline got it. That was what the city was all about. Nobody really knew each other, and yet a refined network of communication existed, in which all who breathed the city's air, could take part. If she proved herself to Vaughan — and there was no doubt that she could — she would be an essential part of that world; but really only a cog in the machine, to make sure the office ran smoothly.

A wind picked up. It lifted some park leaves at her feet and blew them about. She suddenly remembered that there was a letter in her pocket from that morning. It was from an employment agency she had contacted weeks before and forgotten about, she saw as she read down. 'Hotel Receptionist. Starting immediately. The Castlewarden Hotel, Dunduff.' It was the hotel Pat had left; it hadn't closed down. The words jumped out.

She was about to crumple up the page, but her fingers paused. To be able to read the letter better in sunlight, she turned back to face the park. Her companion on the bench was leaving. He raised a hand and waved. Perhaps it was the letter, but she had the sensation, too, of coming out at the other end of something, and that this elderly man was acknowledging her moving forward. He was about to say something: approaching her, his eyes twinkled.

'This is a day in a million. My father used to say *carpe diem.* Make the most of it.' He shook his head on reaching her, as if doubting that the fine spell would hold.

'Would you like another one? We have plenty to give away. You could try the pineapple flavour for a change. I love it.' The yogurt girl was back. This time her eyes took in Jacqueline directly.

'No, thank you. I have a job to do. I must be getting back,' Jacqueline said. This kind of escaping into the temporary welcome of a park, was foolish. Vaughan needed her.

'Seize the day,' she murmured aloud, to hurry herself along. Then she saw the real significance of the man who sat with her in the park: Vaughan was approaching up Grafton Street, and the elderly man had stopped ahead of her, to speak to him. If they knew each other, it was probably a good excuse for her to approach and join in the conversation. She might suggest a tête-à-tête to Vaughan. They could find some intimate corner in a café for a cup of coffee. The elderly man had been fated to help her out, but Vaughan was moving away. She spied a carnation in his button-hole. This was the second wedding in the space of a few days that had been heralded. She raised a hand and called. The elderly man looked mildly surprised as she approached.

'Hello, Jacqueline. This is John, Nuala's father. Meet my ex-wife,' Vaughan said, when she arrived by their side.

'Funny you should say "ex", Vaughan,' Jacqueline interrupted. 'It wasn't an expression you used when you said you missed me being able to organise your life. Only a wife who knows you can do that.' She smiled.

Chapter Thirty-three

One of the things Jacqueline *did* like about her existence as a so-called ex-wife was the amount of freedom the title bestowed. She could lie in bed on weekend mornings, for instance, and watch television. It was not something she indulged in very often, because usually some housework beckoned, but this time there was a black-and-white movie with Ingrid Bergman and a smouldering Gary Cooper filling the screen, and she couldn't resist.

The smell of the sea came in through her open widow. There had been strong winds and lots of rain last night, and she imagined the beach swept clean as a new pin by all this weather, and pulled her duvet closer round her. A feeling of expectation, of a kiss about to happen between the two principal actors, flowed from the television. The last of the swallows leaving for warmer climes made shrill calls outside, and swooped and arched. She glanced out at them; by the time she looked back, the film kiss had come and gone. Maybe it was just as well. She didn't want to set up longing in herself, until she had Vaughan safely beside her, but when the film was over and she got up and showered, she had a sense of tingling anticipation for some time, as though she had been fulfilled by a passionate kiss, bestowed by the man she loved, and more would follow.

'How did your first week go at the office? I haven't had time to catch up,' Auntie Mina asked.

'I can't believe it. Isaac has drunk all the milk again,' Isobel said at the same moment. An Angelus bell struck twelve. They were having an early lunch, but were already late for Vaughan to pick Isobel up. Jacqueline stood, and opened the fridge with a flourish. 'Behold, the cow has delivered,' she said, and pointed to milk at the back, but Isobel continued to growl.

'It's early days yet, but I believe I did well, Auntie Mina. At least Vaughan said so before I left,' Jacqueline told her aunt. She had delayed in responding, not because of Isobel's show of temper, but because her daughter had left a book on the table with the flyleaf open.

Happy Birthday to a wonderful girl. Yours sincerely, Pat, had been inscribed on the open page, and Jacqueline had felt herself frowning. Pat had drawn a smiling face beside his words. It had made her want to grin in return, but that would have been wrong. Vaughan was the only one she wanted. She turned her back on the table, miming *I love you, Vaughan* into the cold-hearted fridge, before sitting down.

'Really, Isobel, you should be more careful. The milk has gone all over the table. I despair of you sometimes,' Jacqueline said to her daughter almost immediately afterwards. A creamy pool had gathered round Isobel's cornflakes bowl, where it had spilled over. 'I can't afford waste like that. This is not your father's house, you know,' she stormed and straight away regretted her words. Isobel glared.

'It's bad enough having to go there and listen to Nuala telling me what to do, without having it here as well.' The unhappy girl slumped in the chair.

'What happens in that house is no concern of mine,' Jacqueline said, but she felt a surge of elation inside. Everything was breaking up with Vaughan's so-called relationship. It was only a matter of time. There was one way the disintegration could be hurried up, though. She remembered that kiss she had missed on the television that morning, and put her hands on her knees and pressed them, to stop them from trembling. 'As a matter of fact, I might have to ask you to stay in Vaughan's place for an extra day next week. I'm finding the work in the office quite tiring. I need to get into the swing of things a bit more. I'll say the same to Isaac, and maybe you might visit Tom: he wants you to stay in his apartment for a few days, Auntie Mina.' She turned in the her aunt's direction.

'Ah, Mum, you can't mean it. I hate that woman,' Isobel burst out.

'Whatever you say, Jackie. Listen to your mother, young lady,' Auntie Mina said, but Jacqueline saw that glint from the past, in her eyes. All Jacqueline needed now was a good reason to invite Vaughan over. She knew what that was too, but although she tried to smile, thinking about it, for some reason her mouth turned down at the corners.

'It's all settled then.' She picked up the milk and put it in the fridge, and cold rushed at her, as if she had been locked inside.

Chapter Thirty-four

Jacqueline was in her silent front room, and a friendly light flooded in. She had loved her house the minute she laid eyes on it, but she knew as soon as he had made his first visit inside the door and seen its elegant, if shabby, dimensions, that Vaughan did too. They had only bought their bungalow in Blakestown because it was a safe place for the children to grow up in, and was near a good school, but she knew he hated suburbia. Having had to take out a new mortgage to give money to her, tied him to it more, and she could see jealousy etched on her face as soon as he saw her new home and its spectacular setting. She would entice him by saying it could be his, she decided. Apart from the flat downstairs, the house was empty when Jacqueline came to her decision. It was either that or let Nuala have everything and steal her children from her, probably. Whatever Isobel said, in the heat of the moment, about hating her, it could be a different matter if the same Nuala bribed the girl with a new coat, for instance, with fifty euro slipped into the pocket. And then there was the time when his girlfriend had persuaded Vaughan to pay for Amy to go to London. If Jacqueline had been mistress of the house, she would have been far more responsible in such matters. She let the criticisms rise in her mind.

It would be all over soon. To enjoy what might be the last time she would be in charge of all she surveyed, she held her arms out and began to move around the room, as if waltzing. In the twenty years they had been married, Vaughan had never brought her dancing; she would change that too, she vowed. It would be a fresh start for both of them.

'You won't believe this. I've found some money in a cavity in one of the walls in the small room at the back of the house I've begun to renovate recently. There are coins you might like to identify. I'd love if you could come over this evening to see them.' Jacqueline made herself sound excited on the phone. She had rung Vaughan shortly after Isobel and Auntie Mina had left, and now was sitting opposite him at the kitchen table. She wore her low-cut red dress, and he was in his shirtsleeves and had the top button open, just the way she liked. She leaned towards him. The smell of roast pork, complete with the crackling he found so irresistible, filled the room. 'I thought we might eat before I show you my find,' Jacqueline beamed. She had lit some candles too, as a centrepiece. They were low and discreet, and when she bent forward they gave her breasts a rosy glow, she knew. Of course as soon as they went upstairs, she would lure him into her bedroom, because there really was no money, and that would be that. Barely waiting for Vaughan to take a first bite, Jacqueline hungrily tucked into her own meal.

'This is delicious,' Vaughan said. 'Having a meal before surveying our treasure trove is a good idea,' he added. Jacqueline thrilled at the word, 'we'. Her husband of old had been won over. She had seen, too, how his eyes had lingered on her full voluptuous body, when she had bent down to take the roast out, for instance, and when she moved close to him to dish out his generous portion of life-enhancing pork.

'I haven't forgotten how hungry you can be, or how you like to lie down afterwards for a short nap,' she said, arching her eyebrows straight after Vaughan spoke, but he had moved one step ahead of her, and raised his wine-glass. The candlelight gave the cheap merlot she had provided a ruby glow.

'To us,' he said. 'I've been searching for an opportunity for you and I to be alone together,' he murmured. This allowed Jacqueline the opportunity to admire the nostrils of that thin nose of his, she'd thought too sharp when they were married. She saw that they flared out in a flattering manner. She didn't even mind that the red wine had caused a dark stain to appear on the inside of his lips, like dried blood; though when they were husband and wife she used to criticise that to herself, too.

'It's the old team again. I have a proposition to make.' Jacqueline let her lower lip stick out, in the way Vaughan had always found sexy — she wasn't quite sure why. Even without drinking much, she was beginning to feel tipsy. 'I want us to live in this house together. It can be all yours, Vaughan. We'll be happy as Larry, just like we were of old,' she gushed. Unfortunately, then she hiccupped — which wasn't so romantic — and she saw a startled, hunted look in Vaughan's eyes.

'Auntie Mina advised me that this would be a good occasion to speak to you, but she never told me about the idea you had in mind.' Vaughan frowned. 'When I said, "as we were before", I meant I would like you to become more of a mother to Isobel and Isaac. I won't take them every weekend, because I know you miss them, and in fact, Isobel has probably told you she's not exactly fitting in when she comes over. My real news, though, is that Nuala is pregnant.'

'Congratulations, that's wonderful to hear,' Jacqueline spluttered. A piece of pork caught in her throat, and she tried to spit it up. Tears sprang to her eyes. Vaughan came round from his side and slapped her on the shoulders.

'I always told you, you shouldn't cook pork. That crackling will be the death of you yet.' His words had the bitter flavour of vinegar on the mouth. Auntie Mina had betrayed her. She had never liked her, since her niece had been a little child. Even so, Jacqueline had a picture of her as an older woman now, and of her caring eyes.

'Perhaps it would be a good idea if you left, Vaughan.' Jacqueline drew herself up to her full height. She dabbed at falling tears with a red napkin, knowing that mascara was running down her face, and that the same napkin was staining.

The sound of pounding waves sprang up the steps and bounced off her, it seemed to Jacqueline, ready to knock her down, as Vaughan hurried away. She took a deep breath. She felt her lungs expand and empty out. Soon, like a weathered beach, she would be empty of love, and maybe of hate too, but at the moment she hated. She hoped Vaughan would crash on the way home and die.

'What are you looking at?' she asked the photograph of Imelda on the mantelpiece, which had confronted her when she went back inside. 'You left us too, without a word of explanation, or even goodbye.' The picture continued to stare. Despite herself, Jacqueline took it up and kissed the dear face. 'At least we had our precious years together,' she said, and sighed.

Another car pulled into the driveway of the old house, she saw through the sitting-room bay-window. It was Pat — Jacqueline knew the colour and make — but she couldn't speak to him in this state, and although very soon he rang the bell a number of times, she didn't answer.

'I'll be in touch,' Jacqueline called out weakly to the closed door, but of course Pat couldn't hear.

Chapter Thirty-five

'He's a bastard. He waited to tell you until you were at your most vulnerable,' Anna said.

'It's true,' Theresa added, munching. 'I'd never speak to him again if I were you. You should send him a solicitor's letter and take him to the cleaner's for all he's got. Tell him you want a divorce, that he's made his choice now but that he was married to you for twenty years, and that a private agreement of a down-payment on a house isn't enough. You'll need a monthly sum to look after his children.' She picked up a spoon and banged it on the table, as if she was a judge making a final pronouncement.

'It's not about the money, is it, Jacqueline? It's about dashed hopes and love and all that,' Annie soothed, and leaned over and pressed her friend's hands. The three women were in Lala's coffee shop on the outskirts of Cloonvara. Jacqueline looked up. Her attention had been arrested by the sound of birdsong coming in the window. A robin was perched on a bare-looking branch, and carolled into a walled garden. Children had left their parents to roam around the enclosure, outside. Laughter came from the serving counter behind her, and she spied two lovers at a nearby table, holding hands. This café was a slice of life, and she was part of it. In the same way, too, all that had happened to her was in the past and should be forgotten about. It certainly didn't matter to the people she was surrounded by. In a few minutes', or hours', time, all the people in the café would be leading their own drama-filled lives.

'I can't bear it. That bitch has taken everything from us. All I wanted was that Vaughan and I would lead a normal existence; that we would grow old, and maybe even senile, together,' she said. She managed a watery smile. *That's the spirit,* she thought, but Vaughan's words returned to her again, like a twisting knife.

* * * * * * * *

It was Monday, some days after meeting her friends in Lala's, when Jacqueline looked out on the grounds of the Castlewarden Hotel, determined to enjoy the view. She hadn't gone to Vaughan's workplace, of course. All that was behind her now. She lifted her face, grateful for a cold east wind. 'You're taking the day off. You need to talk things over and get them off your chest. Otherwise they'll fester away inside,' Bernie had said. She was about to meet her, any minute. Somehow, she had heard about the shocking revelation Jacqueline had been landed with, and had rung her. Her cousin had successfully applied for that job in the hotel. She would dearly love to see Jacqueline, if only for ten minutes during a coffee break, and would meet her, if she waited outside.

A glimmer of sea presented itself on the horizon when Jacqueline looked out. The Castlewarden was an old Victorian residence that had been extended and converted into a hotel. Her eyes wandered over the grounds. A golf course ran up one side of the hotel; she smiled, having a mental image of Bernie slipping out every now and then to put in a few practice shots. Apart from smoking the wrong thing, golf was her other failing, or passion — she didn't know which. Jacqueline leaned against a wall and closed her eyes. There was the crack of a club hitting a ball, the sound of 'Fore!', and then peace descended. Even here, she could get the salty tang of the sea, she decided. Voices passed her by, but she kept her eyes closed. She could see Vaughan that last time she had spoken to him. He had looked anxious, she remembered, and did care that he might hurt her, but that was no good now. The damage had been done.

She opened her eyes to look at her watch. Bernie was late, but there was no problem about waiting. Jacqueline saw a bench and sat down. Autumn had ravaged the trees all around, but the lawns were carpeted by yellow and brown that glowed like lost gold. Soon she would grow old and out of season too, and shed her own beauty, and nobody would care, or want to stick around.

'Fore!' the shout came again, but this time it was louder, and she looked sideways. It was one of the solicitors from Vaughan's office, and he raised a hand and waved. She signalled. Everybody would know the news by now: just when she wanted to forget it herself, she had been confronted by it. Isobel and the other two would be kept in the loop as well, and they would rub it in.

'A penny for your thoughts,' somebody said, and she spun back round. 'You'll get cold sitting out here. It's hard to believe a charming person like yourself is left sitting alone.' For a moment she stared, until recognition dawned. It was John, Nuala's father. She felt her chest tighten, as though this was a trap and she had been run to ground. 'Perhaps we should go inside. I'm sorry about the last time we met. I didn't get a chance to talk to you properly, and now it looks as if our paths have been thrown together again,' the elderly man said, and offered his arm. Jacqueline stood up.

'I believe you've had a bit of a shock.' His face creased in sympathy. 'My daughter told me that Vaughan gave you the news. This can't be an easy time for you,' he added.

As if in a trace, Jacqueline nodded. 'I'm used to loss. It happened to me before, and I can cope with it again,' she said, surprising herself. It didn't come as a surprise, though, to see another familiar figure standing in the doorway of the hotel when she began to walk. Bernie was behind the figure, pushing him out. Wet leaves clung to the old man's shoes as he stepped by her side. Jacqueline remembered the make-believe coins with which she had tried to lure Vaughan; she was being dragged into a false reality here too.

She began to back away. Vaughan had set this up. He wanted to make her squirm and hurt, and to hammer his point home. She would never divorce him. Nuala was getting old; she would probably have a miscarriage anyway. Bernie was pulling her own reluctant companion forward.

'Don't go, Jacqueline. I've been trying to get to speak to you for a long time. I want us to be friends,' Pat said.

He'll probably say he loves me next, the idea flashed into Jacqueline's head. For a split-second, she thought it was Teddy standing before her, as if this, and not the Vaughan conspiracy, was the real plot, and somehow, up in heaven, he and Imelda were conniving together. Well, she wouldn't give in. They had disappointed her before, when she was a child, and she had created her own happiness with Vaughan. She would cling to that forever. Nuala's father was linking her onward, though. Any minute now, Bernie would take out a cigarette and roll it, and God knows what would be inside. Jacqueline had to ignore what Bernie might be doing. Pat had reached her and she had been handed over, as if she was involved in some sort of passing-on of the parcel; like somebody who had been hurt and didn't want to trust in life, but was being made to.

'Hello gorgeous. You don't think I'm going to give up the only woman who matters to me that easily, do you?' Pat said.

Over the hotel, a pale Venus began to glow. 'You mean, hello love. I'm not that easily fooled,' Jacqueline quipped. Beyond her in the grass, burnished leaves shone like hearts of gold.

Leabharlanna Poibli Chathair Baile Átha Cliath
Dublin City Public Libraries

Central Library, Henry Street,
An Lárleabharlann, Sráid Annraoi
Tel: 8734333